Buried Secrets

A Novel by Krissy Baccaro

Copyright © 2020 by Krissy Baccaro

First paperback edition May 2020

Book cover by EbookLaunch
Book design by Polgarus Studio

ISBN 978-1-7346217-1-6 (paperback)
ISBN 978-1-7346217-0-9 (ebook)

www.krissybaccaro.com

For my Poppi

PART 1 - Discovery

Ella

Chapter 1

I spy the cottage through the pines at the edge of the driveway as fragrant autumn leaves drift past me.

It's not the same.

My mind still hears Poppy's whispers revealing the presence of a hidden box in the cottage, urging me to find it. He'd mentioned it once before, but I didn't believe he was serious until it escaped his lips in his last breath. The ache in his voice seemed deeper than the sorrow for that moment.

Where is that box?

And then there's the letter I found suggesting something terrible happened a long time ago. Something sinister. Was Poppy involved?

I tread lightly, cautiously forward, my gaze firm on the charcoal shutters of the bedroom where I'd slept so often as a child. The shutters seem smaller to me now as they peek out between the branches of the old oak standing in front. I slowly proceed and more of the cottage uncovers itself, as if peering from behind a curtain. Soon all of the front windows, the door and the porch are visible, and I stand squarely in front of it. We stare each other down for a moment and I am lost in thought.

I recall how the cottage once stood proudly with its beautiful white Victorian porch and double doors at its center, framed by two grand pillars, enveloped in lush greenery.

Now it slouches, uncertain, sad - a lost soul. Its pillars, chipped in some places and slightly dulled in others, struggle to keep it firm. It reaches for me. I feel it beckoning me, an old familiar friend.

Come in, El.

There's something you should know.

Heavy branches of crispy, golden leaves dance above the roof, and Skaneateles Lake, the cleanest of the Finger Lakes, glistens from behind. Does this pristine lake know it houses a blemish on its shore, clouding its pure waters? It continues to beckon me.

You can do it, El.

I long to be wrapped in its arms again like before, and I ache for happy memories to wash over and comfort me. I wait for my grandparents to welcome me at the foot of the steps. But the steps are empty.

I can't go in there.

But you must.

The cottage is a close friend of mine. Not the kind you see once in a while and you know pretty well, but a friend with whom you share your happiest hopes, your deepest secrets and your darkest thoughts. It once provided endless comfort, stability, and love, the only place I'd seek when I was sad or lonely, a sanctuary to ease the ache and decay within my heart ever since the accident and what happened with Jack. *Don't say it out loud.* It was a constant companion I depended on in my ever-changing life—and not just merely because of its structure or the memories contained within, but because of the two most important people in it.

And now only one. I not only see a difference in this friend, but I feel it deep within my bones. Its DNA is forever altered. And we both stand aloof, the cottage and I, facing each other with a giant, gaping hole in our existence, as together we mourn the same loss.

Our Poppy, the architect of this cottage and the heart, soul, and glue of our family, is gone. We are empty and heartbroken. An uneasy feeling curls in the pit of my stomach and leaves an unsettled darkness I cannot explain as I ponder that conversation about the box just two weeks ago, just before he passed.

Faint sounds of my mother's voice coming from the cottage distract me, but my legs are heavy and anchored to the ground. I choke in the dense air. I am devoid of feelings. Blank. Defeated. And I sense that I'm slipping back into the sadness again. I know I need to go inside. They're waiting for me —to talk about the past and wrap it all up in boxes and send it all away.

A monarch butterfly distracts my gaze and I watch it flit around the flowers in Poppy's garden. Poppy holds my four-year-old hand as together we weave through the rows of vegetables, pointing at potatoes, tomatoes, cucumbers, basil, and lettuce, chattering about the meals we would make. Poppy was proud of his garden and spent hours weeding, planting, adjusting. Spending time with Poppy amidst the fresh soil permeating the air, the sweet, soulful tones of his voice describing the life around us, was unmatched to anything else. Poppy's life centered around eating, and foods were plentiful in our family. The hierarchy in Salvatore F. Perri's world went: God, food, family, food again, and then everything else.

Had I told him how much I loved him as much as he'd told me? Did I do enough for him? Was it really enough? My thoughts are pulled back to the accident, and, in addition to feeling a heavy burden of loss for the love of my life, there rests a heavy burden of guilt. My heart sinks beneath the cumbersome weight upon it—I know the accident was my fault. Jack was not just my loss but a loss to everyone who loved him, especially Poppy. Theirs was a unique and immediate friendship, two kindred spirits bridged between young and young at heart. Had Poppy secretly blamed me for what happened to Jack, like I do?

"C'mon, Ella, Nonna's waiting." Mom's voice, louder now, almost breaks through, but I don't answer, not before I glimpse the tips of Storybook Tree popping out from the far corner at the back of the house. Storybook Tree: the best part of growing up at the cottage as a little girl. For a moment, my legs are light and free from the earth, and I run, almost bouncing around the corner, and stop just short of it. I touch its smooth bark and rub my fingers along the curled edges. I am especially fond of this tree, named by our family for the great stories Poppy and Nonna used to tell us as we sat beneath it. To us, they were the best grandparents in the world.

Poppy built the cottage when they still lived in Buffalo, New York. It was a place where our family often gathered on summer weekends. I'll never forget the day the cottage became their official home. We now had them right at our fingertips. It's funny that, even though it became their home, we never stopped referring to it as "the cottage."

Under Storybook Tree, the adventures of "Ned and Jed" and the chronicles of "Lydia and Matilda" never grew old. As we grew, we'd read our own books under this tree, drifting to sleep in the middle of a warm summer day. But Storybook Tree was not just a spot to listen to stories. Everything sweet, special and important was shared beneath its branches. It's where we came to cry when we'd lost our dog, Duke; where the Ghost in the Graveyard counting began; where we held hands with significant others; and where intimate secrets were told.

Except for one secret. And I need to find it.

What was Poppy hiding in the cottage? What did I not yet know? Would the answers lie among the creeping myrtle and lavender leading to the tree? Were they hidden within the black-eyed Susans or the wispy Leyland cypress trees that scattered along its path? Or perhaps beneath the soft mulch at the foot of the tree where I stand just now?

A fresh breeze coming off of the lake takes up my long dark hair, swirling it about my face. I remove the strands from my eyes and refocus my thoughts. What was it Poppy said about that box the first time he mentioned it, just a few weeks before he passed?

"Hey, El. In case I forget, if there's ever an emergency or if something happens to me, there's a box in the cottage. I want you to find it. Only you."

Find it?

"Oh, sure," I had said. "What, are there diamonds or something in there?"

"It's worth more than diamonds—at least, to me."

I remember thinking, *What could be worth more than diamonds?* He never elaborated, never actually said he was serious. And I never asked. I thought he was being silly. Just being Poppy. Why hadn't he told me about the importance of the box then?

When Poppy's heart began to fail for the second time in his life, the whole family happened to be together for one of our last celebrations of the summer before kids went back to college and families went on vacations.

He'd grown weaker over the past few months but still maintained his usual routines, insisting on cooking dinners and entertaining. He seemed to be struggling, and I noticed that he was sweating a lot and out of breath. He and Nonna had decided a while back that, if his heart began to fail again, he would not go back to the hospital. The doctors said that, other than keeping him comfortable, there was nothing more they could do to improve the quality of his life without putting him at greater risk.

We had just finished dinner and Mom, Nonna, and Aunt Lena began collecting the dirty dishes. Poppy excused himself to go outside and get some air. I followed and spotted him sitting on the bench under Storybook Tree. His curly locks were wet and so was his shirt.

He looked worried, his face ashen. Instantly my stomach tightened, and I felt sick.

"Poppy?"

"Oh, Ella," he strained to say.

"Are you okay? Do you need something?"

"Just more time," he said with restrained emotion. I could not accept this answer. "Whatayagonna do." One of his most famous expressions.

"I can get you some water? Or … should I tell Nonna to call the doctor?"

"Maybe water, but no doctor." His face was drawn, sad.

"How 'bout I walk you back inside, so you can lie down."

"Abriella."

"Yes, Poppy?"

"You've grown to be such a beautiful young woman. You know how much Nonna and I love you. We're so proud of you."

Where was this going?

He gently took my hand, raised it to his lips, and kissed the back of it. Then he slowly brought our clasped hands down to his lap. My eyes fought back tears as I tried to listen to him speak.

"Life is funny, isn't it? We're given so much in life and we don't always appreciate what we have." His words became more labored. I wanted to stop him. Tell him that he was okay. That we were all going to be just fine. But I didn't do that because I wouldn't stop Poppy when he was sharing a piece of himself.

"El?"

"Yes?"

"Are you happy?" I knew he was referring to living without Jack. He'd kept a close watch on me ever since that stormy day.

"Yes, I'm happy, Poppy." Heavy tears rushed down my cheeks.

"I know you've had your share of trials. We all do," he said with downcast eyes. "But always try to be happy. Promise?"

"I promise." I turned and hugged him for a few minutes, not wanting to let go. Then I helped him up and we walked slowly, arm in arm, back to the cottage.

When we reached the back door, my mother's eyes caught mine and together we led Poppy to the sofa. We gave him water and a clean, dry shirt and covered his feet with a blanket while some of us gathered around him and others stayed close by. For the next hour we exchanged sweet words of love and gratitude with Poppy as sorrow filled our hearts and voices.

That's when he took my hand again, pulled me near, and whispered, "Find the box, Ella. It's real. It leads to …" His breaths became labored, his eyelids heavy, but still holding me close he muttered, "Watch who you trust." I swear I saw a slight smile in the corner of his mouth.

"I will." I choked back tears and leaned closer. "Where?"

He struggled to speak, his voice just above a whisper. I couldn't make out what he said. A tear gathered in the corner of his eye and traveled down his cheek.

"It's okay. I'll find it," I said. "I love you, Poppy." *Please don't go.* I kissed his moist forehead and felt his hand loosen. Then our sweet Poppy drifted off to sleep and didn't wake up.

Chapter 2

Hands gently press into my shoulders, and I jump as I'm pulled back to the present. I'm surprised to see Uncle Luca behind me and Aunt Lena at his side. I lean into their warm embrace and we stay like that for a couple minutes. Their scent of leather, tobacco, and pine immediately puts me at ease. They are my favorite aunt and uncle, which is no surprise since Uncle Luca is Poppy's brother and just like him in so many ways. Aunt Lena is a lot like Nonna, too, and she's often mistaken for her sister.

We step apart briefly and Uncle Luca's thumb brushes a tear from my eye. He studies my face and hugs me again.

"I know, Ella. I can't believe he's gone. I just can't." He steps back again, and his eyes are wet. "I know you don't want to go in there," he says, glancing at the cottage and back to me, "but we have to. Nonna needs us now."

I nod, and Aunt Lena dabs her eyes with a tissue. We walk together, arms linked, towards the back door of the cottage. But my thoughts quickly turn to the letter and the box, and I wonder if they know what I know.

We poke our heads through the doorway. Peering into the living room, I see a younger version of us in pajamas watching old black-and-white movies—me, my sister Liv, my brother Sal, Nonna and Poppy. I'd get excited as a child and even as an adult when I knew

I'd be seeing them that day. It was like opening a Christmas present each time; that's how full they made my heart feel. Poppy and Nonna knew my hopes, dreams, and fears and they never judged, always knowing when to listen and when to give advice. As I got older, they'd sometimes seek my advice and often shared old stories about our extended family that not many people knew. I felt special to be trusted with their "secrets." They were my grandparents, my closest friends and confidants.

Poppy had the most generous heart I'd ever known. His presence provided an immediate warmth, comfort, and joy when he walked in the room. He was filled with life and made everyone around him feel like the most important person in the world. Who would have thought that his wonderful heart would be the thing that failed him in the end? "El?" my mom calls again.

"I'm right here, Mom, coming in."

As soon as we walk into the living room, I'm hit with a rush of their scent, an aura that transcends all time and space. A combination of woodsy vanilla, cinnamon, musk, and sugar, perfectly blended, blankets the room. I want to bottle it. But an overwhelming panic fills my chest. I haven't stepped foot into the cottage since his last day.

I can't breathe.

"Nonna, I smell Poppy!"

"Is that a good thing or a bad thing?" my mom laughs. Poppy was well known for being a jokester, and passing gas was one of his favorite pastimes.

"Come here, honey." My mother wraps me in her arms. Nonna shuffles out from the kitchen and I break from my mom to hug her. She is smaller than I remember, and I feel her shoulder blades against my arms. I feel so sorry for her. What will she do now that she's alone? How do you spend fifty years with someone and then, just like that, they're gone?

Aunt Lena and Uncle Luca embrace us both, and then Uncle Luca disappears into the kitchen to pour a glass of wine, as he always does when he first arrives.

"I don't know where to begin," Nonna whispers. She walks to the back window and peers outside.

"Maybe we tackle one room at a time together?" Mom suggests.

I give my mother a look. I am not ready to pull apart the cottage.

"We're just doing a little at a time for now, El, so it's not so overwhelming. Nonna might stay with Aunt Lena and Uncle Luca for a while," she says, looking at Nonna, "until we can figure out what's happening with the cottage."

"What's happening with the cottage?"

"Don't think the worst, El. We'll talk more later."

I don't want to talk about it *ever* let alone later. I turn to Nonna who's staring out the window.

"Nonna, did Mom tell you that I have the scrapbooks and Poppy's oil paintings?"

She nods, holding her gaze on the lake.

"I'd like to hold on to them for a while ... if that's okay?"

"Yes, honey, of course it is," she says.

"Mind if I take the paintings and have them matted and reframed? You know, to honor him. I know it's something he would've loved, but never got the chance to do. I'd like to—"

"Of course, sweetie. That's very thoughtful of you."

"Okay, Nonna. I'll bring them right back as soon as possible." She turns and winks, smiling half-heartedly.

A lonely silence fills the house for the next several hours. Only the soft sounds of clothes being carefully placed into boxes and the tearing of packaging tape can be heard. An uncomfortable, nagging feeling returns to my stomach and I stop what I'm doing to walk about the cottage, imagining the best hiding spots for a secret box.

As I'm about to leave, Nonna asks me if I'd like to take another box of scrapbooks she'd found in Poppy's study. I hadn't remembered seeing them before and happily agree. She shows me to the study and motions to an uncovered box on the floor next to Poppy's desk. It's tightly packed with old photo albums, and I can tell by its bulging edges that it's heavy. I squat close to the floor and hoist it to my thighs, and then one more big lift at my waist. The musty smell emanating from the box makes me cough and sneeze. I slightly bend to kiss Nonna's cold little forehead and tell her I love her before heading to my car.

Holding the box awkwardly in my arms, I completely misjudge the swing of the trunk door. It bumps my chin, and I lose my balance and fall to the ground. The scrapbooks fly out of the box and smash into the ground, scattering several pages over the grass. I quickly sweep everything into my arms, hoping that Nonna isn't watching, and place the separated contents and the empty box into my trunk. I slam the trunk door and quickly glance at the cottage windows, thankful that the curtains are still drawn. As I step toward the driver's door, I notice a few papers remaining on the grass and pick them up—three small, white envelopes which appear to each have a letter inside. The envelopes are sealed and labeled: *Private. Do not open without permission.*

Chapter 3

The poplar trees bid farewell as I exit the neighborhood and turn onto West Lake Road. Their once brilliant colors are muted, and some have lost their leaves. I follow beside a new tree-lined path of oaks and pines until I'm just beyond the little village of Skaneateles.

When I no longer see the lake through the pines, I begin thinking of possible items that one might hide inside a box or in those private envelopes. My mind drifts to another realm, simultaneously shifting into autopilot. The next thing I know, I'm pulling into my driveway and I remember nothing of the drive.

Once the envelopes, loose pages, and photos are back inside the contorted box, I carry it into the house, barely making it to the coffee table before it buckles again. Hercules sniffs the box and wags his tail, waiting for me to kiss his head and scratch behind his ears. Then he runs off, grabs a toy, and tosses it into the air.

I pour a glass of Old Zin, fold my legs beneath me on the sofa, and pick up one of the envelopes labeled "private." Holding it to the light, I can scarcely see slanted, flowing loops through thin folds, and I contemplate opening it.

Do not open without permission.

Permission from whom? Does Nonna know about these? Did Poppy write them?

Not ready to disrespect his wishes just yet, I tuck them into the end table drawer and drag a scrapbook onto my lap. I sweep away the dust with my hand and a moldy smell rises into the air. The pages are stiff and crackle loudly with each turn. Old black-and-white photos of people I don't recognize are sprinkled throughout. Their faces hold the same somber expression blankly staring into the camera.

About halfway through, I begin to see pictures of who I think are Poppy and Uncle Luca as children. I remember seeing similar pictures in another photo album of Nonna's. As I turn the page, I notice a small edge of white paper poking out near the binding of the old leather scrapbook. I pinch the corner with the tips of my fingers and thumb, trying to grasp enough to pull it out. As I pull, the binding begins to shred and crumble, loosening it further, allowing me to place a firmer grip. I continue to draw it out carefully and soon a second corner emerges.

I drag one corner and then the other, back and forth, coaxing more of the paper from hiding. With some added effort, I am able to pluck a small tattered envelope from the confines of the scrapbook. I turn it over a few times in my hands before guiltily opening it.

Neatly tucked inside the envelope is a thin, folded piece of paper, a letter of some sort, about the size of a five-by-seven picture when fully opened. Over time, the folds had become permanent creases, keeping everything locked inside. The fragile note holds a neatly written and smooth, flowy handwriting with a full slant to the right, as if each individual letter had its own special purpose. It reads:

> *My Dearest Gianna,*
> *I cannot believe that, after all these years, I saw you today.*
> *I never thought it could be! I blame my father for what*

happened and I'm sorry that it did. I only wish that so much time hadn't elapsed, and we might have seen each other sooner. But I have no regrets. I will see you again soon.

    Love forever,
    Franco

Franco. Great-Papá? Was this him? But Cecelia was Great-Mamá's name, not Gianna. Or was that her nickname? Or was Gianna someone he knew before Great-Mamá?

I read it again several times before putting it back in the envelope. It snaps to its original fold with ease and I place it inside, curious as to why it's in the scrapbook and what it means. I examine the blank envelope. No address and no date. Nothing to provide further information. I feel as if I've exposed something that was not meant to be seen, like peeking on someone half-dressed or reading their diary. It makes me uneasy, but it also makes me want more.

The next album contains several familiar pictures of my grandparents visiting my sister, brother, and me on Christmas morning when I was probably seven or eight years old. We were in our newly remodeled living room and, although it was still uncarpeted, we were excited to have another room added to our modest home. I long for those dark paneled walls and wooden spindles in the background.

One picture shows a plump Nonna wearing her kerchief tied below her chin, puffy hair sticking out the sides, standing next to my grandfather with his thick head of salt-and-pepper hair slicked back. Both of them are wearing matching black leather jackets and dark pants. Lit cigarettes are held between their fingers, smoke trailing up, ashes falling down. Stylish and young at heart, they never seemed as old as they actually were. My sister, brother, and I stand among a sea of toys surrounding the tree. We have sleepy eyes, bedheads, and big smiles.

Those were the days.

I can still hear Poppy's deep, gentle voice filling the house with warmth while Nonna followed behind him. I knew even then that I was the luckiest girl alive to have grandparents like that.

It was Poppy who taught the lessons about life, He was always checking to make sure we didn't waste time worrying or being petty or angry; encouraging us to listen, love and forgive; to be happy.

"Ella," he'd say, "be happy."

"I am happy."

"You sure?"

"Yes, Poppy, I'm sure."

"Good."

He'd throw that question in every now and then. Maybe because he grew up with parents who struggled to make a good life when they first immigrated from Italy to the United States. They had very little money and it was difficult for my great-grandfather to find work. People were not always welcoming of Italians, and they had to be careful.

Poppy's father, Papá, was harsh and tough on Uncle Luca and him. Papá had unrealistic expectations of his boys, and nothing they did was ever good enough. He was extremely strict and often cruel toward his own family. With Poppy being the oldest, his punishments were the hardest. Any love Poppy sought he found with his mother when she wasn't busy. Because of all he endured, I know that Poppy learned to appreciate what he had in an unpredictable world.

Poppy was a cook during World War Two, which made perfect sense for someone who adored food and cooking for others. He talked very little about the war with us, only about the meals he made.

"The hardest part," he'd say with a catch in his voice, "was not being there when your mother was born. Boy, that was tough." He'd shake his head. "I didn't see my family until I was discharged from the army. Your mom only knew me from a picture she had in her room. She used to go up and hug the picture before bed each night." He paused for a long moment before he continued. "The hardest thing I had to do was leave your mom behind. I'll never forget it."

Next, I come across some pictures that remind me of a brief time when I was a teenager, when Poppy wasn't quite himself. He tried not to be different around us, but I could sense it. When I see pictures during that dark time, I see the suffering in his eyes—a desperate pleading. It's hard to look at them because that's not who he normally was.

I guess everyone struggles, and sometimes they just need time to work things out or have someone listen to them. I'm still learning, too. Looking through these photos, being caught within their memories, I feel a small measure of comfort at my decision to stay at the cottage with Poppy and Nonna at the beginning of the summer.

I reach for the letter I found in the scrapbook, the one between Franco and a mysterious Gianna. I open it and flatten it out on my lap. Next to that one, I place the suspicious letter I found right after Poppy's passing. I found it in the inner pocket of a very old suit jacket when Mom asked me to pull out a suit for the funeral. The jagged edge at the top suggests the greeting was torn off. I keep both letters near as I continue through the scrapbooks.

I didn't do it. Please believe me. I would never hurt her.
   Please don't waste your time on me when the real criminal
   is out there somewhere...
   ~F

My eyes hold each blink longer until they finally remain closed and I fall asleep in the middle of the third scrapbook. A few hours later, I awaken to the soft tapping of rain on the roof. I close the scrapbook and fall back asleep to the comforting, low, rolling thunder in the distance. My dreams consist of Poppy, letters, and war. A conversation about a box. And a woman I vaguely see in the shadows.

Chapter 4

Early the next morning, the sun's brilliance breaks through the parted curtains, and I wake up on the couch in a twisted position. My arms are high above my head and I try to rouse them from their deep slumber. Soon a slight tingling charges through my fingertips, and finally, movement, slowly coming to life again. The scrapbook on my lap had fallen to the floor. I pick it up along with a few loose pictures that had scattered across the floor and set them on the table next to the envelope. A question keeps repeating over and over in my mind: Why would a letter be carefully hidden inside a scrapbook? I want to ask Nonna or my mom.

Watch whom you trust.

The doorbell rings and my heart skips a beat. I'm so jumpy today. I walk past the paintings and cautiously sneak up to the window to peer through a crack in the curtains. I'm relieved to see my best friend, Jamie, waiting at the door holding a bouquet of pink peonies—my favorite. I cry at the sight of her. We hug each other tightly and then she hands me the fragrant flowers. I walk toward the kitchen to get a vase as she removes her hat, loosens her jacket, and heads to the living room eyeing the paintings as she enters. She walks over to the paintings lying against the chair, and then she turns toward the albums strewn across the table. She glances at me with a strange expression.

"What is it?" I say.

"What's all this?" she says, motioning to the items.

"Oh, just some of Poppy's things. Reframing some paintings for Nonna today." I motion nonchalantly toward them.

Jamie nods and smiles, "Maybe I'll come back another time, then?"

"No, it's okay. You just got here. Stay."

"It's okay, El." She smiles, placing her hand on my knee. "You get back to what you were doing. You need that right now. I just wanted to check on you. I'll come by tomorrow and stay longer. Sound okay?"

Jamie is good at always knowing what I need, especially when it comes to needing space. She was right there with me through it all with Jack. There were many times when I needed her and many when I needed to be alone. She always knew. But she has reason to worry, and I know that's what she's doing right now, because I made terrible choices and had no coping skills during that sad time when I refused to let go of Jack.

Her eyes become fixed on the letters lying open on the table. She walks over to it and I meet her there.

"What's this El?" She picks it up, but I snatch it out of her hand.

"It's nothing," I snap. "I'll show you later."

Her face wrinkles and then she stares at her feet.

"I will. Just not right now," I say.

"Promise?"

"Promise."

"Okay," she smiles. "Well, just wanted to stop by and give you a hug." She reaches her arms around me and I do the same.

****

Each oil painting has a distinct life of its own. Poppy had a special gift of noticing life's beautiful moments and, whenever possible, he'd capture it in a photograph so he could recreate it in a painting. He'd spend hours at his easel, his mind captivated in the scene, lost within each stroke. Brush against canvas. Colorful acrylics swirling and dancing, coming to life. A story waiting to be told.

Most of Poppy's paintings were displayed in his home, and some were given as gifts to grateful family members. His warm, creamy, golden earthy tones—greens, browns, and hints of orange—were common colors among his paintings. Sometimes he'd meticulously shadow and shade charcoals and black, providing emotion and depth in his scenes. Poppy's father had also loved to paint, which was the only thing they had in common.

One particular painting of a young woman always enchanted me. She stared off into the distance, her hat falling slightly onto her shoulders, the soft, creamy ribbon still tied in a bow beneath her chin. Deep, brown, mysterious eyes held a pensive gaze at something unknown. Her shoulder-length, unruly brown hair loosely caught behind the ribbon except for one piece curled against her cheek. I asked Poppy who this beautiful woman was, and he said she was just a woman he saw one day and he decided to paint her. I always wondered if he knew her.

A beautiful winery nestled in the center of an expansive vineyard catches my attention next. I lean it against the wall admiring the lush landscaping surrounding the winery. A group of tall, green cypress trees border one side, and thick bushes, shrubs, and flowers surround the rest. Rows of leafy grapevines stand before the vineyard and deep green rolling hills lie behind. You could get lost in a vineyard like this.

I feel along the edges of the frame for a loose edge. I wiggle the edges slightly, back and forth until one edge begins to ease. I pry it off gently and set it aside, similarly working my way around the rest of the frame. As the last edge comes off, a piece of paper comes with it, floating like a feather to the ground. Another small envelope like the one from the scrapbook. I quickly open it and read the note. Other than a few faded letters lost in the creases, it's mostly legible.

Franco,

I can't believe it's really you! Five minutes more and our paths would not have crossed. I know this must mean we're meant to be together. If only timing had been different for us years ago. If only our parents could have stayed friends, things might have turned out differently. But I'm happy that we've found each other now rather than never.

All my love,

Gianna

5 May 1917

1917 . . . What year were my great grandparents married? Perhaps Great-Mamá's nickname was Gianna? Why was this letter hidden within the painting of the vineyard? Was it something Great-Papá did to remember special moments? Or was there something else? He and Gianna obviously knew each other, but in what capacity? I wonder how they found each other and why they were separated. I dive into the next two paintings to see if they harbor secret letters, too.

I move methodically from painting to painting, loosening, unbinding, and exposing, until all paintings stand before me naked. Secrets written on paper, folded and hidden after all these years, now revealed. I'm dumbfounded by what lies in front of me, not quite sure of what it means or its connection to the other letter or the box. Or Poppy.

Another letter is nestled in a painting of a majestic golden castle built into a mountain. Hundreds of steps extend from its base and climb in a zigzag path to the top, resting on the edge of a sparkling blue sea overlooking sand and ocean.

My dear Franco,

Promising you my love and devotion means more than I can express. You're right, we don't need a priest to bless and secure our love and what is in our hearts. I want to be with you every day, but I fear that people will talk. I think they already are.

But I can't deny that my mind is troubled and fights against my heart sometimes. I have some regret for what I'm doing, but mostly sadness that I'm trapped in a life I no longer want or deserve with him. I long only for you. I often wonder, if we hadn't moved from the neighborhood all those years ago, maybe things would be different for us. I'm torn in two. I will see you again at our special place on Friday evening.

Always my love,

Gianna

I quickly find myself at the end of the letter, wanting more, curious to know what happened all those years ago that led Gianna's family to move from the neighborhood. What other life did she have and not want anymore?

I unearth the next letter from behind the painting of a gondolier rowing a gondola over placid blue-green water. The gondola sails toward a quaint walking bridge stretching above the water, connecting a vibrant red building with an emerald green one. The water's path curves left towards other colorful buildings, shadows falling on them as they sail.

Gianna-

Forgive me. I didn't mean to leave so quickly. I'm confused and emotional. Happy yet very worried. I've always wanted to be a father, and to have a child with you is beyond my happiest dreams. But now what do we do? We can't be together in the way we want to. And in a few weeks, I must leave for training for the war. I know that our fate is to be together somehow, but every obstacle is in our way! I love you and no one else. I long for and already miss our afternoons sailing on the canal. I pray I see you again before I go. Leave your letter under the rock this time so it doesn't blow away!

All my love,

Franco

A relentless ringing launches me from the gondola back to my living room. I try to make sense of it and realize there's someone at my front door. From where I'm standing, I see Jamie's car parked on the road and I'm relieved it's not my mother.

I bring her up to speed on everything, starting with what Poppy said about the box and the first note I found. I show her all of the letters—the ones from the scrapbooks and the ones from the paintings. I watch her closely. She scratches her head and starts to say something, but then stops herself.

What is she thinking? Watch whom you trust.

She asks me to place all of the letters side by side, and together we attempt to link them into a timeline. We discuss why the letters might have been written and how Franco and Gianna might have met. What were the unwritten things happening in their lives? There was so much I didn't know about my great-grandparents.

"Franco was headed for World War One, so these letters were written just before he left." I look at Jamie and she nods, so I continue. "Which makes sense, because this letter from Gianna," I hand it to Jamie, "has the year 1917 written below her name. So, Franco might be my great-grandfather, and he must've been assigned to the war toward the end, right?"

Jamie examines the letter, squinting as she reads. Then she lays it on the table and gently presses the paper to smooth out its wrinkles. She looks at me, still squinting.

"You said the date under Gianna's name was 1917?"

"Yes. Why?"

"Because I don't think that's what this says. Look." She rests her finger just below the date. "Do you see it?" She moves the letter under the lamp and smooths out the part near the date. "That's not a one." She backs away and lets me in closer. "It's a three."

As Jamie presses the paper flat near the date, I see it. It is a three, not a one. We look up from the letter at the same time.

"So it's not 1917. It's 1937," she says.

The lines of the number three had been lost in the creases, perfectly folded, hiding its curves for many years, and when finally opened, it presented itself as a one instead— a fat, smudged one. I had missed it.

"So, if Franco was going to war," she continues, "and it wasn't World War One, he must have been preparing for World War Two, right? But didn't you say your Great-Papá's name was Franco?" She glances at me, her brow furrowed. "Isn't he the only Franco we know?"

I swallow hard and sit down to grasp the shocking epiphany. It makes sense and doesn't all at the same time.

"What is it, El?"

"I'm trying to wrap my head around something."

"Around what?"

"Poppy."

My chest begins squeezing in, pushing the air from my lungs. My head swirls, and I steady myself against Jamie.

"Oh my God, Jamie. It's Poppy."

"It's okay, El," she says. "Are you okay?"

"No. Jamie. It has to be Poppy."

She scrunches her brow, still not connecting it.

"Franco *is* Poppy," I say.

"What? Poppy's name was Salvatore."

"Yes. Salvatore F. Perri. The 'F' stands for Franco."

Her jaw drops, continuing to listen.

"Most people called him Sal. Only those he grew up called him Franco."

"Are you saying what I think you're saying?" she says.

"You say it. Tell me what you think I'm thinking."

"If I'm following correctly," she says, "Franco—Poppy—was in love with a woman he grew up with named Gianna. She got pregnant with his baby right before he went off to war. World War Two."

"Yes," I say, "but that's not all."

She tilts her head.

"Well," I continue, "I'm still not sure about the timing of things, like when he married Nonna and when he met Gianna."

"Do you think he was unfaithful to Nonna?"

"I don't know. I assumed Nonna was the love of his life. And now I'm confused." I close my eyes. "I can't imagine he'd do that, but I don't know." I contemplate whether or not to show her the letters that were inside the "Private, Do Not Open Without Permission" envelopes. She's watching me and probably knows I'm hiding something. I sigh and hand them to her.

Dear Franco,

I don't know how to say this. I went to check on Gianna as I've done for you several times before, and this time, I couldn't find her. I stood at the edge of her neighbor's yard in the same spot that gives me a clear view to the living room, but she wasn't there. As soon as the fiancé left, I snuck up to the window, but she was nowhere in sight. I did the three-knock signal, but she didn't come to the door. No sounds, no sight of her or the baby. Something's not right. I'll write again when I know more. Please pray for her safety!

    Sincerely, your brother

    Luca

Jamie's eyes grow wide as she reads the next.

Dear Mama,

    You of all people know better than anyone that I would never do what they are saying I did. Yes, we did meet secretly while I was away. I know it was a risk to do that, but I had to before they moved me again. I love her so much and, although it pains me deeply, I accept where our lives are leading us. I know I can't have her the way I want to, but I would not have ever harmed her in any way. I pray she's okay and hiding somewhere safe. Someone knows something. I wish it were me. Please hug my baby and tell me if you hear anything at all.

    Love, your son

    Franco

First Jamie says nothing, only stares at me, shocked. She takes a deep breath before she speaks.

"I can't believe it," she says. "Do you think he did something to Gianna?"

"No way. But something's not right. Why would Poppy hide

these letters, or even keep them, for that matter?"

"Maybe there's something unresolved? Something he's trying to figure out?" Jamie says. "Or maybe he did do something. Maybe it was unintentional."

"If something bad happened to Gianna, there's no way Poppy could be involved. It's not in his nature."

"We all have secrets, El. Sometimes people do things in a fit of rage and regret it for the rest of their lives." Her eyes catch mine.

"Well, not Poppy." I look away as the knot in my stomach tightens.

Chapter 5

A drive that should have easily been twenty minutes from start to finish soon becomes forty. Impatience rises as every driver who steals the road in front of me drives ten miles per hour below speed limit all the way to the cottage. I tail some for a few seconds before guiltily dropping back. *What if it's an elderly person?*

Butterflies race through my stomach as I race down the last stretch of road before turning onto West Lake Road. I feel badly for the way things were left between Jamie and me, but she shouldn't have pushed it, telling me that Poppy might have done something in a fit of rage. How can she think that? She's probably hurt that I've been avoiding her for the last three days. But I'm not avoiding just her lately, I'm avoiding everyone.

I pull into the driveway, barely shifting into park, and bolt to the front door with the car still running.

"Mom?" I swing open the door. "Can we talk?"

"Well, I've been trying to do that, but you're ignoring my texts. Everything okay?"

"Sorry. Yes. Just want to ask you something." I pinch myself. *Slow down.* "How's Nonna?"

"I don't hear from you in three days, and then you enter in a panic to ask me how Nonna is?" Her arms fly wildly as she speaks. "As expected, Ella. We still have a lot to do here." She motions toward a wall of boxes. "Can you move these to the porch, please? They're ready."

"Sure." I shuffle to the boxes. *I should be helping more.* I kick off my flip flops, grab a box, and carry it to the front porch, relishing the feeling of the soft, worn-in wooden planks beneath my feet, keenly aware of the creaky ones and the differences among them. Poppy was keenly aware as well.

Once, when Jamie and I were teenagers, we tried to sneak out of the cottage after everyone had gone to bed. We were determined to go swimming in the lake, although it was forbidden after dark. I tiptoed from my bed to the bedroom door, being very careful to step lightly, hardly breathing as I did. The moment I entered the hallway and gently pressed the ball of my foot onto the floor, it let out a tiny, barely audible creak which seemed to echo in the silence, completely giving us away.

"Abriella?"

I stopped immediately. Being called by my full name meant I was in trouble. I panicked and fought with myself about answering or ignoring Poppy. We made some silly excuse about getting something to eat and scurried back to bed, knowing that sneaking out of the cottage would not be attempted again.

I slide on the soft floor into the living room and see the curly tops of Nonna's hair from behind the sofa. She looks so small napping there, curled into a little ball, lost among the cushions. A small afghan covers her, gently rising and lowering to the rhythm of her breath. When she begins to snore, I know she's in a deep slumber, and I take the opportunity to talk with my mother.

I wander to where she's kneeling. She's slightly bent over a pile of clothes she's sorting while muttering something under her breath. I squat beside her and she looks up. I smile, pick up a shirt, and fold it. We sit side by side, quietly folding shirts for a few minutes before I say what's on my mind.

"What do you know about Poppy's oil paintings?"

She places a pile of shirts into a box, pressing down firmly with both hands, and looks at me puzzled.

"What do you mean?"

"Is there something significant about them? Or why he painted them?"

"I'm sure they have some sort of significance. You know they weren't all painted by Poppy, though, right? Great-Papá painted some. Why do you ask?" She studies me.

"Just wondering." I say. "So, there's nothing specific that you know about them? They don't represent anything important?"

She stares for a moment.

"I don't think so. I think it's as simple as something interesting or beautiful caught Poppy's eye and he wanted to paint it. You should keep a couple for yourself if you want." She closes the flaps of the box and guides the packaging tape across the seam. "I'm sure Nonna won't mind." She looks at me with droopy eyes, soft wrinkles forming at the edges.

"Actually, the beautiful woman with the hat falling on her shoulders is my favorite," I say. "I don't know why, but I've always loved it. Always wondered who she was. Was she anyone special?"

"That's a pretty one." She smiles, sliding a shirt off the hanger and folding it. "But I don't think it's anyone in particular."

"Mom?"

"Yes?" She slides another shirt from its hanger.

"Do you know anyone named Gianna?"

She straightens her shoulders.

"Gianna," she repeats, twirling her hair. "I don't recall anyone by that name." She turns her head to see if Nonna is still asleep. "Why do you ask?"

"Well, when I took the frames off of Poppy's paintings, the

strangest thing happened." She nods and turns to face me. "Each painting had an envelope." Her eyes widen. "The first one had a letter from a Franco to someone named Gianna, and in another one there was a letter from Gianna to Franco." Her jaw drops as I continue. "Franco was Papá's name, right?" I ask, waiting to see if she'll tell me that Poppy was also referred to as Franco. She nods but says nothing. "So, I'm guessing he's the one who wrote the first letter? But who is Gianna? Do you know?"

Not one word about Poppy.

"That's odd." She shakes her head. "I have no idea." One brow arches. "Where are the letters now?"

"At my house. I'll show you if you want to see them."

"Did you bring any with you?"

"No. I thought it was better to leave them home."

My mom continues twirling the ends of her hair in quick, smooth loops around her index finger.

"If Nonna goes to Aunt Lena's tonight, come over for dinner. I'll show you then."

"Dinner sounds good, but Ella," she pauses, "don't say anything to Nonna about this. She has enough on her mind. It'll confuse her."

"Okay," I say, noticing that something is off in the tone of her voice.

"And I think it's best to wait before removing the frames from the rest of the paintings."

"Why?"

"Just wait 'til I come over."

"What are you girls talking about?" Nonna says in a crackly voice. Sheepishly she sneaks around the corner and shuffles up to us. How long had she been there?

"Just about what Ella's making for dinner," Mom blurts. "You took a nice little nap, didn't you?"

"Who, me? I wasn't sleeping. Just resting my eyes." Nonna always says she's just resting her eyes. Sometimes her snoring would get so loud, we'd have to turn up the volume on the TV. She'd never admit to being asleep, even if she dozed off right in front of you. I'd say, "Nonna, I was right here and saw you sleeping." She'd say, "Nope. I was awake the whole time." And don't ever challenge her on that because she wins every time.

I promise my mother I'll come back tomorrow and help some more. A small feeling of envy rises toward Liv and Sal for living farther away and not having to share in the burden of packing up Poppy's life, angry they're not here to examine the letters with me. They promised they'd move back to Skaneateles after Mom and I so we could all be closer to Poppy and Nonna, especially after his heart attack, but they never did. It was always something—Liv's promotion, Sal's new girlfriend. Time passed and their roots deepened. Now they're there and I'm here.

"I love you, Nonna." I lean down and hug her frail little frame.

"Thank you, honey. I love you, too."

My mother gives me a reminding look and I shoot a reassuring look back, right through my lying eyes.

Chapter 6

The paintings rest against the sofa, stacked one behind the other. I give a fleeting look in their direction but steer myself away, focusing instead on my pressing mentorship papers screaming loudly at me. I should have already submitted them for the residency program at the hospital. My stomach flips at the possibility of losing an opportunity to interview with Dr. Weiss. *This is important to you, right?* Procrastination is both my friend and my enemy. I hope I haven't waited too long.

I loosen my jacket and let it drop to the floor before releasing Hercules from his crate. He jumps and nips at my heels, grunting and sneezing and licking my hands, before unleashing a chorus of howls to welcome me home. My sweet two-year-old German shepherd puppy, given as a gift from Liv and Sal after the accident. He was a rescue from West Virginia who needed love and companionship, much like his new owner. Let's face it—he was the one who did the real rescuing.

He watches as I take the roast from the fridge and slide it into the oven and then follows me to my desk, circling a few times before settling on a position beside me. I sort through the paper clutter, paying overdue bills and completing forms for my residency while frequently watching the clock. *Stay focused.* I leave a message at the hospital and schedule a reminder in my phone to follow up tomorrow. I check the clock again. It's 4:30 p.m., already two hours since I got home, and I haven't done a thing with the paintings yet. Still no word from my mother about dinner; maybe she isn't coming.

I pick up the painting in front, size it up, turn it around, and begin to quickly loosen and pull off the frame, side by side. And just like the first two, tucked within is a letter, another piece of a faraway life. Separately, the letters reveal strong emotion, connection, and love, but together, a story is beginning to unfold in bits and pieces. It's an incomplete story of increasing complexity and uncertainty, and I know there is far more beyond these written words. I read each letter again, beginning with the first, hoping to link them and fill in the missing information. But the doorbell rings, distracting me for a moment. When I answer, it's my mother and she has Nonna with her. And it's only five o'clock.

My heart races, thinking about the mess in the living room, and my mother will know that I disregarded her request of not proceeding with the letters. *It was just one request, El. You can't even do that.* I lead them straight to the kitchen and hastily set a quick snack of cheese, crackers, and wine on the counter, telling them to help themselves—that I'd be right back. I just have to run to the bathroom.

I make two quick trips from the living room to my bedroom with the paintings, frames, and letters and place them on my bed, swiftly closing the door behind me. A loud screeching noise echoes through the hallway and I realize it's the garage door opening. *What now?* I'm surprised and relieved to see Jamie walking through the door.

She places her jacket on a chair and greets Mom and Nonna with a hug. She stops right before me, looks me up and down, and stares into my eyes.

"Everything okay? You seem strange right now and it's freaking me out. And don't lie, 'cause I'll know."

"No, I'm good."

I give her a warning look and pour a glass of wine. I suggest we move to the living room while the roast in the oven finishes cooking, carrying the wine and cheese with me. Knowing it will take my mom a few minutes to get there with Nonna, I grab Jamie's hand and quickly lead her to the sofa.

"I know you've been avoiding me," she says. "I'm sorry for upsetting you." She places her arm around me.

"Thanks," I say, and lean in closer. "I found another letter." I glance up and see Nonna ambling toward the kitchen doorway.

"Really?"

"Yes." I peer again at Nonna.

"Where?"

"Another painting." She stares at me. "My mom doesn't want me to check the other paintings or scrapbooks for more but it's too late.

"Why doesn't she?"

I glance up and Nonna and Mom are almost at the sofa. "Not sure. Can't get into it now." I stand and help Nonna settle into the firmer part of the sofa and bring her a blanket before she can ask.

My mother hesitates for a moment, eyeing me before sitting next to Nonna. She scans the room cautiously and places her wine glass on the coffee table.

"How's my little Nonna?" I say, turning towards her and placing my hand on hers. "I'm glad you're here. Not seeing Aunt Lena tonight?"

"No, honey, she's helping Uncle Luca put away their patio furniture for the fall. It's a big job, you know," she says. "They still have each other." She looks at the floor and mutters something about wishing the Lord would take her now. I pretend not to hear, not wanting to encourage that discussion.

"Yes. Thank God they have each other," Mom says, putting her arm around Nonna. "And you will always have us." She smiles.

My mother's long, dark, wavy hair perfectly frames her face as the waves cascade around her neck and shoulders, just past the golden locket she always wears. I remember how devastated she was when it first went missing a few years ago. She's had that necklace since she was a little girl and said that Great-Mamá had given it to her. A few months later, it was finally found, oddly enough, at Aunt Lena's and Uncle Luca's.

Aunt Lena said she was sweeping the floor and something sparkly caught her eye just outside the kitchen, near the mudroom. After a closer look, she realized it was the necklace my mother had lost. It must have fallen the last time she visited. The necklace probably wasn't fully clasped and came loose as she slid off her coat. Her coat must have taken the necklace with it before releasing it to the floor, further becoming obscured by the ensemble of other coats and shoes that lined those walls. I remember Uncle Luca throwing a fit over the mess of coats and shoes in the mudroom, shouting and reprimanding Aunt Lena for not keeping it neat. He must have been upset that something so valuable to my mother could become lost in his house. It was one out of only a handful of times that I ever saw him appear irrational and lose his temper. All the while, my mother was convinced it was somewhere in our house and looked for it every day, determined to find it. Not a day has gone by since then that she hasn't worn that necklace.

Surprisingly, neither of us bring up the paintings until after dinner and a couple glasses of wine, when she blurts out, "So tell me about those letters you found."

My mother needs no transitions, she gets right to the point. Apparently, she must have had a change of heart about telling Nonna about the letters. I look at my mother, then at Nonna, wondering if we're really going to discuss this in front of her. Nonna appears not to notice what we're talking about. Jamie attempts to change the subject, asking Nonna if she can borrow her sugar cookie recipe. I slip off to my room to get only the first two letters.

I quietly wander back to the living room and sit down on the sofa next to Jamie. She's engaged in a conversation with my mom and Nonna who are sitting across from us. I wait for a break in the conversation while holding both letters, folded tightly in my sweaty palms. They stop talking and turn toward me, and I tell them not to stop on my account. But they insist on keeping their attention on me.

I take a deep breath and begin to explain how I found the first letter in the scrapbook and the second one in the vineyard painting. My hands shake as I take out the letter from Franco, handing it open to my mother. While she reads, I slide the letter from Gianna beside it, so she can smoothly move on to the next one. She looks up at me with her right eyebrow raised.

"Gabby, what's she looking at?" Nonna asks my mother.

"Remember the other day when you gave me those scrapbooks you found in the study?" I say. Nonna nods. "Well, while I was looking at all the pictures, I noticed a little corner of paper sticking out near the binding. I thought it was a picture that somehow got stuck, so I tried to pull it out, and when I finally got it, I realized it was a letter."

"A letter? From whom?"

"It's written from someone named Franco."

"Franco." She pauses. "Your Great-Papá? Why would we have a letter from Great-Papá in our scrapbook?"

"I don't know."

"Who was it written to?"

"It was written to a woman and she wrote back."

"Maybe it's a letter from Great-Papá to Great-Mamá? What's the woman's name?"

"Her name is Gianna," I say softly, hoping she doesn't catch it.

"Oh? That makes no sense." Nonna's skin pales. My mom and Jamie remain quiet, which is very unusual for both.

My mom raises Gianna's letter in her hands. "This letter is dated 1917. Gianna had to have been someone Papá knew before he married Mamá."

Some of the coloring begins to come back into Nonna's cheeks, but her puzzled expression remains. I don't tell her it was really written in 1937, not 1917, and shoot a quick look at Jamie hoping she'll do the same.

"Can I see?" Nonna asks, pointing to the letters. My mother slides them over and Jamie peeks over Nonna's shoulder, reading along in silence.

"I don't understand. What do they mean?" Nonna looks up and I notice the wrinkles around her eyes.

"I don't know, Nonna. But maybe I can find out."

"No. El, just put them away. It's in the past. It doesn't matter anymore," Mom says, watching Nonna.

"*I* think it matters. Why would they be hidden? Maybe there's a connection to the paintings or something important we're not aware of," I say.

"If they were hidden, they weren't meant to be found," my mother snaps.

"Connection to what?" Nonna raises her hands.

"I don't know. I keep thinking about a box that Poppy mentioned. I never paid much attention before. I thought the box was something metaphorical that he was using in some philosophical way—you know how he does that sometimes when he's trying to tell us a message about life? And now I can't stop thinking about the box. And then he mentioned it again right before he died. What if there's a box we need to find? What if these letters mean something? What if we're supposed to do something with them?"

No one says a word. They stare at me as if I'm a stranger they've never seen before. "I feel like I'm being pulled toward something, but I don't know what it is. I can't explain it. I know I'm supposed to find these letters. But what do they mean?"

"I think that's enough," Mom interrupts, glancing at Nonna and glaring at me. "The only thing you should be pulled toward is your residency. These are old letters, written forever ago. A locked box could be anything. It doesn't mean they're connected."

"Doesn't mean they're not."

For a moment, our eyes stay locked on each other.

"Ella, let it go. They're from another lifetime and not something to waste your time on when there are so many other things to deal with right now." She looks at Nonna who's beginning to fall asleep. "We should get going."

At the door she hugs me and whispers, "Please don't search the other paintings."

"I won't," I lie.

As the tail lights disappear into the night, I disappear to my room, pulling Jamie along with me. I show her everything and she is equally as intrigued as I am.

"Why didn't you tell them about the year?" Jamie asks.

"I don't know. I felt funny when I saw Nonna's expression, like she was relieved that it was 1917 and not 1937."

"Do you think you'll tell her eventually?"

"Probably not, unless I discover something that changes that."

Later that night, my mom calls to tell me why she's been acting so peculiar about the letters. She remembers the name Gianna, although she can't remember why. She says there were rumors at one time that Great-Papá had an affair with someone while married to Great-Mamá and that Great-Mamá was forced to raise an illegitimate son as if he were her own. That son could have been Poppy. She said Poppy always felt he wasn't meant to have been born into the family he was born into, although he loved them no matter what. But he would have been devastated if those rumors were true. She also said Nonna played a big part in helping Poppy believe that he was meant to be where he was and that the past didn't matter.

When I asked my mother if she believed the rumors, she said she didn't, and neither should I.

She demanded that I drop it, but I just can't. I intend to search for more letters, and I'm determined to find that box as soon as possible.

Chapter 7

The morning rain falls soft and steady, gently tapping against the window. It descends upon the thirsty earth, darkening its soil and scattering the birds from its grasses. I close my eyes and listen, allowing its rhythm to relax me, until a gust of wind shakes the glass, startling me. Soon soft drops come harder and faster, lights flicker and thunder claps. *It's okay. You're fine. Breathe. It's just a storm.* I draw the curtains closed and move from the window back to the sofa, shaking my head, shaking away the sadness from that day with Jack. The last day we were together. A cumbersome weight of loss and sorrow presses upon me relentlessly and I feel myself slipping away again, but I don't allow it to take me. *Stay busy.*

I pull the letters from my drawer and read them once more, trying to imagine a younger Poppy and Gianna spending time together among the beautiful hills of Italy. I pour over the old photographs again to see if anyone resembles what I imagine Gianna to look like, but there are very few photos taken back when Poppy was younger. And the ones I do find are hard to decipher—posed photographs and serious faces, memories trapped in black and white. Similar haircuts and clothing worn by all the boys make it hard to tell them apart, and the same is true of the girls.

The storm is relentless for the next three days, and I have no desire to leave my house. I study the paintings, letters, and old photographs until they're permanently etched in my brain and part of me. I think over and over again about the box. Poppy must have mentioned where it was, and I hadn't paid attention. Why wouldn't he have told me where it was? *Of course he did. Think. What was it he said the first time he mentioned it? Get to the cottage and find out.*

****

Driving down the long, twisted roads to the cottage reminds me of simpler times. As a little girl, I'd fall asleep in the backseat on our way to visit Poppy and Nonna. I'd sense the familiar stops and turns upon entering West Lake Road and into their neighborhood. Half awake, I'd hear wheels pressing into concrete, then a gradual slowing of the car until, finally, it stopped, just as it does now.

Listening to the soft hum of the idling car, I think about those last few moments with Poppy and Nonna. Had there been something I missed? Why didn't he tell me more about it? Was he waiting for me to engage in the conversation? Maybe he was testing me.

I wander through the spongy grass back to Storybook Tree. A brisk cold and heavy dampness hang in the late afternoon air, and the wind flips my jacket open. Dark gathering clouds roll in from the lake and I contemplate racing to the door to beat the returning rain. For a moment I see myself, younger, with my sister and brother playing in a warm, humid rainstorm, chasing each other around Storybook Tree, daring to stay out in the storm. We loved to feel the ground shake with each loud BOOM, ignoring our mom's distant shouts to "get in here right this minute or you'll get struck by lightning!"

I dash to the back door to get out of the rain, unlock it, and step inside, thankful that Nonna isn't home yet. Lately, she spends her days with Aunt Lena and Uncle Luca, coming home after dinner and going right to bed. I call Jamie and ask her to meet me at the cottage and help me find that box.

The storm passes quickly, and soon a faded setting sun casts a dim glow upon the cottage while the last of the dark clouds sail away and early evening settles in. I flip the switch to the gas fireplace and sit up close watching the dancing flames grow higher and wilder.

Mesmerized by the flames, I contemplate what Poppy expected from his life. I wonder if he regretted being with Gianna, or maybe he never stopped longing for her. Then I think about Nonna. Who did he love more? I want to know what happened in the moments between each letter. He always told us to live in the moment and appreciate time. I wonder if he was able to do that.

I ponder the concept of time and how obscure it is. As a little girl, I wanted to rush through life and be an adult. I wanted to drive, work and be independent, but time moved too slowly for me. Now, I find myself wishing time would slow down, and I long for the past. I long to go back and change the things I regret. I'd stop myself from getting in the car on that stormy night. How different life might be now. Poppy said it wasn't my fault. He said everything would be okay and eventually time would heal my heart. I wanted to believe him, but I had my doubts, even to this day. Did his wisdom come from personal experience? Had he, too, unintentionally hurt someone from his past and regretted it? *Stop thinking like that.*

While waiting for Jamie, I ruminate on these thoughts until a light at the end of the cottage catches my eye. A light coming from the study. Nonna hadn't stepped foot in that room since Poppy passed, but maybe she finally decided to go in there. Nonna and Poppy never left the study light on when they'd leave the cottage. The only lights they kept lit when they were away were the end table lamp in the living room and the stove light in the kitchen.

Some people in my family might think this is a sign that Poppy is trying to contact us, but I'm not so sure about that. In my mind, I begin to wonder if someone else has been in there. I take a walk to the end of the hallway and stop at the partially opened door to the study.

A fragrance of leather and paper mixed with Poppy's scent escapes through the door and pulls me in. This is no ordinary study of desk and simple bookshelves. Instead, it looks, smells, and feels like a little old-fashioned library. Poppy would sit in the middle of the room at his enormous mahogany desk, facing out toward the door, as if he were king of his castle. Thick, dark bookshelves stood tall against the walls behind him. Hundreds of books of all genres filled the shelves, some of which he'd read and others he'd never get to. Nonna's knickknacks are purposefully scattered among the books. A small decorative globe, a green ceramic pear, and a bowling trophy are thoughtfully placed throughout the shelves. I spent hours here in this room as a child, reading on the soft shag rug while Poppy worked at his desk. Now, though, I see the study in a different light and with a different purpose.

I pull open the skinny center drawer of Poppy's desk for a quick look. Calculator, notepad, envelopes. The two side drawers contain nothing unusual. Files, papers, manuals. No boxes.

"Ella! You started without me!"

I jump, relieved to see it's Jamie.

"Are you looking for the box?"

I explain to Jamie how I noticed a light was on in the study and how unusual that was for Nonna to leave it on, let alone the fact that she hadn't been in this room since Poppy passed away. As I'm explaining all of this, a thought occurs that perhaps someone else might be looking for the box. Maybe I'm not the only one who knows about it. *Now you're being paranoid.*

The study was Poppy's private domain, a place where he sought peace and refuge when he needed it. A place where he did his paperwork, worked on paintings and drawings. A place where he would read for hours. Although I feel a little guilty going through his personal belongings, it really makes the most sense to start in this room.

"How 'bout if I start on one end and you start on the other, and we meet in the middle back at the desk?" Jamie says. "What exactly does this box look like?"

"I'm not sure."

"Big box? Small? Colored? Metal? What kind of box are we talking about?"

"No idea. Poppy just said to look for a box."

"And you're sure he wants you to find it?"

"Right before he died, he said, 'Find the box.' And he mentioned it a couple other times over the years. All this time the box has been a real thing. Why didn't he just tell me? He said although there's no money inside, it's worth more than gold to him. Those words exactly." He also said to watch who I trust, but I knew I could trust Jamie.

"What do you think's in it, El?"

"I honestly have no idea." I thought about the beautiful missing Gianna and worried about people pointing fingers at Poppy. I was a little afraid of what I might find, but knew I had to.

Jamie searches the cupboards only to find office supplies, outdated Time magazines, old books, and lots of dust. Nothing unusual. I quickly scan the books on the shelves opposite the cupboards. Nothing noteworthy pops out from here. I do know, without a doubt, that I won't be satisfied until I pull out and examine each book and scour the whole room, every inch of it. I can't miss anything.

Over the next couple hours, we investigate hundreds of books, carefully lifting and replacing the knick knacks on all of the lower-level shelves. The rolling ladder often catches on the rail, but I manage to push it all the way to the edge of the wall where I first started. I begin a new search of all the top shelves, exploring each book, not stopping for anything—not a glass of water, not even to go to the bathroom.

Eventually, I pause at a special section in the center. The books on these shelves are extraordinary. Covered in thick, worn leather with frayed edges, they hold five-hundred to thousands of pages each. Books of kings, queens, and royal families, history, countries, and wars. They fascinated me as a child as they still do now. I affectionately called it "The Olden Days" section. A colorful combination of fiction and non-fiction books together in their own little domain created by my grandfather.

My index finger sweeps across the spines of each book as I read their titles aloud, stopping when I come to *An Italian's Journey*. I separate it from the others, place it on the desk, and hurry back to where I left off. I do the same with *The Coast of Italy*, *The Merchant of Venice*, and *The Name of The Rose*.

Jamie is silent, her eyes zigzagging as I go back and forth from shelves to desk over and over. She asks me why I chose these particular books.

"I've always loved these books," I tell her. "They're old, used, and enchanting."

She looks at me inquisitively.

"Your grandfather and Gianna met in Italy, right?"

I smile. "And for that reason, too." I don't say that an additional reason I've set these books aside is because I see a trip to Italy in the near future.

Keeping mindful of the time while examining the books, I note specific things about the pictures, chapter names, and titles. I flip pages from front to back, waiting for something hidden within them to emerge. Eventually, we stop searching the Olden Days books, knowing we need to keep looking and get out of here before Nonna returns from Aunt Lena's.

As I stand on the ladder, Jamie hands me the two heaviest books, one at a time. I grab the first and shove it into its original spot. I reach down for the next one and something dark from the far reaches of the shelf distracts me. Probably a shadow from another book. I blink a few times but it's too dark to see what it is. The shelves are deep and extend much further back than I expect. Jamie waits, still holding the second book.

"Hold on a sec," I tell her. "Here, take this back." I pull the first book out again and pass it to her. With the extra space, the ceiling light illuminates a larger area on the shelf and I can see that there *is* something else way in the back.

"I think another book fell behind the others," I say. "I'm gonna try to get it."

I reach in, stretching my arm as far as I can. My fingers just barely graze against it. Jamie hands me a flashlight from Poppy's desk drawer and a long umbrella from the coat rack. I shine the flashlight at the back of the shelf and see a large, bulky object.

"I see something!" I yell, anchoring myself against the shelves. I aim the flashlight with my left hand, and with my right I aim the outstretched umbrella to make contact. Back and forth I swipe until, finally, it connects. "I got it! I got it!" My heart pounds fast.

I press the umbrella into it, pinning it against the wall and dragging it toward me. It's heavier than I realize. It comes a few inches more but then I lose contact. I try again. Finally, the point of the umbrella attaches more securely, and I'm able to drag the object almost to the edge where I can finally see it. I drop the umbrella and pull it the rest of the way. It's a black canvas bag with a long strap, and there's something in it.

"Oh my gosh, Jamie!"

I race down the steps with the bag, my heart still racing. I place it on the desk next to the books. Jamie stares wide-eyed and mouth open, mirroring my expression.

I take a deep breath and reach for the zipper.

Chapter 8

The zipper waits in my trembling hand and my mind runs wild thinking of what's inside. Am I really doing this? Maybe this isn't the box at all, and now I've found something that I shouldn't have. I look at Jamie who's staring at me, her brow furrowed. *Just open it.*

Taking hold of that zipper firmly, I carefully drag it toward me. It catches on a few loose threads, causing me to pull back and restart a couple times, until it finally reaches the end of its path. Through the opening I notice something dark. With both hands, I scrunch the bag down around one corner, then two, until all four corners of the mystery object are fully revealed.

My heart skips a beat and I can't believe I'm staring at a small, dark brown, vintage leather trunk. The leather handle on top is well worn as is the old-fashioned hardware which clasps both ends. A musty old attic scent escapes from the bag, filling the room. Butterflies race from my stomach to my chest to my head.

With the trunk fixed in both hands, I tip it slightly from side to side, and its contents slide and stop against the edges. *This is it. This is the box.*

Jamie clears the desk and I place the trunk back down. My fingers rush to the ends of the trunk and my thumbs slide the latches to the left. I hear a soft click and feel a gentle release. My heart pounds so loudly I can almost hear it.

"Ella! I can't believe you found it! Do you think anyone else knows about it?" says Jamie.

"Just you and me." *I think.* "Not sure why Poppy would tell me and not his wife or daughter."

"Or brother."

"Right."

Carefully, I lift the lid and push back until it stops, exposing the contents inside. The first thing I see is an intricately designed, silver, oval, antique frame holding a photograph of a beautiful young woman. Her wavy brown hair falls gently against her lightly tanned skin. She has soft pink lips, slightly parted, and her dark eyes stare off at something or someone in the distance, which I can't see. She has a natural, genuine beauty, almost timeless. I run my finger across her hat, tracing its path where it fell onto her shoulders, the ribbon still tied at her neck. I've seen this woman before. *It's her.*

"Jamie, I think this is the woman in Poppy's painting I showed you."

I hand it to her. She nods, taking the picture and holding it close to examine its details. She shoots me a look, confirming my suspicions, before passing it back.

I flip it over and press firmly against the latch until it's loose enough to pop off the back. Next, I remove the cardboard and peel out the delicate picture. On the back it says:

All My Love, G

"Oh my God, this has to be her. It has to be Gianna. Look at this."

I face it toward Jamie. The woman in the painting was *not* just *someone* Poppy saw in passing and painted, as he'd once said. She was someone he knew very well. Someone he probably even loved. Why would he pretend not to know her? I snap a picture of both sides with my phone before placing it back in the frame.

"He knew her," I say, mostly to myself, while placing the photo back in its original spot in the trunk.

Next to the picture is a small book, like a journal. The soft leather cover is timeworn and threadbare in spots. Its pages bulge at the edges against its weak leather frame, scantily held by a tattered metal clasp.

"Jamie, look at this." I lift it to show her. "I think it might be a diary or a journal."

I turn it around, feeling the ruffled edges of the pages sticking out. It looks as if some of them had been stuffed in and added over time.

"Can you open it?"

The clasp has a small key hole but no key in sight. I try to move the clasp, but it doesn't budge.

"It's locked and I don't see a key."

"Can we cut it?" she says. "It seems thin enough."

I shoot her a look.

"We can probably find something to pick the lock, El," she suggests.

I nod and put it aside so I can get back to the box. As I'm about to take out the last item, I notice a white envelope and quickly pick it up. I lift the unsealed flap and pull out what appears to be a letter. Inside the letter is a stack of money.

"What's this?" I say.

"What is it?" Jamie comes to my side.

My eyes jump from greeting to closing to greeting again. Then I look at Jamie. "It's a letter. To me." I swallow hard and shake my head. "From Poppy."

Dearest Ella,

If you're reading this right now, then two things have happened: You've found the box and I am no longer here. See? I told you there was a box. And now you can see why I said it was worth more than gold. What's in this box represents a very happy and sad part of my life, a special piece that no one else knows about as much as you will.

By now you've probably realized that, like you, I too have lost the love of my life. She was my soul and the air I breathed. One day she was just gone. Many believe that she'd had enough and went off with someone else. Others say I took her life. But neither of these are true. Gianna would never have left me or the baby. Never. No. She was stolen from me. And worse yet, I was to blame, even though there were others who had a motive.

We had a quiet, private relationship, and when it was exposed, it created gossip and many problems. That's the reason why I chose to leave my country that I loved so much, not because of the war (although it was becoming increasingly difficult to live a safe and normal life at that time).

I want you to know this because, now that I'm gone, you'll hear things that aren't true. It will happen. They'll come out of everywhere and nowhere, but they will come. I know that you'll want to prove my innocence, but this is about much more than that. It's about seeking the truth. There are many things I wish I could have told you. I wish I could have taken you to Italy to show you your beautiful roots, but my heart just wasn't strong enough for a trip like that. That's why I'm leaving you this money. Take the money and go to Italy. Spend a lot of time in Tropea and, when you're there, look for a woman named Nina. She will tell you more about what you need to do to find the truth. I never could, but you can. Keep this part between us for now. You'll know when it's the right time to share it.

One thing you need to be aware of is that not everyone can be trusted. And many will doubt you. Some may even try to

*manipulate you. You are one of few whom I trust completely,
and I've known it since the day you were born. You're just like
me, El. Be particular and mindful of who you surround
yourself with, and make sure they are worthy. I love you more
than ever and I'm proud of who you are. I will always be with
you.*

Love forever,
Poppy

Tears flood my cheeks as I read Poppy's words. Not just because of the specific things he said in the letter, but because I begin to feel the weight of his loss. But it's right there, just beneath the surface, where I'm good at keeping things like feelings hidden. I swallow the hard lump in my throat, thinking about how much trust and value he's had in me. I'm torn between outrage that someone would think he could do something violent to anyone, sad that the love of his life wasn't someone he could openly share, and devastated that she was taken from him. I hardly notice that Jamie's been sitting quietly by my side with her arm around me.

"I don't know where to begin with what I'm thinking," I sniff.

She nods and says that she'll be here for me whenever I need her. I wipe my eyes with the back of my sleeve and put the letter aside to examine the last object: a book, maybe a manuscript. The title is written in Italian. I flip through the few handwritten pages near the beginning, noticing the rest that follow are blank.

"Look at this, Jame. I think it's a book. Maybe Poppy wrote it but never finished. It's in Italian. All of it."

"Wow, let me see that." She takes it, flips through it, and looks up and says matter-of-factly, "You'll just need to get a translator."

"No, I won't," I say. "I know Italian. Poppy and Nonna taught me."

"Are you fluent?"

"I can read it fluently, but I'll need to brush up on my own speaking skills."

"Well, what's the title, then?" Jamie says.

"*Agrodolce.* It means 'bittersweet,'" I say.

The cuckoo clock begins its early evening song, reminding me that Nonna will be home soon. When I place the book back inside the trunk next to the photograph and diary, the bottom of the box seems loose, like it's falling apart.

"That's weird," I say. I hand the book to Jamie and take out the other items.

"Is it broken?" she asks.

The sides of the box seem unsteady. While pushing on both sides, hoping to snap it back into place, I observe something strange on the floor of the box: a gap, about a quarter of an inch, along one edge. As I try to wedge my fingers into the tiny space, the bottom pops up.

"I think there's something else here."

I jostle the remaining three edges until I'm lifting away the entire floor of the box.

And yes, indeed, there is one more object inside. Together we stare, alarmed, our thoughts shifting from curiosity to fear. Our bodies are frozen. Our minds attempt to rationalize. Why would Poppy need something like this? Then our eyes meet and ask what our mouths can't: *Why would Poppy need a gun?*

The sun glares through a crack in the blinds, breaking our gaze. This is serious. I know it. Jamie knows it. We say nothing out loud but work quietly side by side, placing the items back inside the box, not bothering to put the floor of the hidden compartment back in place. We are quick, methodical, precise, almost robotic in our movements as we put everything back to the way it was found when we first walked into the study. No one will know that we've been here, let alone taken something.

The floorboards creak. Is someone else here? I glide to the door and listen. Nothing. I take a quick peek outside the door. No one is here. A final check from the doorway and then it's time to leave. We take the box, get into our cars, and drive home, leaving the cottage and its dirty little secret behind.

A text comes in from Mom and I listen as I drive: *Come for late dinner - 8:00 tonight? Aunt Lena/Uncle Luca coming too. Maybe Liv and Sal... lmk. Xo*

I reply to the microphone and it texts back: *Sounds good. What can I bring?*

Mom: *Wine?*

Me: *Sure.*

It'll be fine. Tell them your plan. They can't tell you what to do. I'm anxious to talk to Jamie about everything when we get back to my house. I make a right hand turn onto the main road and, in my rearview mirror, Jamie turns left.

Chapter 9

J amie calls right away to say she didn't follow me home because she needs to prepare for an early meeting in the morning at a law firm she recently began working for. I'm not sure why, but this makes me uneasy.

For the next half hour, we say over the phone what we wouldn't say in the study. She asks if I have any idea why Poppy might have had a gun, and I hope she's not alluding to her earlier statement about people doing things in a fit of rage.

"If he *had* a gun," I bark, "he probably felt he needed protection from something or someone. I don't know who. I can't imagine someone would want to hurt him!"

"Do you think Poppy had any enemies?" she asks.

"No." But then I remember the last letter I found, from Poppy to his mother, which sounded very desperate. I read it over the phone to Jamie.

Dear Mama,

You know better than anyone that I would never do such a thing. Yes, we did meet secretly while I was away. I know it was a risk, but I had to before they moved me again. I loved her so much and wanted to be with her more than I can express, but I accepted where our lives were leading us. I know

I couldn't have her the way I wanted, but I would not have done what they say happened. Someone knows something, Mama. I wish it were me. Please hug my beautiful daughter for me. I pray I see her soon.

  Love, your son

  Franco

We're both silent for a moment and then Jamie interrupts my thoughts.

"Ella," she says, "are you one hundred percent certain Poppy had *no* involvement at all in Gianna's disappearance? Is there even a tiny bit of doubt? That he could have known something?"

"No. No way, Jamie. Listen." I read a small part of the letter again: "'I know I couldn't have her the way I wanted, but I would not have done what they say happened.' He's *saying* he had nothing to do with it. Whatever 'it' is. I believe him. I don't know why you don't. We need to focus on who would have blamed him."

My chest tightens and I fluff my shirt for a whiff of air.

"I'm not trying to be difficult, El, but isn't it possible that Poppy's intense love for Gianna could have become an obsession? And, maybe, it was just way more than—"

"No," I snap. "It is *not* possible and don't *even* suggest it. Please don't go there again, Jamie," I say, while rummaging through my end table drawer for the sealed envelopes that had fallen out of the last box Nonna gave me. I intended to open them all at the same time but didn't get to the last two.

I half listen as Jamie goes on to examine possible scenarios where Poppy might have needed a gun and who would have started a rumor about him hurting Gianna.

The seal of the first envelope pulls away easily.

"Wait. Hold on," I say.

"What? Why?"

The paper inside the envelope looks like a formal document. I sit down on the sofa and examine it, but it doesn't make sense. I wipe my brow and fluff my shirt again. These papers are discharge papers from the army. Dishonorable discharge. My heart sinks.

"Oh, never mind. I thought I was getting another call, but I'm not."

A small white lie. I can't have Jamie thinking she's right about Poppy's involvement.

The other envelopes are warm and slightly moist from being tucked in my armpit. They're rigid and thicker than the others. Both seals separate easily, and inside are several photographs.

"You still there, El?"

"Yes, I found some pictures." I thumb through a few. "I don't recognize anyone, though. They're black-and-white."

Black-and-white photos are timeless and mysterious. They can capture a moment, but the true depth of emotion and story remains a mystery.

"What are they of?"

"Looks like a party. Lots of different people and families."

One picture catches my attention, so I draw it close and study it carefully. It's a woman who's standing awkwardly next to a man. She's sort of standoffish and seems uncomfortable, like he's in her personal space. The next picture shows the same man standing next to her, and they're talking to other people. Another shows a bunch of the same people, drinks in hand, and that same woman off to the side speaking with someone.

"Weird." I say.

"What's weird?"

"They look like random candids at a party. But the same woman appears in every single one of them."

"What's so weird about that?"

"Seems odd. She's in every picture. Either the main focus or in the background. But no matter what, she's there. She looks uncomfortable. Awkward. I don't know. It's almost like she didn't know she was being photographed."

"That *is* weird. Are they from one of those 'do not open without permission' envelopes?"

"Yup."

"Maybe it's blackmail," she says.

"Blackmail? For what?"

"Maybe someone was on to someone else about Gianna's disappearance. But somehow they ended up in Poppy's possession."

"Or were they sent to him specifically?"

"Or maybe," Jamie continues, "and this is a definite possibility so stay open minded, El—maybe the person responsible for her disappearance was the one taking the pictures. You said it seemed like the woman didn't know the pictures were being taken. Do you think this woman could be Gianna?"

Questions swirl through my head, and I think the answers might be in that diary. As soon as I'm back from dinner tonight, I'll dive into it.

Chapter 10

As soon as I step through the doorway, my mother knows something's up. She hugs me, then steps back.

"Hmmm." She scans me up and down and searches for it in my eyes. "What's wrong?"

"Nothing."

"Ella, I've known you your whole life and I know when something is wrong. I see it here." She circles her hands around her eyes. "You've never been able to hide it from me."

"A mother always knows," little Nonna chimes in, shaking her crooked index finger.

"It's nothing," I say. "I'll tell you later."

I pretend a call is coming in and step out to the porch to catch my breath and my thoughts. I know I'm obsessed with this story about Gianna. They'll want me to drop it and move on, but I can't. It's all I think about.

For the next hour, I do anything to delay the discussion about Italy—set the table, make a salad, prepare appetizers, straighten the living room—anything to push it off a little longer, because I know that my overprotective family won't make it easy. I hope Uncle Luca and Aunt Lena will stand behind me and help the rest of my family understand my need to go.

Nonna sits at the head of the table in Poppy's seat. She looks small and meek and seems lost in his chair. Her dark-dyed wispy bangs are swooped up behind her sparkly bobby pin, and she quietly observes her family interacting around her. Sometimes I steal moments like this, too. I watch and listen to their voices, different conversations simultaneously competing, forks scraping against dishes, glasses clinking. It's loud but soothing. A beautiful cacophony of noises: my sister, Liv, talks closely with her boyfriend, John; Aunt Lena tips her head back while laughing at my brother Sal's corny jokes; and my mother dramatically describes the steps in her sauce recipe to Uncle Luca. Everyone has their own melody. An orchestra of voices in harmony.

At one time, another voice overpowered the rest in its commanding yet respectful and soulful way. It had a melody of its own, pulling all the sounds together. Amidst this chorus of voices and competing sounds of life around me, I'm keenly aware that this one voice is missing, and part of my heart breaks again. I quickly refocus on the task at hand: Italy.

My stomach flips each time I attempt to break into the conversation to talk about Italy. How does one begin? "Would you please pass the salt? By the way, I'm going to Italy. Won't cost much, just my residency. Yes, another helping of pasta. I know I'm leaving at the worst possible time, when we should all be together."

Uncle Luca breaks my stare with one of his silly faces. I force a smile and he mouths, "What's wrong?" I wave him off. "It's nothing," I mouth back. But it's not good enough. As soon as Liv gets up and leaves the room, he slides into her seat next to me.

Aside from Poppy and Nonna, Uncle Luca is my favorite human being. He's a second grandfather and an uncle wrapped up into a perfect package. He helped my mother alongside Poppy and Nonna to raise three children after my father died. Jumped right in without hesitation. He's always been there for us. When I was in college, he'd spend hours helping me understand chemistry. He was so patient, tolerant, and understanding and made time for me whenever I needed him. Not once did he make me feel bad for interrupting his day with my problems.

He's intelligent but never arrogant. He's organized and meticulous, two things that I'm not and desperately needed to be in college. When I fell into a depression after losing Jack, three people checked on me the most: my mother, Poppy, and Uncle Luca. If there is anyone on this earth who I can count on to have my back, it's him.

I start to tell him about the letters just as my sister returns to her seat.

"What letters?" she says.

"Are you talking about those letters again, Abriella?" my mother yells from the kitchen.

"Sorry, Gabby! I brought it up!" Uncle Luca yells back.

Even from the other room, I feel my mother's eyes roll back in her head. She walks in with her hands on her hips and gives me a cold stare.

"Let her talk, Gabby," Uncle Luca shushes her.

My mother shakes her head and pretends not to listen as she gathers the dirty dishes from the table.

"Well," I pause, "I'll just get right to it. I've decided to go to Italy. There. It's out." *And not at all like I planned.*

For a second the room is silent. Then Nonna gasps. They wait wide-eyed for me to continue. For once, my talkative, loud, and sometimes overbearing family is quiet.

I take a deep breath and let out a big sigh. "I've been doing a lot of thinking since Poppy died," I say. "But even before he died, I've always wondered about my roots in Italy." I look at the small sea of faces around the table. "Haven't you wondered about that before?"

A few nods, but no one says anything. The only people who have been to Italy in our family besides Poppy and Nonna are Aunt Lena and Uncle Luca. In fact, no one from our family has ever left the states.

"Well," I continue, "that's not the only reason I'm going. I found some things that belonged to Poppy which might also have something to do with what happened when he was younger, and—"

"What things?" Nonna asks, looking at my mother. "Gabby, what's she talking about?"

"I'm getting to that, Nonna." I try to say it politely, but my nerves make it harsh. I clear my throat. "I found some letters written a long time ago between a man and a woman, possibly from our family. Something about the way they were written makes me think something bad happened. It might have involved Poppy."

The feeling in the room changes. A hint of negative energy oozes into the air. My mother eyes me suspiciously as do Uncle Luca and Aunt Lena. They seem defensive. I consider lying but decide against it.

In the awkward silence, I read the first two letters aloud, letters that express a surprise encounter, love, and a longing between Franco and Gianna. I don't say a word about Franco being Poppy or about the other letters yet. I let this hang in the air a bit first.

When I'm finished, I notice Aunt Lena sitting up straight and Uncle Luca's vein quietly pulsating at his temple. Had I said something that upset them?

"What's wrong?" I ask.

They don't reply. They continue to stare at me blankly as if they're staring right through me.

Nonna sits tall and says, "Great-Papá's name was Franco!"

We quickly nod and answer, "Yes, yes, you're right, Nonna. Must have been Great-Papá."

She clasps her hands in front of her. "But sometimes we called

65

your Poppy 'Franco,' too." Quick glances flash around the table.

"We rarely called him that, Olivia," Uncle Luca says to Nonna. "Mostly when we were kids."

"True," she answers.

"I don't get why these letters make you feel like you have to go to Italy right now," my brother, Sal, says. "For something that happened a long time ago. Seems odd."

I want to show them everything I found in the box, but I can't. I want to tell them it was Poppy's one dying wish that he whispered to me and only me before he left this earth. I want to say this is my chance to help Poppy in a way I never could before. Maybe it's a chance for me to do something good, a way to make up for the horrible choice I made that took Jack away. Poppy said to watch who I trust, but now I don't know who I *can* trust. I never thought there were some people in my family more trustworthy than others.

"These aren't the only letters," I say. "I found more in his paintings."

"His paintings?" Sal furrows his brow. "You found them in his paintings?"

I stare at each member of my family one by one. "Some of you already know that Poppy told me about a box he wanted me to find. Well, I found it. In the study."

Their eyes pop open. The air in the room escapes. Side conversations begin. Little whispers, hands to mouths, as if the idea of a hidden box was absurd.

"When were you in his study?" Nonna blurts.

"Earlier today, Nonna. I know I should have told you, but I didn't want you to worry. Or think you had to be there."

She tilts her head. "You kids know you're always welcome any time," she says. "But, Ella, you still should have told me." She swivels her chair toward my mother. "Did you know there was a box, Gabby?"

"No, Mom, I didn't," my mother says.

Nonna faces Aunt Lena and Uncle Luca and they shake their heads. No, they didn't know either.

"These letters you found in the paintings," Uncle Luca says, leaning back in his chair. "Were they all from Franco to this Gianna?"

"No," I say. "Some of them were from Gianna to Franco."

"I don't understand what's going on," Nonna says.

I lean toward Nonna and soften my gaze. "I think something bad happened in Poppy's life. And I don't think he was ever able to fix it or figure it out. I know I'm not making sense. There's more I'm trying to figure out."

"Are you sure this is about Poppy?" Uncle Luca says.

"Everything I've discovered so far seems to lead to him," I say. "But, like I said, I'm still figuring it all out."

"Just ask me," Nonna says, her little eyebrows pointed. "I've known Poppy almost all my life. I'd know if something bad happened."

"I know you would, Nonna," I say. "I think, if this is about Poppy, it might have happened before he met you."

Nonna folds her arms and looks away.

"What was in the box?" my sister, Liv, asks.

"A few pictures and a diary." *Do not mention the gun.*

"A diary?" Uncle Luca blurts. "Did you read it?"

"No . . . not yet. It's locked. But I think I can get into it."

Their faces display a mix of emotions.

"I just need you all to trust me," I say. "Something's not right. I need to do this for Poppy."

"Why you, El?" Uncle Luca almost whispers.

"Because I'm the one Poppy told about the box. And it must have been for a reason."

Liv and my mother shuffle to the kitchen, whispering and mumbling the whole way. They return a few minutes later with cake and coffee, still talking.

"Ella," my mother says, "why now of all times?" She throws the silverware on the table and slams the dessert dishes down next to them. She can't let it go. "What about your residency?" she says. "You're so close. You've worked so hard! What if you lose it?" Arms crossed, she glares at me. "You're telling me you'll throw it all away because you *have* to go to Italy *now*? This is unbelievable, right?" She looks at Uncle Luca who says nothing. *Whose side is he on?*

"Mom!" I bark. "I'm not giving it up. I'll make it work. I have a meeting at the hospital next week."

She looks away, shaking her head. Her ears are a fiery red.

Nonna pleads with everyone to stop me from going. I tell Nonna a little white lie that I want to go to the places in Poppy's paintings as a tribute to him and as a way to help me grieve. I don't share all of my reasons, just enough to buy some understanding.

"Abriella, please don't go, honey," Nonna's soft voice breaks in. She leans her frail body against mine in a side hug and wraps her arms around my waist, her head against my shoulder. She smells of sweet lavender and honeysuckle. I breathe in her scent, wishing it would ease my troubled mind. "Finish what you have to do here first. Poppy would understand."

I turn into Nonna and hug her, feeling bones where it was once plump. She steps back a little and places her small, cold hand against my cheek. "Listen to your mother. She's right, you know." I gaze into Nonna's sweet, slightly faded brown eyes and kiss her forehead.

Then I face Uncle Luca and Aunt Lena who've been surprisingly quiet during this whole ordeal. "What do you guys think?" I say.

Uncle Luca's expression and his posture seem to deflate as if the breath he was holding was suddenly released. He scratches his head and rubs his beard. "I don't think you should go to Italy, El," he says, and I can't believe it. Not even Poppy's own brother thinks I should go. Doesn't he want to know what happened? I think he senses my surprise, because he begins to elaborate. "Your mother's right. Focus on what you need to do here." He stares at me. "Besides, some things are better left alone."

"I'm sorry, Uncle Luca, but I don't agree with you."

"Ella." He sounds serious. "Sometimes, when we dig into the past, we find things we wished we hadn't. You know—open old wounds. Bring things to light that might hurt those we love."

For some reason, the way he says this makes me uncomfortable and sends chills up my spine. Does he know something about Poppy that he doesn't want me to discover?

He continues, "And a trip to Italy could be dangerous. Especially if you go alone. It's just better if you stay here." He dabs his forehead with his handkerchief and half smiles at Aunt Lena who's been nodding in agreement with everything he says.

"I'll be fine, Uncle Luca," I say.

"What's Jamie think of all this?" my mom interrupts.

"She thinks I should stay here."

"Well, that's settled, then," she says.

"Because you all think I should stay, it should be 'settled'?" I air-quote "settled." I catch a glimpse of Nonna off to the side, shaking her head and saying something in Italian.

"I don't know what's gotten into you lately, Ella," says my mother, "but this is not acceptable, young lady."

"'Young lady?' Am I a child?" I throw my hands up.

"You're acting like one."

A fire burns inside me, and beads of sweat gather at my brow.

"I'm surprised at each of you for not wanting to know more about what happened with Poppy all those years ago. And especially you, Uncle Luca. I'd think at least *you* would want to know what would scare your own brother enough to need a gun."

It slips out and there's nothing I can do about it.

"A gun?" Uncle Luca says. "You didn't say anything about a gun." I catch myself and begin backpedaling. "I misspoke. I meant that, from what I've learned, I know he was afraid of something. I think I said what if he needed a gun."

"No, you turned to me and said, 'I'd think at least *you* would want to know what would scare your own brother enough to *need* a gun,'" Uncle Luca says, his eyes shifting.

"Afraid?" Nonna says. "Poppy's not afraid of anything."

"What else do you know, Ella?" asks my mom.

I panic. *Wrap it up!*

I push my hair behind my ears and stand. "I'm not here to ask for your permission, although it would be nice to have your support. But, honestly, I'm an adult, and I really don't need your support. I can make my own decisions."

My mom stares at me with her mouth open. Nonna's little hands flail wildly in the air as she scolds the ceiling in Italian. Everyone is talking at the same time and then, at once, they stop and face me. We're frozen in our spots.

"Honey, please don't go to Italy all by yourself," Nonna pleads. "It's not safe. They'll take you like that!" She snaps her fingers. Nonna always told us to be careful everywhere we went because someone might kidnap us. She worried incessantly.

"No one's gonna take me, Nonna." I reassure her with a smile. "I'll only stay in safe places and check in often while I'm there." I give her a hug, hoping to ease her frightened eyes.

"Oh, dear," she says, her voice fading.

An awkward tension hovers, filling the room with uncomfortable silence. I decide it's time for me to go home. As I leave, no one utters a word about Italy or Poppy or anything related. It's as if the whole conversation didn't exist. But it does. And all I care about right now is digging into that diary and getting to Italy.

Chapter 11

A brilliant sun peers through the curtains and rests upon my eyelids just as the chickadees and nightingales burst into song. I force my eyes closed, but it's too late; I'm awake. I roll out of bed, run a comb through my hair, pour a strong cup of coffee, and sit down on the sofa across from the diary on the coffee table.

I sip my coffee. Bold. Intense. Just what I need.

And there it lies, right beside the diary: the perfect thing to unlock the past. Its length provides a precise grip for easy maneuvering. Its long, narrow end tapers to a skinny little point which is thin enough to press into the hole of a lock. The comb, I decide, is the perfect tool to open this diary.

It's just you and me now.

I fiddle with it, trying to find the exact catch I need. I know what it will feel like, if I can just get it. And then, finally, I hear it: POP. I press hard and force the lock open, then quickly remove the lock and turn to the first page, eyes wide, pulse quickening.

I slide the timeworn, slightly faded pages one at a time. Every yellowed page is filled with deep thoughts and private moments. Stuffed in between the pages are loose papers with more writing. At a glance are beautifully scripted words, neatly written, revealing a thoughtful and purposeful intent. I've seen this handwriting before and know without a doubt that I have Franco's—Poppy's—diary in my hands.

I remain on the sofa, book in hand, all throughout the day, with brief trips to the bathroom or to the kitchen for a snack. Once I begin reading, it's as if the world around me ceases to exist, for I've gone back in time to a faraway land and a lost love. The story that unfolds before me is emotional and disturbing, yet enchanting. The continuous theme woven throughout is Poppy's intense love for Gianna. I even feel it. True love. I remember it well. Giddiness and butterflies. The way it felt to hold his hand for the first time. Kiss for the first time. A warm rush of new love spreading throughout your entire body. Knowing that nothing else matters as long as you have each other. Everyone longs for true love. Maybe someday I'll get a second chance.

I devour the pages quickly, in search of Gianna, to see if the darkness that fell upon her rests in the vineyard or the gondola, or perhaps it ran wild through the quiet neighboring streets of Poppy's little Italian neighborhood with no one knowing, not a soul. *Who was the last person to see you, Gianna? What happened to you?*

The sun has long set, the crickets are chirping, and I've devoured every last word. It is late, and I'm wide awake. I review the notes I scribbled quickly as I read. There's much I still don't know, but one thing I do know is where I'm going and who I need to find.

The next day, I spend a few hours making plans over the phone with a travel agent. We narrow down my stay in Southern Italy between the Amalfi Coast and Calabria, where I discovered Poppy grew up and spent a lot of time. I send her a few pictures of Poppy's paintings. I'm particularly curious about the castle-looking church. She thinks she knows where this castle or church might be located based on some of the locations from the diary.

I share Poppy's descriptions about growing up in the town of

Scilla. He mentions Villagio Del Pino often, and Via Boccata, which I found is the name of a street that he and Gianna often walked through in the village. Via Raffaele Piria, Ristorante Glauco, and Piazza Rocco are also mentioned throughout the pages. These descriptions lead her to believe it's Castello Ruffo, a fifth-century B.C. fortress I'm seeking.

Franco and Gianna would meet in the late afternoons when Franco was out getting groceries for his family. In the diary, he says he'd be gone and back by dinner, so they probably had a couple hours to themselves when they met. I jot in my journal some words he'd written in Italian that I don't recognize so I can look them up later.

I pull the diary onto my lap once more and reread the first entry so I can meet Gianna and Franco for the first time again:

5 May 1937

On my way home from Palermo's Gastronomia today, I stopped to watch some of my friends walking along the path home from school. I don't regret it much, not going to school, because I know I am needed more at home. This is my job now, and much more important than going to school, Mamà reminds me. She also reminds me that I need to find a woman and settle down, and she has her eye on Cecelia, but I don't know.

I almost took my usual route home behind the deli, but instead, I went the opposite way to watch the students walk home. It was my only opportunity to see some of my friends. I am so happy I decided to go that way, because that's when I saw her. I almost didn't see her at all. And I felt like a fool when I bumped into her. I noticed right away something in her eyes that was so familiar to me, and I was surprised when she said my name. As soon as she spoke, I knew it was her.

Gianna Russo. My childhood friend. Our families were from the same neighborhood and stayed close for many years. As kids, we were always running in and out of each other's houses as if they were ours, too. We'd race through the long, narrow, beautiful streets. Flowers scattered throughout. The sun on our backs. If I could only go back.

We talked for a long time, reminiscing about the good old days. I remember feeling so devastated when her family moved north to Tuscany when she was 11 and I was 12 years old. It was like a hole existed in my heart. I had lost my best friend and hadn't even seen her all this time until today. I wonder if she felt the same. We vowed to meet back at Palermo's tomorrow. It will be an eternity till then.

I journey back and forth from the diary and its past to my unfolding expedition and the present.

Most places mentioned in the diary are on or near a body of water that largely surrounds a small town called Scilla. In an entry near the beginning of his diary, when it was still early on in their relationship, Poppy mentions that Gianna lived on or near Via Stretto. A satellite view of this town reveals several small streets lined with two-story buildings; some are houses, others might be apartments or businesses. Many streets and houses look similar to Poppy's neighborhood painting. Scilla appears to be a quaint, pretty little village right next to the Tyrrhenian Sea. I can see why Franco and Gianna would meet there so frequently.

There is much to uncover and explore in Italy. I just hope a two-week stay will be enough time to do what I need to do. And I'm still not entirely sure of what that will entail. The first thing I'll do is find Nina, and hopefully she can direct me on the right path.

What I dread the most about planning this trip is telling my mentor that I might not be able to fulfill my commitment to my residency at this time. This could have permanent consequences for my future—at least with this hospital.

Telling my mother will be next to impossible. Although I told the family at dinner I was going, I'm sure they don't think I'll actually do it. Strangely enough, I'm not as anxious as I thought I'd be. I actually have a sense of calm. *Calm before the storm?* Regardless of anyone's reaction, in exactly one week from today I'll be standing in Italy. *If only Jack were here to go with me.*

"Hey, what ya doin'?"

"Ah!"

I jump at Jamie's voice. I hadn't heard her come in. She does that now that she has her own key. Comes in any time she wants, even though I've asked her over and over to text me first so I don't freak out.

"Jamie!"

"Sorry, I know, I should have texted," she says. "But you haven't left your house in days!" She looks at me, waiting for an explanation.

"It's complicated, Jame."

"What's complicated?" She faces me. "Maybe you're making it that way," she says. "I know you love Poppy and you want to do right by him. I know that, El. But this isn't good for you. You know how you get. You're stuck in your head again."

"I just need to do this."

"I'm worried about you, El. I see it happening again. Narrow-focused. Obsessed. Again. When's it enough, El?"

I begin to sweat, and I'm sure my face is bright red. I stare hard at Jamie.

"It'll be enough when I've found out what happened to Gianna," I say. "When I've figured out why Poppy lied about her. Or why he told me about the box in the first place. It will be enough," I continue, "when I've proven that he had nothing to do with her disappearance!"

My voice echoes against the walls. Jamie shakes her head.

"And I'll know all that," I add, "by the time I'm back."

"Back from where?"

"Italy," I say.

"You're kidding, right? You're not serious." She leans in, places her hands on my shoulders, and stares into my eyes. "Ella. What are you doing? What about the hospital?"

I glance away and back. "I know, Jame."

"You haven't thought this through," she says.

"Yes, I have. It's all I've been doing lately."

"Don't you think you're being a little bit selfish?" she adds. "Feels like it's happening again, El. Can't you see?"

"What's happening again?" My throat tightens.

"You flee," she says. "You stop what you're doing. Turn inward. It's like you're in a closed bubble where no one can reach you. Life goes on around you, but you stay *there*." She runs her fingers through her hair.

"That's not fair," I say.

She softens a little and reaches for my hands.

"El. I get it," she says. "You want to prove to Poppy that you can still help him even after he's gone. But Poppy will understand if you can't do this right now. And what about your mom and Nonna? They need you, too. It's just bad timing."

"I know you're looking out for me, Jame. And I appreciate that. I really do." I pick up the trunk. "Poppy told me about this box for a reason. I need to find out what that was."

"No matter what the cost?"

"No matter what the cost," I say.

Jamie paces back and forth. She walks to the window and peers through the glass. She's sighing and biting her fingers.

"Well," she turns from the window, "if you're determined to do this no matter what, then there's one more thing you need to do."

"What's that?" I say.

"Take me with you."

I don't tell her not to come. That I don't need her. That I can do it on my own. I won't ask her how she'll do it, how she'll get the time off from work so quickly. Because Jamie's smart. She's always known what she needs. She's always known what I need. And I do need her.

PART 2 - Quest

Ella & Poppy

Chapter 12

Ella

The plane begins its ascent, and something within me rises as well. Out my window, beyond the tip of the wing, the houses distance themselves. Streets, neighborhoods, and towns slowly disappear until just the boundaries of land remain through a white, misty veil. Once we're far above the clouds, my body loosens, and my fingers relax. I close my eyes and savor the peaceful feeling within me. But as I let go, another feeling takes hold: fear. Not of plane crashes or lost luggage, but fear of what I might find in Italy. Or what I might not find.

Jamie sits quietly beside me, earplugs in, drumming her fingers to her music. When I stare at the seat in front of me, I can see her in my peripheral vision and I pretend it's Jack sitting there. And for that moment, he is the one going to Italy with me. *Oh, Jack, why can't it be you?*

"Huh?" she says.

"I didn't say anything."

She nods and goes back to her music.

Did I say that out loud?

I study the travel guides and maps throughout each of our connecting flights while Jamie nods off. I re-read my notes about the places we'll go to first, according to Poppy's diary, with frequent checks in my backpack to make sure the diary is still there. Every now and then I give a quick squeeze on the diary to satisfy my OCD. As Jamie sleeps, I read the diary entries again. I keep a novel right beside it, pretending to read it when she stirs. There are just some things in this diary that I need to keep to myself right now.

****

A portly man with a thick goatee, wearing sunglasses and sporting a charcoal beret, pulls up to the curb and waves at us. He waddles out of the driver's side, smiles, and nods while taking our suitcases and placing them in the trunk. He says something in broken English that I can't understand, but I can make out Reggio Calabria Resort & Spa, so I quickly say, "Si."

"Better brush up on that Italian quick," Jamie whispers, which makes me laugh. It's a beautiful ride to the resort, and, eventually, we turn onto a long private driveway that curves around a bend and continues to climb up and around until it reaches the top. Nestled and surrounded by tall green trees and shrubs is our exquisite resort. It's a great, brick building resembling more of a majestic castle. Beautiful pine trees line the cobblestone paths surrounding the resort. When our driver opens my door, I swing my legs out quickly and place my feet for the first time on Italian soil. This is the land that my ancestors walked and, now, so will I. This feels right and resonates deeply in my soul.

"Oh my God!" Jamie yells while sliding out of the car. "It's beautiful!"

We're both beaming as excitement fills us, and we embrace in a tight hug. We even hug the driver before he leaves us with our suitcases at the door of the resort. I don't think my smile can be any wider.

****

While exploring the grounds of the resort, we spy a quaint area off of the back, partially enclosed by an intricate black iron fence. A waiter walks out of the resort and offers us a glass of wine as we settle into the cozy chairs. I begin showing Jamie the itinerary that my travel agent helped create. It's based mostly on the locations mentioned in Poppy's diary as well as other interesting areas I discovered in my research. As I'm explaining everything to Jamie, an attractive couple approaches us, asking if they can join us. I'm a little put off, wondering why, of all the places they could go, they need to sit where we are. Jamie and I exchange quick, puzzled glances.

The woman's long black hair goes down to the middle of her back. She's wearing a sleeveless black pant suit with a flared hem, held together at the waist with a black-and-white swirl-patterned scarf. Her black patent leather heels match her Ray Ban sunglasses, and a bright red lipstick stands out against the black contrast of her clothes.

He wears a crisp, pastel pink dress shirt, dark designer denim jeans with a charcoal, almost black sport jacket and black shoes. His thick, wavy black hair remains in place, even with the wind blowing everything else around it.

"*Ciao*, I am Marco, and this is Sophia," he says in English but with a heavy Italian accent.

"Hi. *Ciao*. I'm Jamie and this is Ella. Abriella is her real name," Jamie says. I give Jamie a look.

"You can call me El." I say.

Marco shakes Jamie's hand and raises mine to kiss. Jamie shoots me a sharp look.

"Do you live around here, or are you visiting?" I ask.

"We're from Tuscany but came here for a little getaway. Something we desperately need," Sophia says, folding her arms.

"I can tell from your accent that you're not from here," Marco says, ignoring Sophia's comment. "Where you from?"

"We're from America. New York. Not New York City. Upstate New York. North of New York City," Jamie interjects, stumbling over her words.

"Ah, I see. We've been to America, but only California," he says. "Why do you come to Italy?"

"Well, my grandparents are from Southern Italy, and I've always wanted to visit," I say, hoping to avoid a conversation about Poppy dying or the diary.

"It's a beautiful place to live—Italy. I wouldn't want to live anywhere else," Marco says with a wide grin. "We love the Amalfi Coast and will visit on our way back to Tuscany. You would love the coast."

"That's actually on our list of places to visit," I say.

Marco's eyes widen.

"We are happy to tell you more about Italy. If not today, perhaps another day while you're here." When Marco says this, Sophia lowers her sunglasses and gives him a warning look.

"Sure, that would be great," Jamie says, and I give *her* a look.

"I'm sure we will see each other again. Nice to meet you both," says Marco as he reaches for Sophia's hand to leave. She stiffly takes his and they glide away down the path. I'm relieved that they only stopped to say hello and not stay, although I got the distinct feeling that Marco would have stayed if he weren't with Sophia.

"Where in the world did those two come from?" I laugh.

"I know, right?"

"Why did you say we'd let them show us around? We don't even know them, Jame."

"I wasn't really serious. But maybe we should."

"Nah, I'm good. I think we can navigate on our own, don't you?"

"I guess. But it might be helpful to have advice from real Italians who know their way around."

"I prefer to avoid having our faces posted on a Missing Persons flyer," I partially joke, and Jamie rolls her eyes. I reach into my backpack and place my hand on the diary—the only Italian advice I need.

Poppy

9 May 1937

Gianna and I have seen each other for each of the last three days. Our meetings were brief, beginning at the gastronomia, where I always buy meats for my mother. We walked along an old path we used when we were children. "Remember when you'd hide behind the cypress trees and try to scare us?" she asked me today. And I did remember spying on Gianna as she walked home from school with her sisters. Sometimes Luca was with me. She laughed saying she always knew I was there hiding and, of course, I pretended I didn't know what she was talking about. Gianna knows when I'm teasing her. She always knows things about me. I love watching her laugh and smile, but I hate that she has to go so soon.

10 May 1937

Today I told Gianna that I love her and that I've always loved her. After walking along the path, I convinced her to come with me to our old neighborhood in Scilla. We walked and reminisced through the streets remembering how we used to run and play through those streets right up until dinner. Being there, I felt as if I were that child again. After a while, we went to the water's edge where the beautiful Tyrrhenian Sea meets the white sands off of Scilla. It is the bluest water I've ever seen. It's like another world; even the air smells different. When I'm with Gianna, all I want to do is touch her. Just reach out and touch her hair or hold her hand, but I haven't allowed myself to do it. How will she react? So, today as we stood on the warm sand, I turned to her and told her how I felt. I just said it: 'Gianna, I love you and I always have.'

She looked at me with smiling eyes and said she loved me, too, then reached for my hands and held them as tears filled her eyes. My heart was full! But there was another look in her eyes that seemed to say something else, and now I'm wondering what her tears really meant. Suddenly, she had to go again. Had I done something wrong?

Chapter 13

Ella

The next day, we venture on a culinary walking tour of Ravagnese, one of the most beautiful towns in Southern Italy. My travel agent says Ravagnese is the perfect place to immerse ourselves with the locals. And I think it's an excellent way to honor Poppy by starting with food.

We first meet Maria and Giuseppe, an adorable older Italian couple who've lived and worked all their lives on the rustic farm that provides foods for their culinary tours. They live in a charming, modest home attached to their family restaurant, and I can see them standing in the doorway side by side awaiting our arrival. We're greeted with warm, tight hugs as if they've known us forever. A few minutes later, Giuseppe begins telling us how much he and Maria enjoy having tours and giving back to their neighbors while, simultaneously, Maria starts explaining how they practice a farm-to-table philosophy by using their own crops and livestock to provide what they need for their meals. They continue their parallel conversations and we're not sure who to follow.

Poppy and Nonna did this all the time. We'd nod our heads, following one of them, while turning to the other one to answer a question or acknowledge a story. It's lunacy, but I love it.

They motion for us to follow, still in full dialogue, and we accompany them through the lush, green countryside while our noses follow a rich aroma of baked homemade bread. Maria points out the beautiful oak, chestnut, and acacia trees as Giuseppe explains the remnants of medieval fountains that scatter the sprawling vineyard.

As we wander through the olive groves, we see beautiful views of the Tyrrhenian Sea and parts of the coast. A sweet scent of tomato and basil wafts into the air and our stomachs desperately grumble and groan. Up ahead, I spot small, globed, golden lights hung in shallow, draping arcs under a wooden pergola, and I know we are close to the farmhouse.

We take our seats among other tourists at a large rectangular dining table beneath the lights and indulge on a delicious dinner of veal parmigiana, salad, homemade bread, and red wine. Everything is beautiful.

For a while, Jamie and I are deeply involved in conversations with different people at the table and everyone is talking at once, much like home. About halfway through dinner, an elderly man sitting across from me leans toward me as if he wants to say something privately.

"So, you're going to Tropea?" he whispers, and must have read my puzzled expression, because he quickly follows with, "I heard you talking to Maria."

"Oh. Yes, we are."

"Where 'bouts?"

"We're following a tour tomorrow to get acquainted with the area, since we're not from around here."

He looks around the table and then says, "What tour is it?"

"I don't remember specifically," I lie.

"You should be careful. Some tours aren't what they seem. The people, I mean. Not always nice to tourists."

Maria notices our awkward conversation and quickly jumps in.

"Sal, are you giving my guests a hard time again?" she says.

"No. No. Not at all. Just making small talk," he says with a wink and tip of his cap.

"Don't mind Sal," Maria whispers. "He lives in town and always comes by for a free meal when I have my tours. He means no harm. He's just trying to be helpful. Just like anywhere, you have to be smart and know what you're doing, right?"

She laughs. Jamie and I nod and look at each other. I wonder how much of the conversation she heard.

"I will say this," Maria continues. "When you get to Tropea, visit Angelina." She hands me a paper with Angelina's number and address. "She owns an inn and knows a lot about Italy. She'll make sure you're all right."

"Thank you," I say, taking the paper from her and passing it to Jamie.

"You'll love it here. And it's good that you came to Italy together," she says in a hushed voice, and gives my shoulders a squeeze as she leaves our end of the table to mingle with guests at the other end.

As we get up to leave, I see Sal watching us. I give a slight wave and he looks away.

"Weirdo," Jamie says.

"Yep." I say as we slip into the taxi and head back to the resort.

I sleep restlessly, thinking about our wonderful visit with Maria and Giuseppe, followed by the strange conversation with Sal. Then a surge of excitement for tomorrow's tour exploring Reggio Calabria and Scilla and finally Tropea. I know from his diary that's where Poppy painted the monastery.

****

"*Buongiorno!*" exclaims our lively tour guide as we step onto the bus. We greet him and notice that the back of the bus is already full, so we quickly squeeze into a spot in the middle. I'm thankful for my Italian upbringing and my knowledge of Italian greetings and phrases. *Buongiorno* is said when greeting someone in the morning. I brought my *Italian for Dummies* book for Jamie's quick reference when needed. Jamie laughs when she notices I covered the book so she won't be embarrassed if she needs to look things up in public. English is not widely spoken in the deep southern parts of Italy. We want an authentic experience from the natural environment and through interacting with the locals.

The tour bus is crowded and smells like sour dough mixed with sweat. We sit near an unhappy family of four, three couples around our age, two elderly couples, and a group of three girlfriends who appear to be around thirty. Our jovial bus driver nods and acknowledges every person who steps on. His little Italian voice echoes through the speakers, informing us that we're driving along the Costa Degli Dei or "Coast of the Gods" and acknowledges the numerous volcanoes along the way.

About thirty minutes into our journey, we stop at a curious little *pasticceria* that at one time was a small house the owners lived in and transformed into a pastry shop. The first level was converted to the pastry shop and the second level was remodeled for the owners' living space. A plump, older woman serves us with a smile, remaining calm and centered for our hot and hungry crowd. We quickly devour our fluffy pastries, eager to begin exploring the Corso Garibaldi shopping district where, just decades earlier, many stars had roamed and shopped.

My mind quickly returns to Franco and Gianna. Had they also wandered through these streets? I scan the area as if I might see someone or spot something significant. Jamie keeps drawing my attention back to the tour guide, but all I really want to do is get to Scilla.

Scilla is known as a romantic little fishing village, and I can clearly see why. The buildings and houses have a warm, golden glow cast upon them, with beautiful flowers and greens cascading beneath the windows. Cobblestone roads stretch across narrow paths, welcoming its visitors near and far. I chuckle at the thought of a young Franco fishing with his brother and friends in Chianalea, the fishing village within Scilla. Scilla is reminiscent of the pictures Poppy painted of his neighborhood.

On the other side of the beach is the restaurant, Il Pirata, which was highly recommended by our tour guide. We gorge ourselves on sea snails, swordfish, and wine in a partially secluded spot with a perfect view of the sea.

"Ella, look!" Jamie points toward a small hilltop where a castle stands overlooking the village. I squint to see it clearer.

"Could that be Castello Ruffo?" I say.

"It has to be," she says. "They said we'd see it here! What else could it be?"

I pull up a photo on my phone and, sure enough, it's a match.

"Castello Ruffo is one of the places that Franco and Gianna used to go to meet each other! It's in Poppy's diary." Goosebumps cover my arms and my eyes well up.

Jamie takes out a brochure from the tour. "It says right here, 'According to legend, many years ago, this is where Odysseus fought against the monster Scylla, and the enchanted princess still lives below the fort.'" She looks up at me. "Did you know they call this area the 'Little Venice of Calabria?'"

"No, I didn't. But it's not surprising," I say. "Look at the little narrow canals running through the village. It's almost like the pictures I've seen of Venice. It's obvious why they chose to meet here. So romantic. I can't wait to get inside."

Poppy

12 May 1937

Today I took my love to Castello Ruffo for a beautiful and romantic view of the sea. We looked down at the coast dotted with terracotta rooftops among the green rolling hills and deepest blue sea. It was too much beauty to take in at once. I took her to the old places where we used to run and play and to our old neighborhood. She recalled one time when she was hiding on me and it took me so long to find her. She climbed way up high in a tree and was making funny noises to get me to look. I jumped at one of the noises, making her laugh so hard that she fell out of the tree and knocked me down. She sure did surprise me that day!

Gianna laughed at me when I told her that Scilla is named after a Greek mythological sea monster, and still doesn't believe me, even though it's true. I love to hear her laugh. We laugh a lot when we're together. When it's time to go, we have no desire to leave this sweet town of Scilla. And then I see that sadness in her eyes that seems to say there's more behind it.

14 May 1937

Le Restaurant Il Feudo del Vicario—I will not forget the wine we drank, the food we ate, and the love I found in her eyes. The golden glow of the light reflecting against her skin, the colorful pink and red flowers and vines surrounding us, wanting this moment to stay still forever.

15 May 1937

Tonight, after I returned from seeing Gianna, my brother Luca and I had finished setting the table and Mamà asked us to go wash our hands before dinner. While we were in the bathroom just around the corner, we could hear the low, accusing grumblings of Papà steadily growing louder and aimed primarily at Mamà. We were uneasy and afraid, and we *didn't want to come out of the bathroom, but we knew we had to. When we finally did enter the kitchen again, it was easy to see the angry eyes of Papà and defeated eyes of Mamà. I saw Mamà standing in front of the stove for a few minutes, not facing us, trying to catch her breath and regain control as she had many times before.*

As Mamà placed the food on the table, she asked me to start dishing out what I wanted and pass the plate to Luca. As we scooped the food onto our plates, we suddenly heard a loud crash, sounding like glass exploding. We stared into each other's eyes, not knowing what to do next and trying to make sense of what happened. What would make our father so upset that he would throw, with such force, one of our pretty dishes against the wall, shattering it into millions of pieces everywhere? As we broke from our fearful stares, we caught a brief glimpse of Mamà, her back to us, shoulders shaking. Papà took his own plate of food out to the living room to eat, leaving us to pick up the pieces. I start to think, Why do I have this tyrant for a father? And I also begin to wonder if he could be the reason why Gianna's family left in the first place.

Chapter 14

Ella

A sea of unending turquoise caresses the white, sandy beach. Small, modest homes of Scilla rest within the mountains and along the coastline. These are the breathtaking views from Castello Ruffo di Scilla. It is surreal to stand on the same balcony as Franco and Gianna and see with my eyes what they saw. I'm captivated by the sense of history and antiquity surrounding me.

"They probably stood right here," Jamie interrupts my thoughts.

"What? Yes, I'm sure they did. I wish I could go back in time."

"Why would you wanna do that?"

"Just to see them together. How they acted. What they said. Maybe I'd find out why they never stayed together. Or how Gianna disappeared."

"Unless she left on her own."

"Poppy's diary doesn't show any indication that Gianna would have purposely left."

"I love the little detective in you," she grins. "You always need a crime to solve."

I can't help but feel offended by Jamie's remarks. Like she's pushing me. Testing me.

"Are you trying to be sarcastic?" I ask.

"No, not at all. Why would you think that?" She laughs, "Because I said 'little detective?'" She stares at me like I'm crazy. "Oh, come on, El. You're being a little oversensitive, don't you think?"

Am I? I shake my head. "Maybe I am." I decide to let it go and not overthink it.

We walk back down into Scilla and stroll through the neighborhoods to kill a little time before we need to leave again. There's no way to really tell which house used to be Franco's and which was Gianna's, so I pretend and imagine them both running through the streets as children and playing until they're called in for dinner.

Two older men are sitting on their porches talking and laughing. They might be old friends or maybe brothers, probably talking about sports or the weather in between cigarette drags. Children play near them while their mothers prepare dinner inside. Maybe, at one time, Franco's and Gianna's fathers were like these two men. I wonder if it was hard for them to say goodbye when Gianna's family moved north. I got a feeling from Poppy's diary that both fathers wanted it that way.

"Jamie, look. Does that say 'Ristorante Rocco?'" I point to a building just up the hill.

"Yeah, it does."

I pull out the diary and flip a few pages until I find the entry. I compare Poppy's written words to the sign on the restaurant and show it to Jamie. "Poppy mentions this place a lot in his diary. They used to come here for lunch. I can't believe it's still around."

Jamie grabs my hand and leads me up to one of the windows so we can peek inside. It's a small room with a kitchen at the back and about ten tables and chairs scattered throughout. It looks recently remodeled. The smell of fried food permeates the air.

"It's so cute," Jamie says.

"They probably came here and talked about everything. Maybe it's where they fell in love."

My voice catches as I recall the exact time and place when I knew I was in love with Jack. It wasn't his words that drew me in or the way he touched my arm or said my name. It was the tenderness he had when he spoke about his father. I could see right into his heart through his eyes as he spoke. The love, admiration, and respect he had for his dad was what swept me off my feet.

Jamie notices and squeezes my hand.

Ristorante Rocco sits perfectly among the neighborhoods where Franco and Gianna grew up, nestled among the houses with a view of Castello Ruffo and the Tyrrhenian Sea. It is magical. I look at Jamie and feel guilty for getting annoyed with her sarcastic remarks and questioning her support. I should know better. She's always been a loyal friend.

"Thank you for being here with me, Jame," I say.

She turns to me and gives me a hug.

"I can't imagine not being here with you, El."

We notice a few familiar faces from our bus heading back, so we grab our things and follow the crowd, excited to head to our final destination and the place I'm looking most forward to, Tropea.

****

"We are entering the Province of Vibo Valentia," our tour guide proudly announces. "To the left, you'll see the twelfth-century cathedral, built on a former Byzantine cemetery. Notice the marble sarcophagi and the painting of the Madonna of Romania, the protector of this town. Farther north," he continues, "over the hills you'll see the centuries-old Santa Maria del Isola. It overlooks the sea—just beautiful."

I chuckle at his cheerful, scratchy voice.

"If you're staying for the day, please be back to our bus by 5:00 p.m. If you're staying in Tropea for an extended period of time, thank you for traveling with us today. While walking through the town or on the beaches, stay in groups and don't go off on your own. Tropea is normally very safe, but lately bands of pick-pocketers have approached tourists, so keep your eyes open. For all of you who have come to Tropea today, we hope you enjoy your visit." He smiles and nods as we exit the bus.

"Jamie! Did you hear him? Santa Maria del Isola!"

"What about it?"

"Remember Poppy's paintings? The one with the castle perched way up high on the mountain?"

"Yes."

"My travel agent says it's not a castle. She's almost certain it's an old church that became a monastery."

"And?"

"The monastery is called Santa Maria del Isola."

"The one the tour guide mentioned just now?"

I nod.

"You think she's right about that?"

"She said it's located in Tropea. Its features are so distinct, it has to be."

Jamie's eyes widen.

"And you know what else?" I say.

"No, tell me." She smiles.

"The monastery is where Franco and Gianna pledged their love to each other."

"Well, then, we should go there right after we go to the beach," she says.

"You read my mind," I wink.

****

I slip off my shoes and feel the warm, soft sand under my feet, cushioning my toes with every step. The balmy breeze embraces me as I walk against it toward the white lounge chairs we rented near the water.

Gentle waves roll in and break before reaching the shore. People splash and jump in them. I'm mesmerized by the beauty of all that lies before me. I drop my backpack next to my sandals and collapse into the chair.

I glance back at Jamie but she's not right behind me as I thought. I stand up and look around. It's difficult to see among all the people. *That's weird. Where'd she go?* I scan the area behind me but don't see her anywhere. I look ahead to see if she ran to the water first. I know how much she loves the water. She's not there either.

My heart begins to quicken. She was just behind me a second ago. The beach is overcrowded with people coming and going; it's hard to keep track of anything. I stare intently, hoping to see her bouncy blonde ponytail emerge from the mass. There are no signs of her. *Oh my God, where is she?* My heart races and I'm thinking the worst. *Nonna was right.* My chest tightens and, for a moment, the loud noises around me are nothing more than muffled sounds of voices and waves.

I hold onto the chair and tell myself to remain calm and rational while I try to figure it out. There has to be an explanation. But panic rises quickly and I feel desperate thinking about the questionable group of young men standing near the entrance to the beach. They were hovering near everyone who exited the bus looking very suspicious. I sensed Jamie's nervousness, too, when she grabbed my arm and started walking faster.

"Jamie!" I yell at the beach. But there's no answer. I yell again, louder this time, hoping she'll hear me.

"Jamie!" My voice breaks. I am a mother looking for her lost child. *Get a hold of yourself. She's probably fine.*

I retrace my steps back in the direction we came but I still don't see her anywhere. *What if she found her way to the chairs while I'm all the way near the tour bus?* I hustle back to the chairs only to see them empty. I look down at the "no service" message on my phone as a drop of water lands on my nose. And then another. The sweet smell of rain surrounds me, but no one leaves the beach or even flinches at the light rain shower. Back home, a drop of rain causes people to scurry about and get inside to beat the imminent downpour. But not here.

I run toward a small group of people I recognize from our tour bus but quickly lose them in the crowd. At once, the beauty that surrounds me disappears and I feel small.

My heart races as I desperately search the sea of people for any sign of Jamie, but panic blinds me and it's all a blur. *What if something happened to her? Nonna was right.* I don't know which way to go. The voices are muffled again. I bury my head in my hands.

"Miss?"

A hand presses gently onto my shoulder and I look up. Someone is talking to me in Italian, but I can't fully understand what they're saying. I shake my head.

"Miss?"

A man stands before me and he's holding my bag.

"You dropped this. Your bag." He hands it to me, and his warm smile disappears when he reads my frantic expression. "You okay?" He bends slightly and I gaze into his kind, brown eyes, easing my panic for a second.

"My friend is lost," I say back in Italian. "I can't find her." My throat tightens the more I talk. "We left the tour bus and walked to the beach. She was right behind me." I look back from where we'd come. "When I turned around, she wasn't there. She's nowhere."

"It's okay. We will find your friend," he says. "I live here. I know this place. I can help you."

I'm not sure how to feel. I don't know him, but without Jamie, I don't know anyone, and I need his help. For the next few minutes, I describe Jamie's hair, her slight build, and beautiful blue eyes.

"What's she wearing?"

"I can't remember a thing she's wearing," I say, disheartened.

"It's okay, let's go," he says, still holding my backpack.

We step in the direction of the tour bus, and I can't believe I'm walking next to a stranger without my best friend.

Poppy

18 May 1937

We climbed to the top of Ruffo del Castello to look out at the sea as we always do at the start of every day together. Gianna looked so beautiful in her flowery dress. I love the way it swayed around her in the wind and the way she felt beneath its silky fabric. We danced to the sound of the waves crashing and the music in our minds.

When we finished, we walked down to Ristorante Rocco for lunch. I couldn't help but notice that Gianna kept looking over her shoulder. I ignored it at first, but it happened a few more times. I reached out for her hand and told her that I loved her and wanted to be with her forever. She said she loved me, too, but her face was drawn, and then, slowly, she pulled her hand out from beneath mine.

I asked her what was wrong, but she wouldn't say. "Gianna, something's not right," I said. "Tell me what it is. You say you love me, but you don't seem sure."

She fiddled with her dress, keeping her eyes lowered. Then finally, she told me.

"Franco," she said, "I do love you. More than anything or anyone."

Her eyes filled with tears and I didn't know what to do. She looked at me as if she wanted to say more, but instead, she stood, burst into tears, and ran out of Ristorante Rocco.

I followed her and grabbed her arm just as she got out the door. She turned to me and said, "Franco, before we saw each other for the first time I . . ."

I wanted to let her finish, but I was also afraid to.

"My parents . . ." she continued. "Shortly after we moved to Tuscany, they became reacquainted with old friends. They . . . introduced me to their daughter. And their son. They arranged for us to be—"

"Don't say another word," I said, closing my eyes to wish it away. "Why didn't you tell me sooner that you were in love with someone else?"

"I'm not. I don't. Love him. Like I love you," she said, her voice strained.

We stared into each other's eyes for a long time. Then we hugged, saying nothing for a while. She said she wants to break off the engagement, but it could come with a price. I am deeply bothered by this for many reasons. First, I cannot imagine losing the love of my life. Second, I believe in loyalty and honoring commitments, and she committed to him before me.

Are we to remain only friends when, in my heart, I feel that she was really mine first?

Chapter 15

Ella

We trudge through the sand toward the tour bus. It's an arduous task for my weary legs. The stranger's big hand takes mine and we weave through the crowd. He's holding my backpack and looking straight ahead. In my mind, I pray that Jamie stopped at the tour bus hoping to find me there.

When we arrive, our tour guide tells us that no one has returned to the bus yet. I take a deep breath to stay calm. Then the stranger turns to me.

"Your friend—maybe she went to the restroom?" he says.

I shake my head. "No, she wouldn't go alone."

The stranger turns to the driver. "Sir, would you please drive us into town for a few minutes so we can look for her friend?"

"She wouldn't leave the beach without me," I say. "She wouldn't. It's not like her."

The driver considers this for a moment, then looks at his watch and shakes his head. "I'm sorry, miss. I need to stay here until it's time to leave. It's best that you stay here, too, where she knows you already are. If you go into town, you might miss her." He seems sincere.

"You're probably right," I say, and glance at the stranger. "I don't know what to do."

"Come," he says. "Let's walk a bit through the town, but we'll stay close by. And then we'll come right back." He seems sincere as well, but how do I know for sure?

"Okay." I point to the backpack. "I can take that."

"It's no bother," he says with a half-smile. Am I sure I want this man to hold my backpack? Or trust him at all? I pull up a picture of Jamie on my phone to show him. It's one of my favorite pictures, taken last summer when we were on our boat at the lake.

"This is her," I say. "Jamie."

He nods and smiles.

"And you?"

"That's me next to her," I say, thinking it's obvious.

"No," he chuckles. "You are called?"

"Oh. I'm Ella." I feel my face flush.

"Nice to meet you, Ella. I'm Nico."

I can tell he's holding in a hearty laugh trying to stay composed and not embarrass me further. For a split second, I relax until a wave of worry rushes back.

As we emerge onto the narrow cobblestone walk, the streets are less friendly than they were when Jamie and I first stepped off the tour bus. The buildings are dark and unwelcoming. The sky is overcast and the shadows blend. I contemplate which direction to go.

An elderly man stands at a corner selling flowers. He waves and motions for people to come see his bountiful collection. His cart contains pots of gardenias and marigolds mixed with wild green vines. He also has several long-stemmed flowers for single purchase or a bouquet.

His charismatic personality easily draws people to him. As we approach, he speaks in low, soulful tones trying to persuade me to buy his flowers.

"*Mi scusi*," I say. "Have you seen this girl?" I show him a picture of Jamie. He smiles and nods. "You have?"

"*Si*," he nods again. "She was lost," he says.

I look at Nico, surprised, and my heart races again.

"Where did she go?" I pant.

He seems confused and points in the direction of one of the connecting roads. Then he shakes his head and points toward another road.

"You don't remember?" I ask.

He shakes his head no.

"Thank you, sir," Nico says, and he whispers to me, "Let's keep moving."

As we turn away, the old man calls us back.

"Wait!" he says. "I do remember! Her friend found her."

"What do you mean?" I say. "What friend?"

"I remember," the old man says again. "After she left, I saw her come back and walk by my cart again. They were in a hurry."

"No, she was alone. I don't think we're talking about the same person. Sorry to bother you," I say, turning away.

"No. It was her," he says with assurance. "The girl in your picture. She came here lost and then her friend must have found her because they walked by my cart together."

Nico and I glance at each other. I don't know what to think.

"What did her friend look like?" Nico asks.

"He was tall, dark hair. Good looking," the old man says.

I wipe the sweat from my eyes. "He? It was a man?"

"Yes. And they were in a hurry. They were rushing toward the beach," he says.

"Thank you, sir," I say, confused and panic-stricken. "If you see her again, tell her to go to the white chairs. She'll know what you mean."

"I'll only be here a little while longer, but yes, I'll tell her!" he yells as we hustle toward the beach.

With each step, I frantically search our surroundings, not wanting to miss a chance to see Jamie. I look at Nico and he's doing the same. Where did he come from? In an effort to capture everything at once, I hardly look straight ahead.

About fifty feet away and just within eyesight of the white chairs, I think I see something, but I'm not sure. I stop walking and squint my eyes to focus better.

"Nico, I don't think those are our chairs."

Nico looks around.

"Yes, this is it," he says. "This is where I found you. Just ahead is where you dropped your bag," he says, pointing.

"Are you sure?"

"I was coming from over there," he says, motioning to a little cabana where a crowd had gathered. They were listening to three men strumming their guitars. I hear the music from where we're standing. I hadn't even noticed that before. "That's when I saw you."

How did you see me in all of this?

We race toward the chairs and, as we draw near, I see a silhouette of a woman sitting sideways, not facing the sea. Her elbows rest upon her knees with her ponytailed head propped in her hands.

"Jamie!" I say, and run toward her. She hears me and quickly jumps to her feet.

"Where have you been?" she yells, throwing her hands in the air. She looks like she's about to cry.

"Where have *I* been?" I bark. "Where have *you* been?"

She looks Nico up and down and her eyes fall on our hands, still clasped from when we weaved our way through the crowd. Nico had taken my hand so we wouldn't get separated. I awkwardly pull my hand away from his tight grip and give her a hug. Relief and worry pour out of me. Exhausted yet confused, I step back.

"What happened?" I say. "You were right behind me, but when I turned around, you were gone. I thought something happened to you! Where were you?"

"Ella, calm down. It's okay," she tries to reassure me. "Don't you remember when we got off the bus? The tour guide recommended we go to the cabana just off the walkway for live music and drinks?"

This is the first time I've heard this.

"First of all, don't tell me to calm down," I snap. "All we've been doing is searching frantically for you since we got here!" My voice and temper rise.

"We?" she says, looking at Nico.

"Nico found my backpack," I say as he slides it from his shoulder to my hand. "I dropped it looking for you. I thought you were lost— or worse! Why would you keep walking without even checking where I was?"

"You did the same thing!" she screams. "And, Ella, I asked you if we could go to the cabana before we sat on the beach and you said, 'Sure.'"

Oh, God. I remember saying "sure" but don't remember what I was agreeing to. I'd been so caught up thinking about Jack that I wasn't paying attention.

"Oh my gosh, Jamie! I'm sorry!" We embrace in a tight hug.

"I'm just glad we're both fine," she says.

"Me too," I say, opening the bag to find my water bottle. "So when you realized that I wasn't with you, did someone help you try to find me?"

"No. I just looked around for you myself," she says, fixing her ponytail.

"Well, then, who was that guy you were with?"

"I wasn't with anyone," she says.

"No one helped you find me?"

"No. No one."

I glance back at Nico to confirm that he's hearing the same thing, but he's nowhere to be found.

Poppy

25 May 1937

Gianna suggested that we give ourselves a few days to think about things, and at the end of the week, we might have some clarity. I reluctantly agreed. This long and torturous week has finally come to an end.

This afternoon, when we met at Ristorante Rocco, I convinced Gianna that, although we could not physically marry each other right now, no one could prevent us from marrying our hearts and souls together. She didn't hesitate for a second. After a walk along the shore, we went straight to the church and climbed its countless steps to the top. After catching our breaths, we admired the incredible view of the sea before walking into the sanctuary.

Once we were alone, we stood before the statues of the Blessed Mother, Jesus, and Joseph and declared our love for each other. We acknowledged that the love between us is true and has always existed. Had our families known, perhaps they would have arranged for us to be together. We held hands before the beautiful sea and exchanged sweet thoughts of our love and devotion, ultimately ending in a kiss. At that moment, our hearts were full.

After we parted, I felt conflicted by the feelings in my heart. I feel strong and content because my heart is connected with my true love. But at the same time, I feel weak because, truthfully, she is not really mine to keep. She is mine in heart, soul, and spirit, which I suppose is most important, but not in the flesh—important in a different way. I can't escape feeling guilty that someone else out there also loves her and doesn't even know this is happening. I'm torn. We must spend as much time together as we can, for I fear it may end one day. I rely on this passage for strength:

Come to me, all who are weary, and I will give you rest. *~ Matthew 11:28*

Chapter 16

Ella

Something doesn't sit right with me about my conversation with Jamie. If the old man at the flower cart said he saw Jamie walking with a man, why would she say she was alone? Perhaps he was mistaken?

I scan the area looking for Nico, who must have felt like he was intruding on my reunion with Jamie and secretly slipped away. I wish I could have thanked him for helping me.

The melodious and vibrant music coming from the cabana seems to have gotten louder since I first noticed. It lulls the people from their hot, sticky chairs to the cool shade beneath its canopy. Jamie and I wander over, and on our way, I can't stop the nagging question circling in my mind.

"So, Jame," I say.

"Yeah?"

"When you were looking for me, did you pass by an elderly man selling flowers from behind a cart?"

"Um," she says, scratching her head, "I think I did. Why?"

"Did you ask him if he'd seen me?"

"I asked a lot of people. Yeah, I think he was one of them," she says. "Why do you ask?"

"Just wondered," I say. "I showed him your picture and asked if he'd seen you. He said no at first, but then he did remember that you were there." I look at her. "Said you were lost."

"I was," she nods.

"But what I don't understand," I say, facing her, "is when he saw you walk by him a second time, he said you were with a man." I dip down to meet her eyes and she's staring at the ground, biting her nails. "Isn't that weird?" I say.

"Yeah, that's pretty weird," she says, looking back at me. "But that could have been anyone. Doesn't mean he actually remembered seeing me. Why are you questioning that?"

"So, you weren't with anyone at all?" I say, my voice laced with doubt.

"No, El, it was just me." She rolls her eyes. "He must have been mistaken."

"Must have been," I say as we near the cabana.

As we enter I watch her closely. I'm convinced that something about her isn't the same as it was when we first arrived in Tropea. She motions for me to follow her to a vacant table she spotted in the middle of the cabana. We sit and order drinks, bouncing our heads to the percussion. I feel its vibration through my soles. Three men happily play their instruments in unison, eyes closed, mouths turned up, fingers busy and heads nodding to the melody as if it's the sweetest tune they've ever played.

I notice that, for the next couple hours, Jamie's eyes occasionally sweep across the interior of the cabana as if she's expecting someone to join us, but they never do.

We stay past the last song they play. The band graciously nods to us as they pick up their instruments and prepare to leave. We continue to sit under the cabana while the clean-up crew makes their final rounds and as the last of the setting sun peeks through the trees.

I'm not sure why we stayed so long. Maybe we're making up for lost time on the beach this afternoon, which is okay. Our visit to the church will have to come tomorrow. For now, I decide not to bring up anything more about the old man behind the flower cart seeing her with a man.

****

When we arrive at Villa Georgio, the owners, a cute older couple in their seventies, are at the door ready to greet us. Jamie and I exchange surprised glances that they'd waited for us long after we said we'd arrive.

Angelina and Vinny are short and plump and walk with a slight waddle. Vinny sports a well-worn beret and Angelina wears a floral apron over her dress, as many of my older aunts did. They're both down to earth and very talkative.

When we first spoke on the phone to arrange our stay, they invited us to cook a meal with them at some time during our visit. They continuously remind us of that while showing us around the villa. I slip my backpack off and place it on the floor, continuing to nod and smile, acknowledging Angelina's stories about how much they love to cook for others.

"Couples who enjoy cooking together, stay together!" she says laughing. She seems to laugh a lot.

We end our tour in the wine cellar, the best place in the villa, according to Vinny.

"We have wine at every meal," he says, trailing close behind Angelina, mostly nodding and agreeing with everything she says.

****

The breeze on the patio the next morning is warm and sweet-smelling. After Angelina and Vinny serve us breakfast, we explain how we got lost as soon as we arrived in Tropea the day before and how unnerving that whole experience was.

"Ella met a man while we were looking for each other," Jamie teases.

"She did?" Angelina says.

I wave off the notion, explaining that it was just by chance that he found me and helped me.

"He actually found my backpack," I say. "Noticed I dropped it and brought it to me."

"What a gentleman," Angelina says.

"I think it's interesting," Jamie interjects, "that of all the hundreds of people on the beach yesterday, that he just so happens to see you drop your backpack. Don't you?"

"What do you mean by that?" I say.

"He must have noticed you when we got off the bus," she says. "He liked what he saw and was watching you. How else would he notice you dropped your bag in such a crowd?" She stares at me wide-eyed.

Angelina's pleasant smile turns slightly pursed. "Ah," she says. "A pretty girl like you will get attention. And you have no man to protect you. Be careful," she says, shaking her finger.

I kick Jamie under the table.

"We'll look out for each other," Jamie says.

"In Tropea," Angelina says, "there's usually no trouble." She looks to Vinny who approves with a nod. "But recently," she continues, "in other areas outside of Tropea, bands of pickpockets are known to work in groups. They approach unassuming tourists and pretend to offer help, but then they lure them away and steal their money! Or other things!" Angelina's face turns a crimson red as she further explains. "Some groups are violent and even assault tourists to get more money, or just to intimidate them—for fun."

At once, Angelina stands erect and shoots her hand right into the air and yells, "*Borsaiolo!*" Pickpockets. As soon as her hand comes down, she bites into it sideways, clenching her teeth tightly on her fingers for a couple of seconds. Her eyes are wild. I've seen this before from watching Nonna. It's the ultimate display of disapproval, disgust, and frustration, and one of many ways an Italian dramatically shows it.

I'm surprised at how quickly she becomes irate over the pickpockets, but later Vinny pulls us aside to explain that something terrible happened to Angelina's sister years ago when she visited from France. He said nothing more.

"We're not as worried that it might happen here. You should be okay in Tropea," Vinny says.

"Vinny, don't pretend," Angelina chides. "You know they've become *grassetto* lately. In fact, they're so bold now, they even do it during the day, in the middle of the streets!" She shakes her head and wipes her brow with her sleeve.

"Oh, Ange," Vinny says flicking his hand in the air. "The neighbors here are like family. We'll protect each other," he assures. "It won't come to that."

"Let's change the subject!" she snaps, looking at me. "You said there was a woman your grandfather wanted you to see while you're here?"

"Yes," I say.

In my backpack, I feel around for the diary that settled to the bottom. I retrieve it and open to the last page where I carefully tucked Poppy's letter to me. The letter I found in the box. With care, I unfold the delicate paper and present it to Angelina as if it's my most precious gem. And it is.

"Poppy, my grandfather, says I should look for a woman named Nina," I say, pointing to Nina's name in the letter. "He said I'll find her here in Tropea, close to the water."

"He didn't say a street name? Nothing else?" Vinny says."Just 'Nina by the water?'" He shrugs his shoulders.

"He needs nothing else, Vin," says Angelina. "There's only one area he could be talking about." She tilts her head and raises her eyebrows. Then she looks back at me. "Nina," she repeats.

At the moment, I can't tell for sure if Angelina is just curious or suspicious, but I have a feeling it's the latter. Then again, many older Italians, if they're like my Nonna, often have suspicions about certain people. And, often, they're right.

"When you go to see this woman," Angelina says, "you'll take Vinny with you." She glances at Vinny, who nods.

"Oh, that's very kind of you, Angelina, but we don't want to bother either of you with this," I say.

"No, no bother at all," says Vinny. "You can never be too sure in a place you haven't been before."

"Besides," says Angelina, "it's good for him to get out." She begins laughing and her whole body bounces in unison with each giggle. Then her smile turns serious and she raises a pointed finger in the air.

"*Sospeto*," she says in a loud whisper, shaking her finger. Yes, she's suspicious just like I thought.

Poppy

31 May 1937

My father did it again. I did all I could to control myself. My sweet mother. My little, old Italian Mamà with her plump cheeks, loving smile, and honest eyes. She makes everyone around her smile.

This evening, she made a delicious spaghetti and meatball dinner with sausage and her delicious, homemade sauce. Everything about the meal was made from her hands, including the bread. In the morning when I woke up, I smelled the baked bread and garlic all throughout the house, making me starved for dinner at breakfast! Some of the neighbors said they smelled it as they passed by walking their dogs. It immediately teased their stomachs, they said.

After a whole day of cooking in our cozy little kitchen, Mamà asked my brother and me to get the table ready and then wait in the living room until she called for us. In strutted my father, the tyrant that he is, and he immediately started yelling at my mother that he's waited too long for his dinner. Then, after complaining, he called her a few names, which I will not write, and sat down to eat. Mamà didn't have to call after us; we were already at the doorway to the kitchen, as if our presence could ever intimidate my father.

We sat down at our places as my mother gently set the food on the table with downcast eyes. My father stared only at his plate the whole time, not uttering a word, and never a thank you.

5 June 1937

I long to bring Gianna home with me, but I can never tell my parents about us, especially knowing that she's engaged to someone else. But even if she were free to marry me, I'd still not want them to know. Without a doubt, Mamà would rejoice that we've found each other after growing up together and then being apart for so long. My father, however, would never accept it. He'd say she is far beneath me. "Stick to your own kind," he'd say in his gravelly voice. And then he'd see to it that Cecelia and I are immediately married.

Cecelia. I do feel sorry for her. I wish I wanted to be with her. I wish she didn't love me and wasn't happy with the arrangement made by our parents. But Gianna Russo has stolen my heart and captured it forever. Nothing can change that.

Although Gianna's and my parents were friends long before they had us, something in my father had changed over the years, and I suspect he was part of the reason that Gianna and her family moved to Tuscany all those years ago. And for that, among other things, I will not forgive him.

If only our relationship weren't so complicated. And now, Luca tells me the townsfolk have been talking about "a girl who's been seen a lot with Franco lately." We must be more careful.

Chapter 17

Ella

A triumphant sun cuts through the stubborn overcast, breaking apart the darkness with its brilliant beams. Parting clouds reveal bits of blue allowing rays of sunshine to highlight the village rooftops, including the public library, Biblioteca Calabrese. Jamie and I stand before it, ready to delve into history, as the sun burns our shoulders and sweat is dripping into our eyes. We walk through the double arched doors awaiting a cool respite, but find none. Angelina suggested we start here first, as this would be the place where we might find records or articles pertaining to Gianna's life.

We sit at a dark wooden table among other sweating patrons, some appear deep into research and others casually reading or working with friends. I take out Poppy's diary and my notebook and review my notes.

Franco stopped going to school at about fifteen years old, and for the next two to three years he'd been staying home to help his father on the farm. One of the diary entries mentions that Gianna was to celebrate her eighteenth birthday just before the end of that school year, so she had to be around that age when she and Franco reunited. I show the entry to Jamie and she agrees.

"If Gianna and Franco were reunited in 1937 and she was eighteen then, she must have been born around 1919," I say.

"Sounds about right," Jamie says.

"So we'll be looking for birth records in that time frame."

"Why do you need those?" Jamie asks. "We know she *was* alive, we just don't know if she's *still* alive, right?"

"I want to see her birth records," I say, and Jamie raises an eyebrow. "I just need to see them. Makes it feel real."

"Okay, whatever you think," she says.

We leave our table and walk over to the information desk. Behind the desk is an older woman with curly greying hair, neatly tucked behind her ears. She's scanning books and occasionally glances up to check the line of people. She chews on her gum in a slow circular motion, much like a cow or horse. Behind her are two other helpers sorting and marking books, dedicated to their task and not looking up at all.

When it's our turn, we explain to the gum-chewing woman that we'd like to look at old birth and death records as well as older articles dated around 1937 to 1939.

"Why do you want that?" she asks.

"I'm trying to find an older friend of the family who grew up in Tropea," I say.

"Hm. If she's a friend, wouldn't you know when she was born and when she died?" she retorts.

"She's someone my grandfather knew and I'm trying to find out more about her."

"So, why the 1937 to 1939 articles?" she says. "Was she famous or something?" She glances at the clock and rolls her head around as if to loosen a tight muscle.

I feel myself shifting from one foot to the other and I take one cleansing breath to sustain my patience. I can already tell she's not interested in anything I have to say. I ignore her questions and dig through my backpack to retrieve my notepad, Gianna's picture, and whatever else I might need for this woman. Jamie elbows me and I ignore that, too.

"I have a diary," I say into my backpack.

"A diary?" says the woman. "Should you be reading someone else's diary?" she adds between chews. I purposely keep my head down to prevent it from whipping up and spouting something sarcastic. I still need this woman's help.

"I'm not sure how a diary can help anyway," she continues.

Sweat forms in my armpits and runs down my back, and I quickly feel my composure begin to slip away. *Stay calm. Poppy would stay calm.*

"Is there something I can help you with?" says an amiable and somewhat familiar voice. I slowly lift my head from the bag to see if it's me they're speaking to, and I see him. Now I know why Jamie has been so quiet. And why she elbowed me. I wonder how long he's been standing there. I stare into his deep brown eyes, dark waves cascading around them. I feel one corner of my mouth slightly turn upward. His eyes relax and he smiles.

"N—Nico?" I say.

"Yes," he says, nodding. "Nice to see you again!"

"What are you doing here?" I say.

"I work here," he says.

"Here?" I think how stupid I'm sounding. Of course he works here. He's standing behind the help desk.

"Yes, while I go to school," he says.

"What are you studying?" Jamie asks.

"You remember my friend, Jamie," I say.

"Yes. The lost one." He laughs. "I'm studying law." When he says this, Jamie's jaw drops.

"So am I," she says. "Well, I've actually just passed my exams and recently started at a law firm back home."

As they continue talking about law schools and bar exams, I notice that the gum-chewing woman has slipped away, and I feel disappointed that I may have lost an opportunity. Nico glances from his conversation with Jamie and our eyes briefly lock again.

"What was it that you came here for?" he asks.

I begin to explain once more about Gianna and wanting to find records and articles.

"I see," he says. "What records are you looking for?"

"Birth and possibly death certificates," I say.

"Hmm. I'm sorry, but those kinds of records are no longer kept here," he says.

"We were told that we could find them in this library," I say, disappointed.

"Yes, a long time ago they were kept here," he says. "But now they're kept at the Registrar of Vital Statistics. Everything in one place."

I look down at my notepad and add this to it.

"Where's *that* located?" Jamie asks.

"Not far from here. I can show you," he says. "But wasn't there something else you needed? Maybe I can still help?"

"Well, yes," I sigh. "I'm also looking for local news articles around the years 1937 to1939, in this area, Vibo Valentia. But closer to Tropea, near the sea."

"That's very specific," he says. "What do you hope to find?"

"Um, a distant relative," I say, "Someone we lost track of."

"Something might have happened to her," Jamie adds. "Something sinister."

I elbow Jamie.

Nico tilts his head as if trying to figure out if Jamie is serious, and then he walks around the edge of the counter, motioning for us to follow. He's wearing khakis and a white t-shirt that defines his muscular shoulders. He smells of leather, earth, and mint. Jamie notices, too, and she makes an exaggerated sniff of the air and smiles.

Nico brings us to an area of the library where people are diligently working, each plugged into some kind of electronic device. Some are reading, some listening, and others writing, often stopping to look up at their screen and then quickly scribble their thoughts on paper. He sits in front of one of the computers and types something in the search box. He waits for a response and then his fingers begin to madly dance across the keys.

"I've minimized a few of the local news sites that date back to 1937 in or near Tropea. We also may have more articles in the back from older newspapers. I can show you when you're finished here if you'd like."

"Yes, we'd love that," says Jamie.

"Yes, thank you, Nico."

He nods and smiles.

"I hope you find your relative," he says. "And I hope there's nothing sinister." He winks and Jamie laughs out loud.

"I'll be here until three o'clcok," he says, walking back to the front desk.

I check my watch. Two more hours.

Jamie and I jump right into our search, side by side on our own computers, combing through article after article but finding nothing relevant. I'm growing weary and discouraged and beginning to feel that this has all been a big waste of time. Every now and then I think I see Nico walk around the corner to see if we're still here, but that could just be my imagination. Soon I'm daydreaming at the screen, still scrolling, not really paying attention, until I think I see something. *Wait. What was that?* I stop immediately and scroll slowly back up to where I think it was. And then I see an article: "Local Woman Missing: Community Comes Together."

"Jamie!" I yell, and a few eyes shoot in my direction. I mouth "sorry" and turn my computer toward Jamie so we can read the article together.

Poppy

17 June 1937

Many of the townsfolk continue talking about a girl that I've been seen with, and they are speculating about who she is. They do not know her name, but they have seen us together. I fear that rumors might begin spreading, so we must work harder at keeping our time together more discreet. Already we are meeting less often. We know that our innocent reunion that began as friendship has blossomed into something much deeper. But do they?

27 June 1937

I took Gianna to the vineyard today as I knew it would be safer for us there than in town. We were immediately captivated by its rolling green hills and beautiful plants and flowers and grapevines.

We walked hand in hand along the path toward the back of the vineyard. No one else was around, only me, Gianna, and the nature that surrounded us. She took my hand and led me further down the path into a wooded field, still part of the vineyard, but not often used. The trees and vines above the path grew together and connected, creating an arched ceiling. Little rays of sunshine pierced through the small open spaces between the vines. She continued to walk ahead of me on the path, our hands still clasped, and then she stopped at a grassy area.

She turned toward me, ran her fingers through my hair, and stared into my eyes. I held her waist and pulled her in. Her lips parted slightly, and she leaned in closer, placing hers on mine. Soon, our bodies moved in unison on the soft grass. Only the birds knew we were there.

Chapter 18

Ella

I stare, dumbfounded, at the screen. My peripheral vision disappears and I'm alone in a tunnel that seems to deepen. *Is this it? Is this the one?* My eyes sweep from title to subtitle again and again: "Local Woman Missing: Community Comes Together." The words can't come fast enough. I devour them one by one in rapid succession, but it's not sufficient. I need more. My breaths are shallow and my heart accelerates.

After reading it twice alone in my head, I read it aloud in English next to a silent Jamie:

> "The search for Gianna Russo of Vibo Valentia continues. She was last seen leaving her home on Via Carmello a week ago Tuesday to go for her morning walk around 9:00 a.m., says a neighbor. Over the course of the week, some witnesses claim to have seen her on Via Rosa coming from the beach. Others say they spotted her at the old sanctuary, Santa Maria dell'Isola. Authorities are checking all leads and tips. More than 100 people came out today to help in the search, including her mother and father. The search has recently been expanded to the coastline and nearby farm areas."

I look up from the article at Jamie, whose jaw has dropped. I snap a picture of the article with my phone and jot down Via Carmello, Via Rosa, and Santa Maria dell'Isola on my notepad.

"I can't believe we found something," Jamie says in slow, monotonous tones. But she quickly adds, "Let's keep looking," and together we continue to scroll through the remaining articles.

Several headlines suggest a changing state of affairs developing in Italy at the time:

> "Italian Regime Banned Marriages between Italians and Abyssinians"
> "Soviet Union Accuses Italy of Torpedoing Two Russian Ships in the Mediterranean"
> "German Chancellor Adolf Hitler Meets with Premier Benito Mussolini in Munich"
> "Italy Withdraws from the League of Nations"
> "Mussolini: Civil Rights of Italian Jews Cancelled"

The headlines produce a slight sickness in my stomach, knowing what was to come in our world's history.

Very few local articles appear among these headlines. The article I found about Gianna was the most explicit and detailed.

Jamie enables English translation on her computer and pulls up the article I found about Gianna. While reviewing the articles that follow, she catches another smaller article off to the side, almost unnoticeable. "El, look at this one," she points. "Came a month after the first one on Gianna."

I notice that the title is a light font, almost the same as the article. We could have easily missed it. I read it aloud, "'Authorities question two suspects but have very little to connect them to the case. Although the search has been called off for now, the investigation will continue.'"

"Two suspects?" she says as we exchange curious glances. I snap a quick picture and jot down "two suspects" in my notepad.

The last article I almost miss simply states: "Vibo Valentia woman, Gianna Russo, still missing. Her whereabouts remain a mystery."

"Oh my gosh, El," Jamie says, and swivels her chair to face me. "I can't believe it. We actually found something."

I rub my eyes and lean back in my chair, absorbing our discoveries. Behind Jamie I see Nico talking with the older librarian, his back to us. Her hands on her hips, she leans on one leg, and shakes her head. Her eyes are narrow and her hair bounces as she speaks. *Is she scolding him?*

"I know, Jame," I reply. "I don't even know where to begin with what I'm thinking right now."

Nico and the librarian turn toward us. She squints as Nico points in our direction.

"Two suspects," Jamie says. "Who could they be?"

"There's got to be more somewhere," I say as Nico and the librarian stride toward us.

Jamie notices my distraction and follows my gaze. "What's going on?" she asks.

"I have no idea."

The librarian, who is slightly ahead of Nico, takes measured steps in our direction. Her calf-length flowy skirt gathers between her legs with each step. Nico follows behind her, rolling his eyes. He cradles two books in his right arm, while his left hand rests in his pocket. Something tells me to minimize the site on my computer, which I quickly do.

When they reach us, the librarian removes her glasses and flashes a fake smile. She clasps her hands together and eyes my computer.

"Girls," she says, "how are you coming along with your research?"

"Fine," we reply.

"Oh, good. Now, what was it exactly that you were looking for? A woman, I think you said?" We stay silent, watching her.

"I'm sorry I couldn't be of more help earlier," she pivots toward Nico, "but I'm so glad that Nico was able to help."

We nod our heads "yes."

She faces us again. "So did you?"

"Did we what?" Jamie asks.

"You know—find what you were looking for?" she says, tilting her head.

"No," I blurt, "unfortunately, we didn't."

Jamie catches on and nods in agreement.

"And we were here all this time for nothing," Jamie feigns annoyance.

"Yes, you were here for a very long time," says the librarian. "That's too bad," she says, folding her arms at her waist. Although she's frowning, I feel that she's secretly smiling inside.

Nico stands impatiently next to her. He runs his fingers through his hair and then shakes his head, loosening his waves. He glances at me with apologetic eyes.

"Well," she continues, "you're more than welcome to come back tomorrow."

"Tomorrow?" I say, looking at my watch. "I thought the library was open 'til five."

"We're closing early today," she says, "for Inventory." Something seems off about this woman. Nico, now standing slightly behind her, shrugs his shoulders. She looks back at him, "Right, Nico?"

"Yes, that's right," he says.

The librarian turns to leave, expecting Nico to follow, but before he does, he faces me and relinquishes the books he was holding. "Here are those books you wanted me to find," he says loudly. "It was nice to see you again."

"Oh, thank you," I say, taking the books. "Nice to see you, too."

He holds his gaze on me for a few seconds and then turns to leave.

When he's a few feet away, Jamie whispers, "What books did you ask him to find?"

"I didn't ask him to find anything," I say.

I watch him follow the librarian all the way from where we're standing to the Information Desk. He strides past the other working patrons. A few lift their heads as he passes. Some join in following him as he exits. I notice a warm feeling expanding within me and brush it off to examine the books. One is titled *Southern Italy* and the other is *Santa Maria dell'Isola*. I turn the second book toward Jamie so she can see the cover. "It's the sanctuary mentioned in the first article," I say. "Remember? Some of the witnesses said they saw Gianna there."

Jamie's eyes widen and she nods her head, taking the book from me. A curious piece of paper sticks out at the top, so I pull it out. It's a note. Jamie looks on as I read: *"I would like to see you again…maybe I can help you. ~Nico"* His number scribbled beneath it.

"Are you gonna call him?" Jamie asks.

"I don't think so," I say, and shove the note in my pocket as we join the checkout line.

Poppy

5 July 1937

Why does my father laugh and play around with visitors and friends, but with his own family he almost never smiles? He's a paranoid man who believes in conspiracy theories and the notion that one should keep their friends close but their enemies closer. I think he really believes he has enemies. Maybe he does. It's easy enough to see why many friends have slowly drifted away. He destroyed the few friendships that he and Mamà had with others—good people no longer wanting to be around us because of him, leaving Mamà to feel even more isolated than she already is.

Mamà is the kindest person you would ever want to know. She is joyful, loving, and sweet to everyone and she warmly hugs Luca and me all the time. I know we are her pride and joy. I often wish Mamà would marry a different man, anyone other than my father who clearly doesn't deserve her love. But she is loyal and true no matter how badly he treats her, and she makes him feel loved and welcomed regardless of the lack of love she receives. Is he even capable of feeling loved?

9 July 1937

As Gianna and I were leaving the vineyard and just on the edge of town, I couldn't help but feel that we were being followed. I can't explain it, other than a heaviness of someone's presence that stayed with me through the town. I kept looking over my shoulder and around corners but never actually saw anyone, that is until we arrived at the point on the path where Gianna and I say goodbye and part our separate ways. As I kissed Gianna, I saw someone disappear into the shadows behind Rocco's where we used to meet. Whoever it was must have noticed that I looked in their direction, because they disappeared at the exact same time. I told Gianna what I saw and made her promise to be careful and aware of her surroundings as she walked the rest of the way home. Who could that have been? Am I becoming paranoid like my father?

13 July 1937

Dinner was silent again, which is what I had hoped for. A quiet, disengaged father is better than the alternative. Only the gentle placing of glass upon wood, forks scraping dishes, mouths chewing, and occasionally a swallow or gulp could be heard. No voices. As if ghosts sat at the table instead.

But in the moment I was beginning to relax and think that we might actually have a peaceful dinner, my father pounded the table with his fist, jolting us from serenity. Our bodies froze as we sheepishly looked at my father. He lifted his gaze from his food and stared at me. Staring with no words. When he finally spoke, he said, "You need to join that Royal Italian Army, son. Things are getting worse. They need men." I didn't know what to say. I just stared back, knowing that a response was expected and it better be the right one. My face was hot and I felt my eyes well up.

"Okay," was all I could manage. I bent down, pretending to look for something I dropped so I could hide and wipe away my tears.

"Okay?" he yelled when I popped back up.

"I will," I said, and he gave a nod. I fought back more tears of helplessness and anger at not standing up for myself. Not saying, "I don't want to join. It's still a choice so why should I have to? What about Gianna?" It was an eternity before dinner finally ended. I am distraught and filled with grief.

Chapter 19

Ella

L eaves whisper through the branches and the sun fades into the clouds as we emerge onto the property of Villa Georgio. I look out my window at the lengthening shadows surrounding the villa, thinking about Gianna. Could she still be alive somehow? If they never found her, does that mean she's still out there living a whole life that no one knows about? I slide my hand into the front pocket of my jeans feeling for Nico's note. My fingers find the paper but I don't take it out.

As soon as our driver drops us off in front of the villa, we are immediately greeted by a savory bouquet of fine cooking. Baked bread and garlic are released into the air, and I'm back in Poppy and Nonna's kitchen. So many memories of their cooking together. As Nonna mixed herbs and spices into the vegetables, she'd take a few and pop them into her mouth and would continue doing that throughout the entire cooking process with all of the foods. After Poppy said the blessing, she'd say, "I'm just not that hungry today," while the rest of us smiled and winked at each other, knowing she'd already eaten a full meal before we even sat down.

As I set the books Nico gave me on the bench by the door, I spy the dining room table filled with large serving plates of food. Burning candles glow from their place at the center of the table set for four. We walk through the main doors to the dining room as Angelina places bottles of wine in the middle of the table next to the candles. She's practically jumping up and down as she waves us over to join her.

"Come. Sit," she says.

"For us?" I say.

"Yes, of course. Everyone is welcome," she says.

Jamie and I are starving, so we happily sit next to Vinny while Angelina pours the wine.

After the second bottle of wine, Angelina asks us to tell her about the woman who Poppy wants us to find.

"Her name is Nina," I say.

"Near the water, right?" Angelina asks.

"Yes, that's what Poppy wrote in his letter," I reply.

"If she's near the water," Angelina says, "then I think I know where to start." She lifts her eyebrows. "You're going tomorrow, yes?"

"Yes, tomorrow after I go to the Registrar of Vital Statistics for the birth and possibly death certificates," I say.

"Oh, you didn't get those today?" Angelina says. She furrows her brow as if contemplating the reasons for this.

"No, they no longer keep them there. They said—"

"You mean Nico said," Jamie interrupts, trying to be funny. I don't think it's funny and I shoot her a look.

"Nico? The young man from the beach?" Angelina asks, smiling.

"Yes, apparently he works there," I say, and for some reason I feel my face flush. "He's the one who told us that we needed to go to some record of vital statistics office."

"He wants El to call him," Jamie winks.

"Just to help," I say. Angelina, Jamie and Vinny look at me as if they're aware of something that I'm not. I quickly begin justifying my thoughts. "He was really nice and wanted to help us. And he was a lot of help. Even gave me a couple books. There's nothing more to that, so . . ." I don't finish, but I think they get it.

"Okay," Angelina says. "As I was saying, you'll want to take Via Violla most of the way. That will eventually run into Via Bella, and at the end of Via Bella you could go left or you could go right." She pauses to see if I'm following, and I nod. "Go left and it will lead you toward the sea. If you go right it will lead you toward vineyards and fields." As she speaks, her fingers trace an imaginary map on the table. I write down everything she says. *Vineyards and fields. The same vineyard that Franco took Gianna to?*

"And the steep hills! Don't forget those, Ange," Vinny says. "We'll be climbing forever," he jokes, glancing at Angelina for confirmation, and she nods.

"And right at the crest," Angelina says, spreading her arms wide, "are green rolling hills of vineyards, fields, and farmland. As far as the eye can see."

"But don't we have to turn left just before the hills?" Vinny asks. "And walk down a narrow street, more like an alley. What's that called again?"

"Yes, you're right, Vin. And the narrow street is Via Rosa. It almost doesn't even look like a street," Angelina replies.

"Ah, yes. Via Rosa," he repeats. Their eyes briefly meet and I sense something shift in the room.

"Is everything okay?" I ask, looking from Angelina to Vinny and back to Angelina. Angelina glances from me to Vinny.

"It was a long time ago, Ange," he says, and she gives him a warning look before continuing.

"Yes," she pauses. "A very long time ago, Via Rosa was not an area you'd want to go to, especially alone."

"People say the *malocchio*, the evil eye, is known there. Many

Italians from way back were afraid of having bad luck, and the scariest thing of all is the *malocchio*. You know what *malocchio* is, right?"

"Yes, I do, but I don't think Jamie does." I look over at Jamie who's been unusually quiet.

"I have no idea," Jamie says.

"*Malocchio*. Say it like this: *ma-loik*. Try it." Angelina says to Jamie. After Jamie repeats it correctly, Angelina gives her a big approving nod. Nonna taught me that there are varying pronunciations of this word, depending on where in Italy you were from. "It's the look," Angelina continues, "that one gives to another if they're jealous or envious. Those who are extremely beautiful are more susceptible because others may be jealous of their good looks."

Angelina studies both Jamie and I as if trying to assess our risk based on our looks. She shrugs her shoulders and continues.

"If you're the person giving the *malocchio*, you can cause harm to another person. It's like giving someone bad luck or putting a curse on them and causing them pain, headaches, or misfortune. Can be intentional or unintentional," Angelina says.

"Sounds like voodoo," Jamie says under her breath.

"The negative power of envy will lead to bad luck," Angelina says.

"Some even believe," Vinny jumps in, "that if someone says something *positive* about another person or highly praises them, that they may fall victim to the *malocchio*." He makes a funny expression with his mouth as if the mere thought disgusts him.

"Seriously?" Jamie says, also seemingly disgusted or embarrassed.

I remember Nonna talking about the *malocchio* once when my cousin brought her six-month-old baby to visit last summer. The baby was lying on her back on the couch, looking up at me as I was leaning over her making silly noises. I told my cousin she had the most beautiful baby in the world. Suddenly, Nonna appeared out of nowhere making the sign of the cross. She looked at me and put her finger to her lips. She was shushing me. I thought it was really strange but blew it off as one of Nonna's many unusual quirks.

But now, after what Angelina is saying about the *malocchio*, I know that Nonna must have been trying to ward off any unintentional or intentional envy.

"Do you have a necklace with a *corno*? You know, horn? Maybe gold?" Angelina says.

"No, but I think Poppy had one," I say.

"Well, you might want to wear one when you visit Nina. To keep away evil spirits," she says, and then quickly adds, "Italians also wear a horn as a symbol of pride, you know."

I nod, noticing Angelina's Italian horn necklace layered on top of a cross necklace, and I wonder which reason she wears hers. *Did someone put a malocchio on Gianna?*

"I can figure out if you have the *malocchio*," she says, "and how to get rid of it." She smiles at me in a proud and reassuring way.

"I'm pretty sure we won't need to worry about *that*," Jamie quips.

I give her a look. My phone vibrates and at a glance I see a text from Uncle Luca. I open it: *Hope you're having a great time in Italy! Find out anything interesting yet?* I smile thinking how lucky I am to have an Uncle like him. Always taking care of our family.

****

Early the next morning, Vinny isn't feeling well and decides he's not strong enough to escort us to Nina's. They beg us to wait until he's better, but time on this trip is going fast and I still have much to do in the next week or so. We decide last-minute to go to Nina's before making a trip to the vital statistics office. We dash out the door to catch the taxi, waving to Angelina and ignoring her pleas to stay. But before we reach the car door, she shoves something in my hand and runs back inside. Once inside the car, I open my hand and see a gold necklace with an Italian horn. I stuff everything I might possibly need, including the necklace and Nico's note, into my backpack.

The taxi drops us off close to the area where our tour bus did a few days ago. It was as if we were plunked down right in the middle of a painting which had come to life. Some houses stand so close together there's less than a few inches of space between them. Others are connected like apartments. Each has separate entryways adorned with baskets of flowers as I'd seen in many pictures and on our tour through Scilla. Some of the entrances to the houses have stairs leading to a higher level while others are right off the street. This pattern of alternating entryways repeats all throughout the hilly neighborhoods. I don't know what to look at first. My eyes are drawn up to the curvy iron rails that frame all the upper balconies with just enough space to seat two people.

The houses in the next neighborhood we cross are very different. They too stand close together, but they're more humble and simple. The buildings slightly behind them are more compact. But regardless of the differences in houses and neighborhoods, one thing remains the same: the cobblestone roads beneath our feet and the quaint, old world charm of a small town with friendly people just waiting to chat with you.

Up ahead is the exact spot that Angelina told us about. We follow her directions and remember to go left toward the water. We encroach upon a small road that we almost mistake for a driveway.

"Are you sure this is it?" Jamie asks. I review the directions I'd written and peer down the dimly lit road.

"Yes, this must be it." I take hesitant steps forward and Jamie reluctantly follows. The air is stagnant and I can't help but wonder if the fresh air just a few feet away ever moves through it. A small sign, almost faded, reads "Via Rosa." My heart skips a beat. I direct Jamie's attention to the sign and she gives a concerned look that matches how I feel.

Had Via Rosa become lost or forgotten over time? Poppy said that parts of Southern Italy struggled for years to remain as strong as the

North, even after World War II. It seems as if most of Southern Italy ·
had regained its strength and beauty, all except for the little
dilapidated street of Via Rosa.

The doorway of each dwelling, spaced about ten to fifteen feet
apart, has a small streetlight right above it. Most of the lights flicker
while others are unlit.

"Keep going?" Jamie asks.

"Keep going." I say. And for the better part of an hour, we knock on
every door asking if there's a Nina living there. Not one person on one
whole side of the street is named Nina nor do they know anyone named
Nina. I note who isn't home in case we need to return tomorrow. Most
of the people we meet are kind and willing to talk, but some answer the
door with caution, questioning our intent and connection to a Nina. I
wonder if they're telling the truth or keeping a lie. When we reach the
end, we cross to the other side and begin again.

About halfway down, the wall dips slightly left just before a
meager staircase of only four steps leads to an arched doorway. The
bronzed light above it flickers. Two shutter slats from the window
near the door quickly open and close.

"Did you see that?" Jamie whispers, and I nod. Our eyes remain locked
on the window, and a few seconds later, from a small uncovered space near
the edge of the shutters, an eye is peeking back at us.

Poppy

20 July 1937

*Is he testing me? Why is my father so different with me than he is even
with Luca? He always has something to say about my clothes, my grades
when I was in school, or my friends. He never sees the good I do but
readily points out what I don't do right. He smiles at Luca, but not at*

me. To others his face might not reveal a smile, but I see it. My father's face is always serious and stern. His features slope down in a hopeless expression. But sometimes I can see a very minuscule crease in his left eye that arcs ever so slightly upward when he looks at Luca. That's his smile. But not for me.

Every day for the last week, my father pushes and reminds me about joining the army. I don't feel that it's something I can avoid now. And it might be the only thing I can do right in his eyes. Does he want to get rid of me? When he brings it up, Mama's eyes fill with tears and she leaves the room.

I dread telling Gianna and avoid doing so every time we meet. She has already talked about breaking off her engagement for me.

25 July 1937

Today in the vineyard, Gianna seemed anxious, not relaxed and at ease as usual. I could sense that something wasn't right. When we sat on the bench farthest from the winery, she took my hands in hers and looked right into my eyes. A nervous feeling crept inside my stomach.

"I have something important to tell you," she said, half smiling. I waited for what seemed an eternity before she finally said the words. But before she uttered a word, she took my hand, brought it to her belly and rested it there. Then she looked up at me. It took me a second before she said it. "I'm pregnant."

"What? Oh my God," was all I could say at the moment. I've always wanted to be a father. But now? I must have hesitated for too long, because her smile became serious.

"Are you upset? I know it's surprising," she said, glancing at the ground. "But are you happy? Because I'm happy."

"Yes, of course I'm happy!" I said, and hugged her tight, not wanting to let go. I pulled away a little, though. "But I'm also worried. Everything is so complicated."

"We'll be okay. We'll be together soon, right?" she said. All I could do was nod and hug her again. I couldn't tell her what was really on my mind.

Chapter 20

Ella

Jamie reaches for my hand and gives it a quick squeeze. I squeeze back as we continue our staring contest with the eye. The shutters blink and then it's gone, but a second later it's back again. I lightly rap on the door causing it to disappear for a third time. The shutters remain motionless. I knock once more and the door opens sharply about three inches wide. Within that space the eye appears once again revealing wisps of frizzy hair on a partial face. Slowly the door sways just enough to expose the other eye and a chubby face on an older woman with a crooked smile. Wispy, loose greys fall haphazardly around her plump cheeks, their curled ends fraying at her jawline. She scratches her jaw and tucks a curl behind her ear. Her cropped pants and short-sleeved shirt are partially covered by a floral apron. Old leather sandals can't contain her wild toes poking through the spaces in all directions. *Nina?* Silence fills the space between us as we awkwardly stare at one another for what seems like forever.

"*Ciao*," she says in a raspy voice, and I notice some of her teeth are missing. Jamie scopes out the woman's home, trying to peek beyond her to see inside the house.

"*Ciao*. I'm looking for someone named Nina," I say to the woman in Italian. "Are you Nina?"

She immediately glances to the floor and then peers outside behind me. I turn to follow her gaze but find nothing.

"No, I'm sorry," she says with downcast eyes.

"Do you know of anyone named Nina? Who might have lived here?" I ask.

"No. No Nina here," she shakes her head. I can't help but feel so close to finding her. I fumble around in my bag and retrieve Poppy's diary, promptly turning over the cover. I take out Gianna's picture and present it to the woman.

"Have you ever seen this woman?" I ask.

She takes the photo from my hands and pulls it in closely. Her eyes twitch as she studies it. And there's something else. Surprise? Recognition? I can't decide which, but more resides in those eyes. The woman pushes the photo back into my hands.

"This is not Nina," she says.

"Not Nina?" I repeat in English for Jamie.

"Excuse me, but did you say this is not Nina?" Jamie asks.

"I'm sorry I couldn't help you," the woman says. "I have to go." She starts to close the door, but I stop her.

"Please, just wait," I say, and she pauses, still holding the door against my hand. "If you know this woman is not Nina, then that must mean you know who Nina is?"

She says nothing but furrows her brow. Her brooding eyes have much to say. And then, reluctantly, she opens the door wide, motioning for us to come in. I start to follow but Jamie pulls me back.

"Are you sure we should go in?" Jamie whispers. "We don't know her. She seems weird, El."

"I have to, Jame. This might be our only chance. I have to find out," I say.

We step into her simple home consisting mostly of one room. A

141

small kitchen, not much larger than the sitting room, is off to one side and a short hallway with two closed doors side by side are on the other. If I were to stand in the middle of the room and hold my arms out straight at my sides, I might actually touch the walls on both ends. The air has an old attic smell mixed with garlic that's been sitting around for too long. Bare walls on the inside are in almost as much need of repair as those on the outside.

I place my bag on the old woman's tattered sofa, being careful that the buckle doesn't catch in the small holes. Jamie and I sit next to each other as the old woman places a pitcher of water and three glasses on a little table between us. She fills each of the glasses halfway and then plops herself onto the chair across from us. She folds her arms and rests them on top of her belly.

"I am not Nina," she sighs, shaking her head, "but I knew her. Very well." Her eyes fill with tears and she blinks quickly, looking away. We wait anxiously for her to continue. "I'm Maria. Nina was one of my closest friends," she says. *Was?* The woman raises her glass and takes a sip. She places it back on the table and inhales deeply. "We grew up together. Like sisters," she says.

"What happened to her?" I ask.

"She passed on," she says, "about a month ago. Cancer." She shakes her head. My heart sinks into my stomach. *I'm too late.*

"Did she live here? With you?" Jamie asks.

"Oh no. Not with me. She lived a few houses down," she says, pointing. "I miss her so much."

"I'm so sorry," I say, restraining myself from asking the roaming questions in my head.

"Why are you looking for Nina?" she finally asks.

"My grandfather wanted me to find her. I think she knew something about the woman in the photo," I say. "He was in love with her." I trace the frame's edge with my fingers.

"Did something happen to this woman?" Maria asks. "What did you say her name was?"

"Gianna," I say. Maria's eyes flicker.

"And your grandfather? What is his name?"

"His name is Franco. Salvatore Franco Perri," I say.

Maria takes out a small rag from her pocket and wipes her brow.

"They grew up together south of here in Scilla," I continue. "He passed away recently and—"

"God rest his soul," she interjects, making the sign of the cross.

"Thank you," I say. "So, before he died, I think he'd been trying to find his old friend, Gianna. I guess I'm doing what he couldn't."

She glares at me intently. "The book you have with all the writing," Maria says, motioning toward my hand. "Can I see it?"

"No, I'm sorry but you can't," Jamie blurts. "Not until you tell us what you know."

Maria pauses, staring off into her kitchen. She is pensive, as if contemplating and choosing her words precisely.

"Your grandfather. He went to war, didn't he?" she asks. "Became a cook?"

"How did you know that?" I say.

"And he must have made it through the war!" she chirps. "Of course he did, because you wouldn't be here if he didn't."

"Yes. He served in the Royal Italian Army," I say.

"That's all. That's all she's saying," Jamie interjects and gives me a warning look. "You've said enough, El. Let her tell us what she knows."

I nod at Jamie, still dumbfounded by what I've heard.

"So he must have gone to America," Maria says, "to look for her."

"I don't understand—"

"You have his eyes. I knew there was something about you."

I feel my eyes squinting, trying to comprehend, but she's not willing to give it all to me yet.

"I looked for her, too. We all did," Maria continues. "Ever since that day she left and never came back." She wipes a tear from her cheek. "Some say she's up in the north country still hiding. Some say she left for America with a lover." She shakes her head and blows her nose wildly into her rag. Then she lifts her eyes and stares into mine. "Others think he killed her."

I clench my teeth and glance at Jamie who's scratching her head.

"How do you know all this? Who are you?" I ask.

"I know this because I was there when it happened," she says. "I was always there . . . with *her*. Until that day," Maria says, reaching for the photo. "May I?"

I hand it to her.

"I know this because I'm . . . Gianna's sister."

Silence fills the room. I hear the wheezing of my own breath but nothing more.

Impossible.

Both of Gianna's sisters died in childbirth.

It's true. I read it in the diary.

Poppy

5 August 1937

This was not a good day. After many agonizing weeks and increasing pressure from my father, I decided it was time to enlist in the army. Some of my friends have already enlisted, and with the threat of an impending draft, despite my fears, I felt it was the right thing to do.

Telling Gianna was impossible. My stomach was in knots all day until we met.

"Franco, no!" she cried.

"Gianna, I have to. It's my duty." I tried to sound convincing. "It will be a short tour, I promise. And I'll be allowed to visit. Once in a while," my voice caught. When tears began to fall steadily on her cheeks, I questioned everything I'd ever considered about joining. All of my doubts and fears returned and I no longer felt willing to go.

"But what about the baby?" she sobbed. I wiped her tears and placed my hand on her belly.

"I will be here for you and our baby," I said. She brought my hand to her lips and kissed it and then gently cried into my cupped palm. And then I said what I dreaded most of all.

"But I need to also tell you something that I know you won't understand," I said. I gazed into her confused, beautiful, brown eyes. "I don't see any other way right now."

"What is it?" she said.

"If someone finds out that you're pregnant, being that you're unmarried, it could make your life very bad," I said, my eyes filling quickly. "I only see two choices, Gianna."

"No. I will not marry him! Is that what you're suggesting? How could you suggest that?" she cried. "After everything . . ."

"But you haven't broken off your engagement yet. Like you said you would," I said.

"Don't you think I want to?" she yelled. "It's complicated, Franco! You of all people should know that."

"Do you trust me?" I asked. She nodded. "Do you believe that I will do anything I can to protect you and our baby?" She nodded again. "Then it's either that, or else we need to get you away. Somewhere safer." In that moment, she looked more beautiful than I'd ever seen her look before. I gently cupped her face in my hands. My thumbs brushed her tears away. I pulled her in and brought her soft lips to mine. Our hungry kisses melted the world around us. If only for a moment.

15 August 1937

It is done. I am officially part of the Regio Esercito, 286th *Engineer Combat Battalion of the binary infantry division. I will depart for basic training in three weeks to Maddaloni. I have no idea where they will send me after that, but I think it may be to Greece or Africa. I've never operated a gun, or any machinery such as that, and that terrifies me. I am afraid to leave my home, especially my family and my heart and soul, Gianna. I will meet Gianna later tonight. We will go to the vineyard and to our favorite spot.*

Chapter 21

Ella

The dense air thickens, and beads of sweat gather in the small of my back. I press my shirt against it to absorb the moisture. Jamie's fingers remain stuck in her hair as if someone froze her as she swept her fingers through. Her eyes lift to meet mine and neither of us speaks.

"They think *who* killed her?" Jamie finally breaks in.

"Hard to say," Maria says. "Maybe her husband. Maybe Franco. Or maybe someone else."

The tightness in my throat rises and I leap to my feet.

"No," I blurt. "Franco did not kill her. He loved her and wanted to be with her more than anything. I know he didn't kill her. That's ridiculous!" I yell, forcing my hand out as if to dismiss the thought.

Maria's otherwise pleasant expression turns grave.

"Now, listen," she whispers, "I didn't say *I* believe Franco killed her." Her eyes scan the small room and wander toward the window. She pulls her body away from the couch and leans in to the middle space between us. I resume my position next to Jamie on the sofa. "I'm saying what people were talking about at—"

"Did people actually think that?" I interrupt. "That my grandfather snuck away in the middle of one of the worst wars in history? To come all the way back down to the tip of southern Italy?" I feel my voice and temperature rise, but I can't stop myself. "To kill the love of his life? And then what? Dispose of her somewhere that no one's ever found?" I pant, "then sneak all the way back as if nothing ever happened? No one saw him? No one noticed. Why? Why would he do that?"

Jamie's hand rests on my back. My face is hot and my palms are sweaty.

Maria, still leaning forward, continues to stare, waiting for a chance to jump in again, but I don't let her. "Anyone who's ever known my grandfather would know that there's not a single bone in his body that could ever harm anyone."

"Sometimes," Maria adds, "we do things we never thought we'd do when we're desperate. Or provoked." I begin to stand again but she motions me to sit. "I'm not saying *I* think that. But that's what the neighbors whispered among the houses. Back then."

"So what are *you* saying, then?" Jamie asks.

"Most people didn't know about Franco and Gianna because they were so secretive. But I knew." She takes out her rag again and dabs her forehead. "She told me everything." Her face relaxes, and the left corner of her mouth slightly rises.

We stare, waiting for more. The shadow of a bird descends and rests on the window ledge, takes a quick peek through the crack, and flies away. The fan facing us works tirelessly, spinning its blades to produce a monotonous squeal but little to no moving air.

"It's sad, what happened," Maria continues. "So much stood in their way. Everything they did to be together . . ." she trails off for a moment, lost in the memory. "But more people wanted them apart than together." She shakes her head as if remembering. "When we were little, Franco's father—your great-grandfather—started to see something he didn't like about my family. And once he made up his mind about us, he pushed us away."

"What do you mean?" I ask, remembering that my grandfather alluded to this in his diary but never really had proof. Just a feeling.

"Oh, Franco's and Luca's father was a terrible man," she says, screwing up her face. "He never really showed his angry side when we first lived next door. But the closer our families became, the more agitated he grew. He stopped allowing us to play together. 'Girls shouldn't play with boys,' I'd hear him yelling at them. And he was vicious when he yelled. His voice became deep and dark and it'd turn to a raspy groaning sound." She places her hand across her chest. "I used to plug my ears when he'd yell at his family. Gave me nightmares sometimes."

Maria loosens her shirt in the hopes of wafting in some air and fans herself with her hands. Then she refills our glasses with water. I take a sip, noticing it's like warm bath water, and quickly put it down.

"Then one summer day," Maria continues, "I'll never forget it: My father came home from work and told us to pack everything up, that we'd be moving the next day." She stares into the upper left corner of the ceiling, gathering her thoughts, pulling from her memory. "At the time, I thought it was because of the growing tension from the war. Maybe he wanted to move us to a safer area. Not long after, I learned from eavesdropping on a conversation between my parents that my father *did* want to keep us safe, but not from the war." She drags her gaze from the ceiling and fixes her eyes on mine. "He wanted to keep us safe from your great-grandfather."

I swallow hard, remembering my mother telling me how cruel my great-grandfather was. And then, later, finding out just how bad things were for Poppy and his family when I read about it in Poppy's diary. Poppy often reflected and questioned why his father treated his family so harshly. But sometimes he'd treat Luca with kindness and randomly other people outside of the family. I remember reading that his father often pushed their friends away, further isolating his family. While it breaks my heart to hear it again, it also fills me with pride that Poppy overcame the ever-present obstacle of his father, not allowing his difficult upbringing to prevent him from becoming the loving person he was.

"I often wonder," she continues, "if he noticed something small developing between Franco and Gianna and wanted to put a stop to it. Even when we all played together as children, I could see that there was something special, different, between Franco and Gianna. I bet he saw it, too."

"What do you think he did that was so bad to make your family ultimately take all of their belongings and their lives and move?" Jamie asks.

"I don't know," Maria shakes her head.

"Are you saying that Franco's father might have something to do with Gianna's disappearance?" Jamie continues.

"I just don't know," Maria faintly utters almost to herself.

We sit in silence for a few moments, absorbing the details of our conversation. Jamie whispers in my ear, reminding me to show Maria the pictures I'd taken of Poppy's paintings. Maria's eyes brighten when she sees the monastery and the neighborhood scene.

"Is this the neighborhood you grew up in?" I ask.

She nods. Her eyes are wide. I zoom in so she can see the details. She traces the edges of the buildings with her index finger and then travels with it along the road. She is a child again running through the streets. I swipe to the picture of the vineyard and she flaps her hands wildly.

"That's right here! Nonno Scorno's Vineyard!" She smiles so wide that her cheeks have pushed up into her eyes, creating two crescent moons. "It's right up the hill!" she exclaims. "That's where *your* grandfather Franco and *my* sister, Gianna, went to get away. To be alone."

The rolling hills in the opposite direction of the sea, just as Angelina mentioned.

Maria rises from the chair and tells us to wait right where we are; she'll be right back. She shuffles off to one of the rooms near the back of the house and we hear her rummaging through things like a little mouse. My phone vibrates next to me. I missed two texts, one from my mother and another from Uncle Luca. I can't wait to tell them what and whom I've discovered.

When Maria returns, she's holding a shoebox, its sides held together haphazardly by tape. She moves the pitcher of water and glasses to the floor and places the box on the table. Then she sits back down into the rounded indentation she had left on the seat of the chair. She reaches into the box and takes out a handful of photographs. She places them on the table and spreads them across, some overlapping others. Near the top of the picture pile, I see a familiar face. I know right away it's a picture of Poppy, and right next to him is Uncle Luca. I'd seen dozens like this in Poppy's old photo albums. They look about nine or ten years old, their skin darkened by hours of playing in the sun, their smiles wide. Both are wearing shorts and tank tops. Three girls are standing next to them wearing sundresses, also smiling, their long dark hair flowing past their shoulders. They're all roughly the same age, maybe a couple years apart at most. I now know the girls are Gianna and her two sisters, Maria and Sienna.

"This," Maria's chubby finger points at my grandfather, "is Franco, your grandfather. And this is Luca. And here is me. And next my sister Sienna. And there is Gianna." She looks up and smiles. "Oh, how we played all the time. We'd run like wild through the streets and then into each others' houses and play some more." Her hands fly through the air as she explains.

Next, she draws two photos from the pile and carefully places them on the table apart from the others. One is a picture of Gianna holding an infant, and the other one is Gianna standing next to a man I've never seen. Then she sits back and rests her clasped hands on top of her belly.

"Do you see the baby in that picture?" she asks us.

I nod, picking it up while Jamie studies the other one.

"This is the baby of Franco and Gianna," says Maria.

Prickly goosebumps scatter across my arms and head. I pull the photo close to see the baby's features, to determine who she looks like more, but it's hard to decipher in black-and-white.

"I always wondered what happened to their baby," I say.

"How is your mama?" Maria asks.

"My mama?" I repeat. "She's good. . . ." Jamie and I exchange confused glances.

"She's healthy and happy, then?" she says.

"Yes," I say, stretching it out.

"And your father. How is he?" she asks, and I'm confused by these unconnected questions.

"He died when I was little, so I never got to know him," I say. I notice that Jamie is now staring at Maria with an odd expression.

"I'm so sorry. God rest his soul," Maria says. And then she tilts her head and raises her hand to her chin. "You don't know," she says, looking at me.

Jamie mirrors Maria's gestures.

"Don't know what?" I say.

"Franco and Gianna's baby girl. What do you know about her?" she asks.

"Not really anything more than that," I say. "Poppy's diary ends before the baby becomes a child, so I don't know what happened after that."

"Do you know what they named her?" she asks.

I search my memory of the entries. "Yes. They named her Bella," I say, and Maria nods slowly.

"Yes, that's right. Her name is Bella." She pauses for a moment and adjusts her position on the chair before continuing. "But Bella wasn't the baby's full name," she says.

"I don't know what you mean," I say.

"Bella," she continues, "is short for Gabriella," she says, still tilting her head and now squinting her eyes to see if I understand.

Suddenly Jamie slaps her hand down hard on my thigh. We look at each other and, at that moment, it registers.

"That can't be," I stammer. "What you're trying to say. It can't be."

"It is, though," Maria says. "Their baby—"

"No, don't say it," I blurt, causing her to pause briefly.

"Gabriella," she croons, "is your mother."

My heart skips a beat. "Then—"

"Yes." She reads my mind. "Gianna would have been your grandmother."

But what about Nonna?

Poppy

25 August 1937

I was told today that I will head north for Maddaloni in three weeks to begin my basic training before embarking on a tour to Greece. Some of my friends are excited to go and serve our country. But not me. I'm afraid. I fear the growing tension with Germany, and there is talk that Mussolini may align with Hitler. But my father now actually smiles when he's telling someone that I've joined the army. I sometimes see his teeth when he's yelling, never when he's smiling. So now I'm finally making him proud. Or is he just happy that I'm leaving? I can never tell. It's unusual to be spoken of by my father in a positive light. He talks about me more than he does Luca now! But I worry about leaving Mamà alone with him. I won't be there to protect her from him, and I'm uncertain I can depend on Luca for that. Luca is mostly concerned with himself lately.

Gianna refused to see me for a few days after our last meeting when I told her I was joining the army. It broke my heart when she pushed me away, but I gave her space to think and hopefully she'll understand. We reluctantly decided that, after I leave, Gianna must go on with her planned wedding as soon as possible and raise the child as if it were the product of that marriage. This hurts my heart immensely, but it is the safest decision for all of us. For now.

7 September 1937

Luca pulled me aside today and told me that when he went into town this morning, a few people in the market asked him about me and Gianna. A woman told him people are saying I am involved with a married woman! A married woman? She isn't married, but I suppose she's close enough. Not long after, a man said he knows Gianna's husband (although he didn't say her name) and he fears the husband may know about us too. People should be more concerned about their own business and stay out of mine. Sadly, I'm less anxious about the townspeople talking than I am about my father hearing their whispers.

10 September 1937

Gianna and I walked among the cypress trees along the path we frequented when we knew each other as children. We were quiet as we walked, listening to the burbling river as it followed us. I led her off the path to a secluded area and we sat beneath the shade of an old oak tree. Birds gathered on its branches and peered down at us while we talked. As I told Gianna of the stories Luca heard, her eyes grew wide and she began to tremble. I took her hands in mine and tried to reassure her that they couldn't have known it was her. She pulled her hands away and shook her head, staring at the grass.

"I also have something to share with you Franco." she said. It seemed like forever before she continued. She reached up and pushed aside the stray hairs that had fallen along my brow and then situated herself so that she faced me squarely. "When I left you the last time we were together, I was distraught." I nodded, remembering. "As I walked, I felt a growing presence near me but I didn't see anyone," she continued. "I thought it was my emotions getting the best of me."

"Do you think you were being followed?" I asked, my chest tightening with each word. She didn't acknowledge my question but proceeded with her story.

"I can't explain it. It was like a heaviness all around me. Almost on top of me. I just wanted to disappear," she shook her head, "but still had a way to go before I reached my house."

"You must have been terrified," I said, angry at myself that I didn't walk her home. I couldn't walk her home.

"Every step I took was dreadful. My body was filled with fear," she panted. "When I reached my door, my mother was standing there asking where I'd been and why I hadn't told her where I was going. It was so unusual, Franco, for her to be there like that. And then she told me that he was looking for me."

"Who? Who was looking for you?" I barked.

"My fiancé Carlos."

"Do you think he was the one following you?"

"I don't know," she lamented. "I don't think so, but I don't know for sure. He came by later that night and seemed normal. Like nothing ever happened."

"Oh my God. This isn't good," I said. "We have to keep you safe, Gianna."

"I know," she said, "but what does that mean for us?"

"I don't know," I said. Although I did know, I just couldn't say it. And just like we usually do after these kinds of discussions, we sat in silence holding each other until, with heavy hearts, we had to leave. This time, I told Gianna of another way she should go home, and I pray it's safer.

Chapter 22

Ella

The sounds around me float away. They're tucked in the background, a low muffled murmur. Maria's mouth is still moving but her words are suffocated in the dense air. Jamie has been listening and observing the seriousness of our conversation, not yet knowing its full weight. She shifts her attention to me and then to Maria each time we speak, picking up on small nuances but nothing more. She faces me with her jaw dropped. I know she's waiting for me to interpret Maria's revelation, but I can't say a word.

Maria picks up the photo and gently waves it in front of me so I'll look again and acknowledge what she's telling me, but all I can think about is Nonna and my mother. *Does my mother know?* I remember what Poppy said in his diary about his parents and Luca bringing the baby to America and raising her until Poppy had finished serving in the army. Could that baby be my mother? I mean, it makes sense, but it doesn't.

Jamie's hands are on my knees and she's lightly shaking them to shift me back to the conversation.

"El?" she says.

"Sorry," I say, taking the picture from Maria. I place the picture in Jamie's hands and indicate the baby. "That baby is my mother," I say solemnly. I see the connections and questions rising in Jamie's eyes.

"She is your mama, *sì?*" Maria says.

I peer into the eyes of the happy baby Gianna holds, her soft curls touching the bottom of her mother's chin. She is snuggling into the curve in Gianna's neck. I bring the picture in closer again and trace her small, almond-shaped eyes and nose with the tip of my finger. A familiar expression emerges, and I catch glimpses of my mother's face. Poppy's face. *My face?*

"*Sì*, she is," I say. I search every inch of the picture as if I might discover something else, perhaps hidden in the background. I've only ever seen one baby picture of my mother and it always made me sad that she only had that one. It's probably why she took hundreds of pictures of me as a baby. But there *were* more pictures of my mother, they had just remained in Italy with Gianna and her sisters.

"Do you have any other pictures of the baby?" I ask, not yet ready to refer to the baby as my mother.

Maria nods and smiles as she sifts through the pictures on the table, pulling out two. One is a picture of Gianna holding her baby. She looks to be about six months old. Their foreheads and noses are touching and Gianna's eyes are closed. She is in love with her little girl. In the other picture, Gianna is outside sitting on a porch swing, her baby sleeping in the crook of her arm. Gianna smiles at her photographer, her hair swept to the side, falling over her shoulder.

"She's like you!" Maria exclaims, holding the picture next to my face.

"How can you tell? She's just a baby," I say.

"Right here," she says, pointing to her eyes and nose, and I can't deny it.

Then she does something strange. She looks at the ceiling, makes the sign of the cross, and mutters a quick prayer. For someone named Grace, I think.

"Grace?" I say.

"Oh no—just a small prayer. Happy for this moment. I said 'gracious.'" One tooth peeks through her crooked smile.

"What's this one?" Jamie picks up a picture of Gianna next to a man. The man has his arm around her while she appears awkward and stiff, not smiling and not natural like in the other photos.

"Eh," Maria shakes her head and makes a face. "The husband, Carlos. I never liked him."

"Why?"

"*Diavolo*. No good," she says stiffly. "Always on her. He didn't like it when she'd leave the house for anything. He tried to control her. But I wouldn't let him. No," she continues, "she only loved Franco. I think Carlos knew she didn't love him. But people talk and talk. And he was a jealous man." Her eyes widen.

"Was she afraid of him?" Jamie asks.

"Surprisingly, no," she says. "He made her angry and sometimes nervous, but not afraid. Except one time they had a big fight. I don't know what it was about and Gianna wouldn't say. I just knew it was something bad. Gianna and the baby came here and stayed with me. She told him she needed to take some time away. I didn't think he'd let her, but he trusted me. They stayed for a whole week!" she says, her hands fly through the air as she speaks.

"Did she go back to him?" I ask.

"Not right away," she says, "and not for long. It was maybe one month and she was back with me." She begins digging through the photos again and teases out another picture.

She places the now-familiar face of Gianna in front of me. Two men stand behind her in the background. One is someone I don't know, the other I think is Uncle Luca. The man is talking to Uncle Luca, but Uncle Luca's gaze is on Gianna.

"Is this Uncle Luca?" I ask, pointing. "I think it's him, but I'm not sure."

"*Sì*, it's Luca," she says, shrugging her shoulders. I examine her closely and notice something adrift in her eyes.

"And who's the other man?"

Maria takes the picture back and scrunches her nose, examining. "I can't remember. What was his name?" she asks herself, searching the ceiling.

"Didn't Uncle Luca sometimes check in on Gianna after Poppy went to war?" I said, recalling a diary entry that mentions this.

"Oh, yes. In the beginning, he came over once in a while," she says, her eyes lighting up. "I loved it when he visited. Luca and I were always close. Not like Franco and Gianna, but almost," she says, reaching for her glass. "Then, he came more regularly, once a week," she continues. "Sometimes the three of us strolled along the path near the coast after lunch." She pauses for a moment, bringing her hand to her chin. "Even when I couldn't go, they still went," she says, looking away.

"So Gianna and Luca became close as well," Jamie says, her elbow propped on the arm of the sofa, her head resting in her palm.

Maria nods. "Luca would stay for dinner too," she adds. "He'd hold the baby, sometimes feed her, help around the house. It was nice to have a man around again."

"I'm not surprised," I say. "He's a very selfless man, always wanting to help the family."

"But I didn't like when he tried to persuade Gianna to join the Resistance," Maria says, furrowing her brow. "I told her, 'No, Gianna. If they catch you, they'll beat you, or worse.' You'd think she'd learn after what happened to my husband. The German and Italian armies watch everyone," she continues, her eyes shifting back and forth. "They listen and they watch. If you say something they don't like? One day, you don't come home." She blinks hard.

I've read of private groups that banded together during World War two to secretly fight against the harsh rulings of the Germans and Italians who had quickly become allies. They'd spread the word about fighting against the war, sometimes hiding coded messages in books or other objects, sometimes hiding people and sometimes hiding guns. It was their way of doing something heroic and regaining control in the midst of chaos and harsh rulers. It was very dangerous.

"But I started to see something different in Luca's eyes," she says."Kindness and a genuine caring was still there. But something else was there too. His passion for helping became a preoccupation, almost a fascination, that he couldn't let go of."

"Like an obsession?" I ask.

"With what?" Jamie adds.

"Not what," she answers, "whom."

"Sounds like he was just being overprotective," I say. "If he promised Franco he'd watch over Gianna, that's exactly what he was doing."

"He must have loved you and Gianna an awful lot to be there like that," Jamie says.

"Everyone loved Gianna," Maria says with a tone I'm not sure of, but it makes me uncomfortable. Then she takes the picture with Luca standing in the background and looks at it again.

"I always thought Luca was so cute when we were little," she says, looking away. "When he got older, he grew *agitatore*—you know, getting into lots of trouble. But that didn't stop the girls in town from liking him." She takes a swig of water and places the glass down hard. "In fact, they liked him even more.

"I often dreamed that Luca would come for me once Franco found Gianna, but that never happened." Her mind wanders away again. Jamie and I sit quietly, waiting for more details of the story to emerge.

"I told Gianna about the neighbors," she continues. "I warned her that they would talk about Luca coming to visit so often. I said they'd talk just like they did when she was sneaking off with Franco. I feared that her husband would hear about it, too, and he did."

"What happened when he found out?" I ask.

"Oooh. It was bad," she says, shaking her hand. "He was in a rage. Came over waving his gun around, looking for Luca. He thought I was letting them have an affair. Right here in my own house!" she says, her face turning red. "It took a lot of convincing to calm him down."

"You must have been so scared," Jamie says.

"I was terrified," Maria says. "After that, Luca was even more worried, obsessed about Gianna's safety. I'd see him standing in the road across the street, watching. Sometimes even at night when her light was on in the bedroom. One time, when I saw him out on the grass, I opened the door and said, 'What do you want, Luca?' But he didn't even answer. Just turned around and left. I told Gianna how strange I thought it was, but she didn't seem to be bothered by it."

Something glazes over in Maria's eyes. I'm not sure what, but it takes her out of the present and places her back in the past. A mixture of concern, fear, and regret wash across her face. I sense it and I see it. The shadows begin to fall and I know we've probably overstayed our welcome, but I need to know what else she knows. Maria blinks and rises briefly to turn on a light. Then she sits back down in her chair. I feel that more is coming.

"I told her not to go for a walk that day," she says. "I had this feeling, right here," she circles the area above her heart, "that something bad was going to happen. I can't explain it. It was so strong.

"Gianna said I was overreacting. That everything was fine. She'd just be gone a half hour and she needed to get out of the house," she panted. "She didn't want to take Bella with her and asked if I would

watch her. Said she wouldn't be alone—Luca would go with her."
Maria gets up and walks into the kitchen, still talking. I watch her
pull a new rag out from one of the drawers and begin blotting the
drips of sweat pouring down her face. Upon reentering the room, she
stands directly in front of the fan and pulls her shirt out over it.

"I told her that would be worse," she continues. "Didn't she
understand the danger she'd be in if her husband saw them together?
Didn't she care?" Her eyes are brimming. Jamie and I look on. "She
was so naive," Maria says, shaking her head.

"About an hour later, Luca walked up the driveway. When I saw
him coming, I ran outside and asked him where Gianna was. He had
no idea what I was talking about. Said he was coming by to pick her
up for a walk. I panicked. I said, 'She left over an hour ago to go on
a walk with you!'" Maria puts her hands on her hips. "He said, 'With
me?' And I said, 'Yes, with you.' Then he started to panic. Started
looking around. His hands were shaking. He was scared." Maria
becomes very animated, throwing her hands into the air and shaking
her fist at the ceiling. "I asked him again, 'So you didn't see her at all,
then?' And he said, 'No, I was supposed to come here to pick her up
first.'" She trails off, dabbing the corners of her eyes. "It was a blur
after that," she says, blowing her nose.

"So do you think Luca was the last one to see her alive?" Jamie
asks.

"He says he wasn't. But I don't know." Maria walks up to the
window and peers through the crack in the shutters. Then she walks
to the kitchen to refill the pitcher. She fills her glass and drinks the
whole thing. Her breath is shallow and she's murmuring something
to herself that I can't comprehend. Jamie looks at me, waiting for
translation, but I just shrug my shoulders.

Silence fills the room all except for the ticking of the clock. I look
up; it's already five o'clock. How fast the hours flew. We needed to

be out waiting for our driver fifteen minutes ago. As we stand to leave, Maria stops us.

"You said you're close to your Uncle Luca, no?" she says in a heavy whisper.

"Yes, very. Why?" I ask.

"Talk to him. See if there's anything he remembers," she says. "We never found her. Maybe she's still—"

"Okay," I say, placing a hand on her shoulder. "I think he would have already told the authorities everything he knew, but yes, I will ask him."

"Please," she adds as she walks us to the door. She seems gracious and thanks us for coming. But I think she wishes we hadn't.

As we turn to offer a final farewell, we see Maria standing in the doorway. Her shoulders are shaking, her face buried in her hands.

Poppy

15 September 1937

Gianna and I went back to Castello Ruffo today, probably for the last time. Of all the places we meet, Castello Ruffo is our favorite. We gazed into the brilliant blue sea right out past the Straits of Messina. I wanted to take Gianna and sail out onto that water straight to Sicily and never come back.

The wind swirled around us as we stood at the edge of the castle, picking up our hair and the edges of our clothes. The waves below us crashed and fell against each other, its currents so strong. It was dangerously beautiful and captured the torment in my heart. Standing against the stone wall with Gianna in front, her back against me, my hands resting on her thickening waist, I just wanted to remain there and shield us from the passing of time and things to come. I was confused and bewildered, feeling peace one moment and craze the next.

The rhythmic dance of the white-tipped waves pulled at me, lulling me, testing me. We were so close to those waters. Just a slight tip forward and it would swallow us at once. And we would be together. Gone, but together. Gianna woke me from my trance when she called my name. "Franco," she said over the waves, "this is our spot." She waved her hand at the blue expanse. "This place. It represents our love. And how we found each other."

She's right. This is where we are most at peace together. I wiped a tear from my eye before she could see it when she turned around. Guilty for what I'd been thinking. Sorrow filled my heart. We stayed there for a few hours just watching, reminiscing, talking, dreaming. Planning and hopeful for a promising future that I could only dream about but could never really happen. We went to dinner at Rocco's and came back to watch the sunset, not caring about who might see us or how long we were gone.

And then, no matter how hard we tried to put it off, the most dreadful moment had come to say goodbye. We sat quietly on a bench near the water. I reached into my pocket and pulled out a small jewelry box I'd been holding onto all day. I gave the box to Gianna and told her to open it. When she did, her eyes filled with tears as a combination of joy and heartbreak spread across them. She lifted the delicate gold necklace I had specially made for her. At the center of the chain is 'F & G' with a small heart next to the G. I flipped the necklace over so she could see the faint inscription: "my one true love." I told her the heart represents our baby.

"No matter what happens and no matter where we are," I said, "this represents our love and our bond forever." She cried as I put it on her. It looked beautiful resting against her golden skin.

We held hands walking home, and when it was time to let go, we embraced hard and kissed passionately one last time. Forever. Make it last. Remember this feeling. Don't let go. "I will come back for you one day," I said.

"Promise?"

"Promise." And then we turned in opposite directions and walked slowly until our fingertips no longer touched.

I didn't sleep at all that night.

20 September 1937

The day has finally come. All that I hold dearly in my heart has been left behind. All that I've ever known: the comforts of home, family, food, love—gone. The ease and joy of life and freedom that I took for granted will not exist in my new world. How will I do this? How will I survive? What will happen to everyone I love while I'm gone? Will they remember me? As I go on and do what I must to fight for Italy, I will keep them alive in my heart and fight to return to them. Fight for Calabria. Fight for my family. Fight for Gianna and our baby. Fight for the life I once had.

Chapter 23

Ella

I rise in the morning with the birds and throw on yesterday's jeans. I pull a sweater over my head and tiptoe, diary in hand, down the hall to the veranda, hoping not to awaken anyone. Upon entering the veranda, it appears much larger with no one there to occupy the tables and seating areas strategically placed throughout. The waves roll in and gently collapse against the shore in a quiet, relaxing rhythm. I traipse to a sofa on the other side and sit among a sea of crisp white pillows strewn across dark wood. Fresh flowers adorn the tables, and lanterns of various sizes are scattered at the edges of chairs, doorways, and archways. It's a perfect setting for my muddled mind.

Lush green vines stretch and wind along the sides and top of the archway, pulling forth a fresh, sweet scent of lemons. Thoughts of Jack pop into my mind, as I increasingly mourn his absence each day, especially now. I pull up his picture on my phone, widening and zooming closer to his face, his eyes, his lips. *I miss you so much. You should be here with me.* I push the sadness back into the lower, darker region of my heart where it might remain for a day at most before bubbling back up to the surface again.

A bird flies overhead; its wings gently lift it upward until it's higher than the trees and lost in the sky, like the bird that sat on Maria's window ledge, peeking in while we whispered about Gianna. It makes me think of Nonna and what she's been hiding all these years from my mother. What else could she be hiding? Why did everyone think Maria and Sienna were dead when Maria is very much alive?

And Gianna—who would have thought that the beautiful painting I'd always loved and admired was actually my grandmother? *Nonna is my grandmother.* Why had Poppy pretended that the woman he'd painted was no one he knew? Was he trying to protect himself? Or someone else? What happened between Poppy leaving for the war and my mother being born? Could Uncle Luca really know something?

I tuck my fingers into my pockets to warm them up and feel an edge of paper. Nico's note. I guess I really don't need to call him now. He said he'd go with us to the registrar's office, but now there's no need to go. If Gianna's own sister thinks she might still be alive, there won't be a death certificate to look for. But maybe Nico can still help me in a different way. I take the note from my pocket and quickly type in his number before I'm able to change my mind. He answers with a start. My stomach flips.

"Yes? Hello?" says a quick and raspy voice. Did I dial wrong?

"Um, hello? Nico?" I say. "This is Ella. From the library?" Silence. "Is this a bad time?"

"Ella? No, it's not a bad time." The voice is stronger now, and bits of Nico begin to emerge. I glance at the time and realize it's only six o'clock in the morning.

"Oh, Nico, I'm so sorry," I say. "I didn't realize the time! You were asleep. Let me call you back."

"No, Ella. Please. Stay," he says. "I'm awake. I hoped you would call."

"You did?"

"Yes. I—I hope the books were helpful."

"Well, I haven't had a lot of time to look through them yet, but I plan to."

"Oh, that's okay. How was your visit with your friend on Via Rosa?" he asks.

"It was very interesting," I say. "I wonder if maybe we can meet somewhere? I'd like to get your opinion on a few things."

"Yes of course," he pipes up. "Where would you like to meet?"

I pull up the calendar on my phone. A slight rush of panic spreads as I realize my time in Italy will soon come to an end and I still have so much to do.

"Why don't you come with Jamie and me to Nonna Scorno's Vineyard later this afternoon," I ask, hoping that Jamie won't mind.

"Nonna Scorno's? The old vineyard?" he asks. "That's close to where you were yesterday."

"Yes, it is."

"Sure," he says, "I'm happy to meet you there."

"Thank you, Nico," I say as butterflies race through my stomach. "I'll text you later when we know the time."

"*Ciao!*" he says.

I end the call and Jack's face pops back into view. A pang of guilt squashes the butterflies. I place my phone down and notice Jamie waving from the doorway of the veranda with a funny look on her face. She walks to the sofa with a carafe in one hand and two cups in the other. She places them on the coffee table, sits down, and props her feet up next to the cups.

"Who were you talking and laughing with just now?" she says.

"Me? No one."

She gives me an "I'm not buying it" look and folds her arms across her chest. I roll my eyes.

"It was Nico. And we weren't laughing." *Were we?* She starts to talk but I cut her off quickly. "I know what you're thinking, Jame, and you don't have to worry. I think he can really help us at the vineyard today. He knows a lot about the area and its history. We need someone like that."

"You invited him to come with us? To the vineyard?" she says, her voice rising. "Without asking me first?" She shakes her head and starts to get up.

"Hold it, Jamie," I demand. "This is not about you. This is about my grandfather. This trip is for him. I don't even know to what extent Poppy knew about the things we know. If I think Nico will be helpful to us, then that's all that should matter, don't you?"

"Fine, Ella," she pouts, pouring us both a cup of coffee. "Your Uncle Luca called me, by the way."

"He called *you?*" I say, looking at my phone to see if I missed another call from him.

"Well, he said you hadn't called him back, so he tried my phone," she says. "He seemed a little worried. You should call him back, El."

"I know. I plan to tonight. Why would he be worried?"

"I don't know, probably because he hasn't heard from you?" she says. "I told him you'd call him back after we go to the vineyard, so make sure you do."

"You didn't tell him anything else, did you?"

"No, I left all that for you," she winks.

"I'll call him later," I say feeling conflicted about sharing what Maria has told me.

"*Che sorpresa!*" says a deep, soulful voice. We turn our heads to see Marco walking toward us followed by an annoyed Sophia. Jamie glances at me and we both feign happiness to see them. Marco leans in to offer a hug, so I rise and we embrace over the table. He does the same with Jamie. Sophia stands next to Marco and gives a slight nod.

"So nice to see you again!" he says.

"What a small world!" I say. "Are you taking a cooking class at the villa today?"

"No," Sophia scoffs. "We're here as guests. Like you." She rolls her eyes and runs her fingers through her long shiny hair before resting her hand on her hip. Jamie kicks me under the table.

"Oh, how nice," I lie. "You'll love it here. Angelina and Vinny are so—"

"Yes, they're lovely. We've met before," Sophia interrupts with her bossy, beautiful Italian accent.

"We stayed here last year and loved it so much we came back," Marco says, eyeing the diary. "Looks like something interesting."

"Oh, it's just a journal," I say, resting my hand on top of the diary.

"So old and worn. You bought it this way?" He reaches for it and I sweep it onto my lap, cradling it like a child with a special blanket.

"Actually, it is an old journal that my grandfather gave to me to bring on this trip."

"Ah. To write about Italy?" His arms widen to the beautiful surroundings on the veranda. I love how he says "Ee-taly."

"Yes. *Si*," I say.

"I can tell you so much about Ee-taly if you like. I—"

"Marco, we should go," Sophia blurts. She taps his shoulder and then her watch.

"Ah, yes, we should," Marco says. "We're going sailing. You should come!"

Sophia stares blankly at him.

"Maybe another time," Jamie adds.

"*Va bene! Arrivederci!*" he yells as Sofia pulls him away.

"I hope we never see them again," Jamie says, laughing.

"Me, too," I say. "So weird that we're all here at the Villa."

****

As we approach the streets that lead to Nina's neighborhood, Nico directs the driver to the parking lot of an old church around the corner from Nina's street. We walk a short distance until we come to the now-familiar area that Angelina first mentioned when she told us how to get to Via Rosa. Instead of turning left toward the beach, we make a right and begin walking up a steep, narrow cobblestone road. We tread carefully along the delicate path, stepping over missing and badly cracked stones where the passage of time and neglect have ensued and unruly weeds disturb a once-beautiful journey to the vineyard.

We follow the broken path to the top and slightly left. A few steps more and we're surrounded by a magnificent view. As if we've walked through a dark magic tunnel and emerged into a glorious world, neatly tucked and carefully hidden behind the neighboring roads of the village. I immediately understand why a younger Poppy might have brought the love of his life to this spot, away from both of their conflicting worlds. I imagine a young Franco and Gianna walking arm in arm along the paths, sitting on the benches, wandering near the woods.

Miles of plush green stretch before us like a cashmere blanket laid across bumpy, rolling land. A mostly-smooth blanket, slightly wrinkled at the edges. About halfway to the center stands the winery, a two-story brick building with arched doorways and windows.

"This is it!" I yell. "This is where Poppy and Gianna met all the time. Right here," I say, spreading my arms across the wide expanse.

"Once it was even more beautiful than it is now," Nico says. "Can you imagine that?"

Jamie and I shake our heads no; we can't imagine something more beautiful.

Nico takes the lead and we follow him past the scattered green cypress trees toward the winery. He motions that we should go into the winery, but I wave them toward the back to the spot where Franco and Gianna went. Wispy red and yellow flowers, very much like the ones in Poppy's painting, wave in the wind as we pass.

Nico stops walking. "These hills were once part of an old farm." He waves his arms to indicate everything beyond the winery. "And the farmer used to own this winery," he says about the land before us that stretches for miles. Tiny houses dot the hills.

"I can't believe it," I say, taking a few steps back. "Hold on a second." I take out my phone and scroll to a picture I took of one of the paintings. I hold the phone up and adjust my footing to match my view of the picture. With the exception of a few mature trees and houses, it is almost an exact match.

"Look at this," I say, and Jamie and Nico quickly come over. "Hold it right here," I say, handing the phone to Jamie, "and then look out there." I motion to the edge of the winery and surrounding hills. Their eyes widen as they compare the painted picture with our actual view.

Nico looks at me. "Your grandfather painted this?" he says, and I nod yes, smiling. I open the diary to where I tucked Gianna's letter to Poppy saying how thankful she was that their paths had crossed. The same letter I found hidden in the painting of the vineyard. As Nico and Jamie read the letter, their eyes grow wider.

They look at each other and then at me. And then behind me. I turn to follow their gaze, squinting to focus on the young couple standing about fifty feet away from us. The man waves wildly and walks toward us.

Poppy

10 December 1937

    It's been three months of heavy combat training as a machinist. I barely sleep at all even though my body is exhausted from constant daily challenges. I've recently begun individual training to learn about different metals and types of machines. I spend part of my time in a classroom environment and part of it out on the field and hardly have time for anything else. I've written one letter to Gianna and one to Mamá. I wish it didn't take so long to get there.

    We had our first emergency today. Gino, the cook, suddenly became ill. The emergency medical team came and took him for evaluation. He was sick and in so much pain and we were worried, wondering if he'd been poisoned or had something contagious. Just a little while ago, we found out it was appendicitis and he can no longer perform his duties as our cook. They will not allow him to stay, so, eventually, he will be honorably discharged. I'm glad he's okay, but I'd be lying if I said a part of me didn't wish it happened to me so I could be honorably discharged and go home, too.

    But then the strangest thing happened. The sergeant came to us and asked if any of us could cook. I was the only one who raised my hand. He asked me where I learned to cook and what kinds of meals I've made and seemed impressed when I started talking about food. Not long after that discussion, he came to me with a decision to move me from being a machinist to a cook. If there's anything to be happy about being in the army, it's this. I only wish I'd known about it before I sent my letter to Gianna. A cook! Imagine that!

25 December 1937

    Cooking for the men gives me some sort of focus but little solace in a place like this. Everyone loves the hot meals I prepare and the Sergeant Major seems to like me. He smiles and tells me the food is good. But maybe he's smiling because he gets to eat first. Although I'm glad I'm not on the front line, preparing to fight, boredom is now setting in and that makes time move slowly.

Today is Christmas but it feels like every other day. I've missed the beautiful build-up of anticipation that this holiday normally brings throughout the month. I've missed Gianna's growing belly and Mamá's daily cookie baking. I've already missed so much.

Chapter 24

Ella

My eyes strain to see beyond the hot, hazy film of humidity between us, but as they draw near, it's unmistakable and unbelievable. *What are they doing here?*

"What the . . ." Jamie whispers through the side of her mouth. "They're everywhere."

"Who *are* they?" Nico asks as they're almost upon us.

"*Questo è bellissimo!*" Marco says, spreading his arms wide as if welcoming us to his land. Sophia follows slightly behind, one hand clasped to his.

We stand there motionless, speechless.

"You're kidding me," Jamie huffs under her breath.

"You know them?" Nico asks.

"Not really," I say.

When they reach us, Marco releases Sophia's hand and greets us with a firm embrace as though we're long lost friends who have been apart for years. We awkwardly hug back. Marco slowly scans Nico up and down before turning his attention to me. Sophia adjusts her high ponytail and bats her eyes at Nico.

"Hello again," I say, unable to hide the sarcasm in my voice.

"*Ciao!*" Marco exclaims. "It's so funny," he says, "when we returned to the villa after sailing, we saw Angelina and she said you were at an enchanted vineyard today." He continues, "And I thought, maybe we should go see this beautiful vineyard, too. And when she said it was Nonna Scorno's Vineyard, I was surprised. But also excited," he says, "because it really is beautiful." His smile widens. "And definitely enchanting. Isn't it?" I stare too long, searching for something in his eyes, my shaky smile surely revealing the doubts in my mind.

"Why were you surprised?" I ask.

"I was just gonna ask that," Jamie says, her gaze fixed on Marco.

"Well," Marco continues without answering the question, "I'm glad we came to this beautiful place." He pulls Sophia closer to him. She smiles half-heartedly.

"It's a little bittersweet, too," he says with a grim expression. "A pity—what they say happened here. You must know, too, Nico."

"Know what?" Nico says.

"Marco," Sophia blurts, "please don't start with your stories again."

"Know what?" I ask.

"*Non importa.* Never mind," he says, waving his hands.

"No, you said something happened here. Please continue," I say, glaring at Sophia. "Did you mean recently?"

"Oh, no. It was a long time ago." He pauses, studying us intensely. *Is he glaring at me?* I recognize something deep inside his eyes but can't determine if it's good or bad. A moment later, he glances at Sophia, then at the ground, then back to me.

"There's an old story," he begins, "about two young lovers who came to this vineyard all the time. They'd walk along the paths, drink some wine, and eat the food. They came every single day, usually staying until just before dawn. They were lovesick and dreaded being without each other for long.

"Something happened to her lover and she became distraught and depressed without him. She came to this vineyard every day, hoping he'd be there. A short time later, she came here with another."

"Another lover?" Jamie asks, furrowing her brow.

"I think so," Marco whispers solemnly, as if imparting sacred information. I glance at Nico who has slowly crept up to my side.

"Have you heard this before?" I ask Nico.

"I've heard something similar," Nico says, "but I always thought it was just a story. No one's ever proven it's true."

"One day," Marco continues, "something strange happened when she came to the vineyard with this other man. Something bad."

"What do you mean?" I ask.

"That day, the man she'd been coming with left the vineyard by himself," he says, "even though they walked in together. Do you understand?"

"No one actually saw her leave," Sophia interjects, "so they just assumed he did something to her."

"Did he?" I say. "Or could she have left before him?"

Marco shakes his head and looks at Nico. "You've heard this, right?"

"I heard that two men were deeply in love with a woman and fought over her," Nico says "Were they brothers?"

"Yes, I believe they were," Marco says.

"Or they might have been close friends, like brothers," Sophia says, flipping her hair.

Marco shakes his head. "One of the two men was off somewhere far away. He heard about the affair between the woman and his brother and came back for her. But not in the way you think. It was somewhat sinister."

Something grips my heart and squeezes it tight. I place my hand there to soothe it.

"But they don't know who it was that came back?" I say. Jamie wanders to my side and stands next to Nico. A hand rests and circles the small of my back. I look at Jamie and hers are tucked in her back pockets.

"Why would he come back to kill the woman he loves? It doesn't make sense," Jamie points out, her voice sharp and edgy.

"Why do lovers do these things?" Marco says. "Jealousy? Anger? Fear? I don't know."

I stare at Marco, trying to analyze and decipher his story. Compare the details to the ones I've come to know. Connect it to my story. *Is it my story?*

"Do you think this is about the missing woman you were trying to find in the library?" Nico says gently. "A family member, right?"

I nod. "Yes, possibly my grandmother," I say, acknowledging this for the first time. Nico's eyes widen, and then the light inside them disappears. *Does he know something?*

"El," Jamie says, "do you know how many people—young lovers—have probably come to this vineyard over the years?"

"Not like that," Marco interjects. "Not every day. Most don't even know about this vineyard. Only the locals. And that's not many."

"What else do you know about them?" I ask.

"Some. But not everything. No one knows everything," Marco says. Sophia glares at him. He gives her a reassuring look but she shakes her head and kicks at the grass.

"Some say they were brothers," Marco continues. "Some say friends. It's hard to know. And, as Nico said, they quarreled over this woman. Ruthlessly. One of the men was stronger, wiser, more cunning than the other. He thought *he* deserved her. As if he owned her. When she refused to choose him, he became enraged. He was blinded by his rage. And then, instead of releasing her and letting her go, he made her fear for her life. Beg for her life. Finally, after much torment, he pulled the trigger.

"After that, the man was beside himself. So much rage and regret, but also intense jealousy. He pointed the gun at his brother and held it there for a few seconds, but instead of shooting, he ran," Marco says, "and never returned. It was a mess."

The overhead clouds cast an ominous glow, and a quick gust of wind throws my hair back. All is silent except for the faint, muffled sounds of a train. Nico points to the sky.

"The locals say that on a clear night you can see three stars in the shape of a shallow arc over the vineyard. One for each of the lovers." He traces a large arc with his arm.

"They also say," Marco adds, "on stormy nights, if you listen closely, you can hear her screams mixing with the wind."

Sophia elbows Marco.

Jamie faces me. "It's just a legend, El," she reassures me.

Marco's eyes meet Nico's for a second before facing me as well.

"Well, that depends," says Marco. "Do you believe it's just a legend made up for fun? Perhaps to teach a lesson? Or," he points his finger at me, "do you believe that a legend grew from a story that was once real? I guess it depends on what you choose to believe."

"I don't know what to believe," I lament. *Is this just a story I'm chasing? If it's real, what is it saying about my grandfather?*

"I think you've said enough," Sophia says, "and it's hot out here. I'm going inside to cool off."

We agree and follow her into the winery, dazed and bewildered. Nico stays nearby and seems to be watching me closely.

At the bar, the bartender asks Nico, "What can I get for you and your lovely girl?"

Nico and I glance at each other. The corners of his mouth rise to show a full set of beautiful white teeth. I look at the bartender apologetically while Nico chooses something from the wine menu.

I smile and laugh awkwardly as a warm wave spreads to my face.

"To Italy and friends!" Nico raises his glass and we all clink our glasses together.

"And to the stars above," Marco adds with a wink.

By the time we finish our third bottle of wine, we're all laughing and leaning into each other, brushing shoulders as we talk intimately about nothing. Nico watches Marco a lot. Quick glances every now and then, as if he doesn't trust him or he's waiting for something to happen.

Soon the small room is packed as the dinner crowd arrives and I have to strain to hear Marco talk. He leans in and we're standing uncomfortably close so that our noses are almost touching. Nico swoops in with a bottle of wine causing us to separate as he fills our glasses. He stays right between us the whole time, listening to Marco drone on about his trip to the coast, not stopping once to take a breath.

Sophia and Jamie are whispering off to the side as if they're best friends. Nico repositions himself so that he's standing slightly behind me. He rests his hands on my hips, subtly pulling me back little by little, until he's created an awkward space between Marco and me. I think he's being protective. And I like it. His hands remain there until I step aside.

Suddenly Marco straightens and moves closer. "My mother said she was young," he barks, swaying. "This girl, when she went missing. The neighbors talked about it. Whispered about it to each other." We stop talking and turn our attention to Marco. "This girl wasn't from around here," he proclaims. "Not supposed to be here. With him. All the mothers forbade their daughters to go out alone after that. After he got rid of her. And her baby—"

"No. Not her baby. He didn't kill her baby," I say.

Jamie elbows me gently and mouths, "Let him talk."

"If he can't have her, no one can have her!" He slams his hand hard on the table and we all jump. My heart quickens and my palms are sweaty. I gulp the last three sips of wine and pour some more.

"He was a fighter, you know," Marco slurs, "I didn't mention that before, but one of the men was a fighter in the war." My heart sinks. "He snuck away during his tour to take care of things. Then he went away again. Sailed the oceans." Marco turns and faces me, his eyes wide. "He got away with it! And they never found him." He staggers, almost tripping over his feet. "Probably lived a great life somewhere far, far away while the rest of this town picked up the pieces." We stand, mouths agape, waiting for more. *A fighter in the war. Like Poppy. No. Not like Poppy.*

"They tried to find him to bring him to justice," Marco goes on to say, "but never did. He was too quick and too clever." He places his hand on my shoulder. "And that's why the neighbors still hear her cries at night. Maybe her spirit is still out there, restless, wandering. Or maybe she really isn't dead at all!" he laughs. But his smile quickly fades. He grabs my arms and stares at me with a strange expression, almost pleading and desperate amidst his drunken state.

"And that is why you *must* stop looking for her," he says. "Let her rest in peace. Let her be. Let them all be."

"Marco, don't," Sophia says, but he brushes her off.

"The neighbors are talking again. About you this time," he says, still gripping my arms.

My heart beats rapidly and sweat gathers on my brow. Nico is at my side again, one hand on my back. He faces Marco and steps toward him, fists clenched tightly at his sides. His jaw twitches and a vein near his temple throbs. Marco relaxes his grip and steps back. Jamie whispers something to Sophia.

"What are you trying to do?" Nico demands.

"No disrespect," Marco says, raising both hands. "I just think she should know," he looks at each of us, "you all should know that the locals don't like having the past dug up again. It was hard for them then and it's hard for them now."

"What makes you an expert on the locals?" Nico asks.

"I'm from this area," he says. "My grandparents lived here. My family is here. They're the ones we visit when we come to this part of Italy. I know the stories."

"How do they know I'm here? How do they know what I'm doing?" I say.

"Oh, they know," Marco says.

"Marco, that's enough," Sophia insists.

I don't trust Marco, but I suspect something odd. A feeling. A sense. That there's some truth in his story.

"I need to go back to something you said a few minutes ago," I say. He nods, waiting for me to continue.

"You said the neighbors *still* hear her cry with the wind." I say. "Do you mean they heard her screams back then?" A wave of nausea courses through my stomach.

"*Sì*. Someone did," Marco says. "It was all they talked about for days—her poor mother going door to door looking for her, asking if anyone's seen her daughter and granddaughter." *Granddaughter.* "Some remember an angry old man coming to the girl's house only days before, yelling at the girl's mother . As if he knew her."

"Who was the older man?"

"No one knows," he shakes his head, "or they didn't say."

"What else? What else do you know?" I say.

Sophia puts her arm through Marco's and pulls him back a little. "Marco, let's go," she says. "You've had too much to drink. And you've said enough." She positions her body between his and ours so we can't see or hear what she's saying. Marco nods, relenting, as

Sophia steps aside facing us again. "I'm sorry but we need to go now. He doesn't know what he's saying."

Marco waves and staggers out as Sophia leads him to the door. His eyes are two small slits and he's smiling. As they turn the corner I faintly hear him say something to us: "Let them be."

Nico brushes the hair out of his eyes and then reaches over to push aside a strand of my hair that caught on my eyelashes. I look at him and he awkwardly retracts his hand, shoving it in the pocket of his jeans. The butterflies return for a moment but I quickly shoo them away. Jamie's hands are on her hips watching us.

"You know this is a big coincidence, right?" she says. "I mean, what is the likelihood that Marco's story is the same one as Poppy's?" She looks at us and Nico shrugs his shoulders.

"To me," Nico replies, "what I've heard tonight sounds a little bit like what Ella's been saying about her grandfather and the woman in the photo. But I don't know all the details."

I look at Jamie through watery eyes.

"Two men, possibly brothers but maybe friends," I say. "One was a fighter in the war who was deeply in love with someone he left behind. Jamie. The box, the diary. Oh, my God, the gun. Could it be?" I say, starting to pace. "What happened to my sweet Poppy all those years ago?" I cry as tears run down my cheeks.

"Oh, El, no. Don't think that," Jamie says, and places her hand on my arm.

Nico just stares helplessly at me. I stare back into his eyes, but it's more of a daydream that I can't release myself from. Jamie must think I'm infatuated with him, but I'm stuck between reality and fantasy. Truth and lies.

Nonna's words begin echoing in my head, "Ella, you know there's no such thing as coincidence. You are meant to be where you are. Pay attention. Embrace it. Learn from it. Then do something about it."

Poppy

4 January 1938

A new year has emerged although it doesn't feel any different to me. Just another day. But I received a letter from Gianna today! The envelope smelled of her perfume, and when I opened her letter, my heart leapt at the sight of her handwriting and a picture of her that she included. I couldn't stop staring at her eyes and studying every part of her face, her hair. And the pretty sparkling necklace I gave her delicately rested at the base of her neck, F&G with a heart in the center. My stomach fluttered at the sight of it. She'd worn it, at least for the picture. I knew she wouldn't be able to wear it often if at all.

Gianna told me how much she loved and missed me all throughout the letter, even until the very end when she also mentioned that she had, in fact, gotten married. I knew it was coming. It had to come. She's pregnant; it was the only way. But seeing those words: "It is done. I'm now married to Carlos. Carlos believes it's his baby. At least our baby will have a proper family—that is, until we can be together. You still want that, right?" Those words pierced my heart and soul, creating a small hole that I fear cannot be repaired. How will this work? How can we ever be together?

10 January 1938

I'm still reeling from Gianna's letter. I sleep with it and her picture under my pillow, breathing in traces of her perfume as I fall asleep. I cannot write back just yet, but I will. I worry that Gianna will have a hard time during childbirth. Luca recently told me that both of Gianna's sisters died while giving birth to their first born. How tragic and heartbreaking. I can't imagine a loss like that. I want to talk to Gianna about it but Luca says it's not something the family ever discusses and that I should never bring it up to Gianna. I asked him how he knows but he says he can't say. Some day when the time is right I will ask her. In the meantime, I will pray that it doesn't happen to Gianna.

It is tense where I am. All around me, hostility and fear increases as we prepare for an upcoming mission. The air is thick and heavy, and it's quiet. An eerie quiet. I feel that something bad is going to happen. But all I can do is wait.

Chapter 25

Ella

My own words are crushing. To think them is one thing, but to say them out loud is entirely different. They weigh heavily on my chest, deflating the little air I had left from the shallow breaths used to spit them out. All I can think about is the gun we found in the box. *It can't be.* I'm frozen. I feel my face wrenching into an ugly cry, but nothing comes out.

Nico and Jamie are at my sides talking. I hear their faint voices telling me to breathe, it's okay, just breathe. Something releases inside of me and I gasp for air as tears stream down my cheeks. They wrap their arms around me and I cry in their embrace, not embarrassed at all to be crying onto the shoulders of someone I hardly know. Yet it feels like I've known him all my life. Jamie offers a tissue and Nico leans back to give me space.

"Listen, El," Jamie says, "let's not come to any conclusions yet. Maybe we can talk to Angelina and Vinny about it. If the locals know this story, maybe they know something, too."

I nod, wiping my tears.

"It's hard not to draw conclusions," I say on our way to the car.

The ride home is slow and quiet. I feel my eyes blinking longer each time until the sparkling streetlights become one long blur. I awaken to the slam of the driver's door and realize that my head had fallen onto Nico's shoulder and my right hand is on his chest. Instinctively raised to an old position. I straighten up, relieved that Jamie and Nico were also asleep.

"Thank you for coming with us today, Nico," I say leaning toward the rolled-down window in the back seat, "and sorry if I came across as crazy." I smile, shaking my head.

"My pleasure," he says, "and you're not crazy."

Jamie and I step onto the curb so the driver can pull out and take Nico home. As they drive away, Nico mouths something. I scrunch my eyes and shrug my shoulders to show him I don't understand. He raises his hand to his ear and mimics talking on the phone.

"Oh," I mouth back, nodding. "Okay."

Jamie looks at me. "He's sweet on you, El."

"No, he's just being thoughtful." I wave my hand as if I'm waving away the thought. "He's like that with you, too."

"He was always there at your side," she says, "and I don't think he liked Marco being near you, by the way."

"Really?" I say, secretly acknowledging that he *was* always near me. I remember his gentle hands on my hips, pulling me away from Marco. Something inside me liked that feeling, but then I dismissed it and pulled away.

"And I think you not only know that," she says, tilting her head, "but you like that, don't you?"

"What? Oh, no. I'm not ready for that yet." A conflicted feeling swells in my heart. "Besides, he lives in Italy, for God's sake."

Jamie says nothing back, but she doesn't need to. Her right eyebrow is raised in its highest position.

"It's okay, El," she says softly. "But you'll have to move on eventually."

I swallow hard and look away as a raindrop taps my nose. And then another. A heavy sprinkle ensues followed by a familiar scent of rain. A smell I used to love. We make it inside the villa just before the downpour. It's quiet and dark except for a few scattered accent lights along the hallway to our room. I fall into the soft comforter on my bed and close my eyes. The pouring rain grows louder as I slip into sleep.

> *. . . I am holding his hand and he is smiling and watching me as we walk from the brick building to our parked car. A glint of the moon's light shines through the trees. A warm summer breeze blows the long hair off my shoulders, swirling around us on the dimly lit street, rustling the leaves on the low-hanging branches, and picks up another scent on its way back. The sweet smell of rain coming. "A perfect night," I say, still holding his hand, and he pulls me in and kisses the curve between my neck and shoulder. I breathe in the woodsy-mint scent of his cologne and freshly laundered shirt and I could stay in this moment forever. "I'll drive," I say.*
>
> *"You sure?" He stumbles.*
>
> *"Of course."*
>
> *I am in better shape to drive tonight. Our hands detach as we break toward opposite sides of the car, but our eyes remain locked until we get in.*
>
> *The road is dark, the streetlights farther apart. Cool, misty air rushes in through the partially opened windows. Rain begins its descent. One drop, then another, falling separately, unevenly. I glance at him asleep next to me. He is smiling, his head against the glass. I squeeze his hand and return mine to the wheel. The raindrops quicken and tap dance upon us, and for a moment, I am lost in its rhythm. A relaxing, beautiful rhythm that is both comforting and calming. I long to be home*

in our soft bed, listening to the rain pattering against our windows as it lulls us to sleep.

Soon the raindrops are quick and heavy, beating hard and unruly. And now it has no rhythm. I should have worn my glasses. I ease up on the gas and attempt to reach for the glasses in my purse. The car swerves, sending my purse to the floor. I quickly return my hand to the wheel, trying to straighten, and we swerve again.

The windshield wipers push waves of water back and forth in a futile attempt to keep up, and I can scarcely see the white lines on the road. I know I should be pulling over, but we are close to home. I sense a detachment of wheels from the road, and I no longer see the road or anything else. A deluge of water empties its rage from the sky. My hands are one with the steering wheel now. Adrenaline races through my body and terror fills my mind. And then a deafening and fearful silence surrounds me, and I float through nothing. Waiting . . .

. . . I am weightless and flying fast. Glass shatters and metal bends as we are thrown over and over into rock and road. I scream for him, but he doesn't answer. And I am crying but I can't hear my voice. My thoughts get lost in the wreckage . . .

A voice breaks through. A slight rocking motion. Where am I?

"El?" it asks, and then demands, "El! Wake up!"

I bolt upright into Jamie's arms leaving sweat marks on the sheets below me.

"Shhh, it's okay," she says, examining my face. "You were having that dream again, weren't you?"

"How did you know?"

"You were calling his name." She swipes my hair behind my

shoulders. "I thought those dreams had stopped."

"They did. Until we came here." I rub my eyes, still clinging to the foggy edge of the dream. "It was so real," I say. "Just like it was happening all over again. I gripped that steering wheel so hard. I tried to straighten it," I say, noticing red marks on my palms where my fingernails pressed and squeezed in my dream. "That eerie feeling of floating. Flipping . . ."

"It's okay, El. You're here now. You're okay," Jamie says, softly caressing my arm.

"I tried to reach out for him but—"

"I know," she says, hugging me. "I know."

"He just slipped away," I say, extending my arm, still trying to feel for his hand. Tears pour down my cheeks from the heaving sobs that can't be seen but come from deep within my soul. *Don't fall into the sadness. You've worked so hard.*

"Why am I dreaming of this again?" I say angrily, wiping my tears. "I don't want to keep remembering it."

"I think . . . well . . ." Jamie says.

I purse my lips and give her a look. "You know you can't do that and not say."

Jamie takes a big breath and sighs. "I know it's a stretch, but . . . maybe it's Nico."

"Nico?"

"Just hear me out. You haven't had that dream for, what, six months? Nine? Maybe longer? We come to Italy and meet Nico. He was at your side every minute while you were trying to find me at the beach when we first got here. Remember? He was holding your hand and you didn't even notice until I said something about it. Then at the vineyard, it was so obvious. Probably the most obvious. Like I said, everywhere you went, he was right by you. I think he was jealous of Marco."

"No. I think he's just being protective."

"Okay. But why? He hardly knows you."

"I don't see the connection between my dreams recurring and Nico."

"You blushed and smiled every time he came near you," she says, "and every time I mention that he likes you, including now."

I reach my hand to my damp cheeks. *Am I blushing?* "How is that connected to the dream?"

"You're fighting it," she says, "because you want to like him."

I shake my head. "No. I would never do that to Jack." I catch myself, surprised at my words.

Jamie gently holds my arms and faces me toward her. "You will always love Jack. No one will take his place. No one needs to. He can have that place." She pauses for a moment as if she knows I need to absorb this. "But it's okay to find love again, El." Her eyes are sincere, warm, honest. They hold a genuine love for me as her best friend. She has a deep understanding of who I am and where I've come from. No one else besides Jack knows me like she does. "I'm not saying that Nico is or even should be the one to love. I'm just telling you that you are fighting some kind of feeling for him, and it's because you're holding on to Jack. And that makes you feel guilty."

Just then, everything inside me weakens. My body and mind are loose and I close my eyes to conflicted feelings of peace, comfort, and fear.

My phone vibrates. It's Nico, but I let it go to voicemail. I notice another missed call from Uncle Luca.

****

"Hi, Uncle Luca, it's El!"

"Oh, hi there, Ella, how are you?" he says. His voice sings like a bird.

"I'm fine. How are you guys?" A rush of eagerness passes through my chest. I can't wait to share what I know. Find out what he might know.

"We're great, honey. How's Italy?"

"It's amazing!" I say. "I love it so much, I don't want to leave."

"We knew you'd love it," he says. "Aunt Lena says hi and she loves you."

"Hi, Aunt Lena!" I say.

"We can't wait to hear about your trip, Ella," he says. "A couple more days, right?"

"Three days," I say, wishing it wasn't true. I search my mind for other things to talk about but it's suddenly blank. "Uncle Luca . . . um . . . I was wondering if I could ask you something."

"Of course, anything," he says.

"Remember that woman, Gianna? From the letters?" My adrenaline spikes and I begin to pace.

"Yes," he says. "Why do you ask?"

"Well, I found some information about her."

The line is silent. Have we lost connection?

"Are you there?" I ask.

"Yes, I was waiting for you to continue," he says, his voice serious. Formal. "What information? How do you know it's true?"

"I'm sure it's true," I say, not sounding sure.

"What makes you so sure?"

"Because it . . . came from her sister, Maria."

I hear a strange breathy noise. A knot tightens in my stomach.

"Impossible," he says. "She's not alive."

"But she is!" I say. "I went looking for Nina, but the person—"

"What the hell?" he whispers. "Did you say, Nina? How do you know about Nina?"

In his voice I detect shock and something else. Fear?

I begin to shift the wording of the letter, slightly altering its intention. "Before I left, I found a letter from Poppy to me, and it said if I go to Italy someday I should find Nina."

"Another letter? He said to find Nina? You never told me that," he says.

"It—it was right before I left. I didn't think it was anything I needed to share right away." The knot in my stomach squeezes harder.

"I see," he says, his voice relaxing, loosening a bit.

"I was surprised," I say. "Even more surprised when it wasn't Nina who I found but *Maria*."

"And you're sure it really was Maria?"

"Yes, I'm sure." Silence resumes, but I wait.

"All these years we thought Maria was dead. Is . . . Sienna alive?"

"No, unfortunately, she passed away just before I got there."

"But she's been alive all that time, too?" he says. "I'll be damned."

I hear Aunt Lena in the background saying something to Uncle Luca, followed by a muffled conversation as Uncle Luca covers his phone to talk to her. A few seconds later he's back. "So, what was it about Gianna you wanted to ask me?"

I inhale, hold my breath, then exhale to the count of four. "One of the things Maria mentioned was that *you* might have been the last person to see Gianna before she went missing. But you didn't mention that when we were talking about it at the cottage. You acted as if you didn't know her . . . as well as you did."

"Oh, Ella," he sighs, "of course I knew her well. Our families were close at one time. Then we went our separate ways. As you know, Poppy and Gianna reconnected and then the three of us became close again.

"But I was *not* the last one to see her. I remember that day clearly," he says. "I was supposed to see her, but she never showed up at the park where we'd meet before our walks. I waited a while and finally left the park and went to Maria's to—to see if maybe I misunderstood or got the wrong day or something. You know I was watching out for her while Poppy was at war, right? That's why we went for walks together."

"Yes, I knew that."

"So why are you digging all this up, Ella?" he says with an edge. "Sweetie," his voice softens, "you're delving into things that were difficult to understand *then*, let alone now."

"I'm doing this for Poppy," I say. "And he more-or-less asked me to."

"What do you mean?"

"I mean he told me there was a box and I found it. He must have wanted me to find the diary, the letters—everything. I still don't know exactly why, but I think he wanted me to finish something he couldn't."

"A diary? What else have you found?" he says, and then the muffled voices return for a moment.

"Well . . . Maria showed us a few pictures of you and Poppy with Gianna and her sisters. You were all so young. And I saw some pictures of Gianna and her baby and—"

"She had pictures? The baby—did she talk about the baby?" he says.

"Yes, she did."

He sighs, "So then you know."

"Yes, I know. Nonna isn't mom's biological mother. Gianna is," I say. "It'll be hard to tell her that, but—"

"That's not what I meant."

"What did you mean?"

"I mean, yes, you're right, it will be hard to tell her, but I'm not sure it's really necessary. She thinks of Nonna as her mother and, technically, she was her mother. She raised her. Maybe we should leave it alone," he says.

"I can't lie to my mother, Uncle Luca."

"No, I don't want you to lie. That's not what I meant. This is hard to process right now. Is there anything else you've discovered while you were with Maria?"

"No. Not with Maria."

"What do you mean?"

"No, I meant there's nothing else." *Except for the stories from the vineyard. First, there were three, then there were two and then one. One man. Where are you, Gianna? Who saw you last?*

Poppy

15 February 1938

Something terrible happened. After serving stew to the soldiers, I finally sat down to eat when we got some devastating news. Our men had just embarked on a mission to invade an area in northern Italy (I cannot name it). The men were exposed to terrible conditions for an unusually extended period of time. We were worried and hadn't heard anything for weeks.

Just now, Sergeant Major told us that several of our men on the ground were killed or severely wounded in a surprise attack. He also said that the ambulance with two of our men was in that attack and he wasn't sure if they were alive or dead. I don't know what's worse: to be dead or taken as a P.O.W. I have already lost too many friends. I cannot believe this. I can't take it all in. Another thing that's hard to believe is, had I not become a cook, it would have been me in that ambulance.

11 April 1938

Luca wrote me a letter. He said that Gianna is married (which I knew) and she had a baby girl! Oh, my gosh, a baby girl!! But he didn't know her name. When I read that, I almost passed out. Thank God both Gianna and the baby are healthy and doing well. I wish I could hold them both in my arms. I should be there with them, not here.

Luca is the only person who knows about Gianna and me. And he's the only one I can trust with it. I remember when I first told him that I'd found Gianna after all those years and that now we were together and loved each other, he laughed! I couldn't figure out why, and then he admitted that he also had a crush on Gianna when we were little. No surprise. He always liked what I liked.

Luca said he would keep me informed about how Gianna and the baby are and anything new. He also said that Mamà prays the rosary every day for me before she goes to bed. Papà is still a tyrant around the house, barking orders and belittling them.

I still can't believe Gianna is married and not to me.

Chapter 26

Ella

Jamie and I sit quietly side by side after listening to my conversation with Uncle Luca on speaker. I reflect inward, hoping that Jamie stays silent just for a few more minutes.

Something in Uncle Luca's voice was off. His smooth, glassy voice that usually warms and comforts me was rough and uneven. A voice normally brimming with confidence and assurance had an edge of uncertainty, uneasiness. It wasn't apparent at the beginning of our conversation, but as soon as I mentioned Nina and Maria, a slight shift occurred. I know I wasn't imagining it because Jamie and I glanced at each other at the exact same points while he talked. But maybe I'm overthinking it. Probably nothing other than genuine surprise at hearing about Maria and Sienna being alive. But why wouldn't they be alive? I heard it again at the end of our conversation. A change. A deviation in his voice. What wasn't expressed in words permeated the air between us.

My skin itches as if tiny bugs begin to divide and multiply throughout my limbs, neck, and head. I feel them crawling through my mind. I have to move. I need to do something but I don't know what. Where do I go next? What can I accomplish with three days left? How do I prove or disprove something I still can't fully grasp?

Poppy could not have hurt Gianna. The very thought makes me nauseous. And if he did, would I actually expose him? But then why would he send me on this journey, knowing where it would lead? Does he want me to reveal what I find because maybe it was something he couldn't do himself? Is that it? Did he go too far? He couldn't have Gianna, but couldn't live without her?

Maybe it was an accident. And then, when he realized what transpired, it was too late. They'd blame him. Say it was his fault. Turning himself in wasn't an option—he had the baby to think about. He'd already lost so much. He couldn't lose his child. *Don't even think of it.* But why? Why would he hurt Gianna if he deeply loved her? *God, please don't let it be.* Is there something I missed in the diary? Something I overlooked?

"I need a few minutes to clear my head, Jame. Gonna sit on the veranda and look through Poppy's diary again."

She's been so quiet since we hung up. Probably knows I'm dissecting every part of that conversation.

"I'm not pushing you away," I say. "I just need a moment."

She gives a gentle squeeze of my shoulder as I pass by and leave the room.

The warm breeze coming off the sea is comforting. I close my eyes and breathe deeply before opening the diary. Once I'm inside Poppy's world, I detach from mine. I'm one with his words, woven into the fabric of his story. Skimming some areas, re-reading others, combing through his words, analyzing his tone to determine what's not written—what he purposely left out.

"*Come stai?*" a gentle voice breaks through. I raise my eyes, leaving my mind in the diary.

"Marco," I say, surprised to see him standing so close to the table. His smile is wide, his hair swept perfectly to one side, impeccably dressed as always. He's holding a beautiful bouquet of white and yellow flowers. "I'm fine, thank you. Were you standing there long?" I say.

"Not long. A minute? Maybe five?" he says, pushing the bouquet out toward me. "These—for you."

"For me? Why?"

"Lilies are very popular in Italy," he says, pointing to them. "Yellow roses represent friendship. And these," he gently brushes the tops of the smaller, delicate white flowers, "are white poppies for, you know, your grandfather."

I lift the flowers to my nose and breathe in their sweet scent, and then I gently run my fingers across the white poppies.

"They're beautiful. How thoughtful. Especially the poppies. Thank you, Marco," I say. "But why?"

"I feel a little bad about how I behaved at the vineyard," he says, slouching. "I was having so much fun and had a little too much to drink. I talked a lot about nothing. You know. Said too much."

"Oh, don't worry about it," I say, waving my hand. "But . . . what you said at the vineyard about the men and that woman—did you make that up?"

"I also brought you these," he says, gesturing toward the bouquet, ignoring my question, "just for being you. You're so kind and so happy. You laugh at life. You love life. And you love your family. You would do anything for them. It inspires me."

"Yes, I would do anything for them," I say, nodding. I touch the bouquet. "These are beautiful . . . and unnecessary. You and Sophia shouldn't have done that."

Marco's smile disappears. "Oh, these . . . are just . . . from me," he says.

"Oh. Um . . . I . . ."

He jumps to the chair beside me and puts his index finger up to my lips. "Shhh. Say nothing. There's no need."

I lean back slightly. "Marco, what are you doing?"

"There's no need to say anything," he smiles. "I know you feel it, too."

"Feel what? We had a great time at the vineyard, but—"

"What we have"—he points to me and then to himself—"this."

"'This'?" I make the same gesture.

"Don't pretend, Ella." He places his hand on top of mine and stares into my eyes. "Don't deny it."

I stare back, trying to understand where this is coming from. I slip my hand out from under his and look away toward the entrance to the veranda where Nico is standing, watching us. He's frozen mid-stride as if he's seen something unexpected and needs to retreat. I stand quickly as he turns and walks away. Marco shifts, looking back at the doorway. I glance at Marco.

"I'm sorry, Marco, but I have to go," I say as he grabs hold of my hand.

"Wait. I have more to say!" he yells.

"I can't," I say, running toward the doorway, leaving Marco and the flowers behind. I race down the hallway to the front entrance of the veranda and down the steps toward the driveway as Nico's car speeds away. "Nico!" I yell. But it's too late.

Angelina approaches the doorway leading to the front porch. "What happened?" She opens the door, climbs down the steps, and puts her arm around my shoulders. "What happened?" she repeats.

I shake my head. "What a mess," I say as we turn and walk back inside.

What just happened on the veranda with Marco was completely unexpected. I'm worried about what Nico thinks he saw.

Angelina leads me down the narrow corridor to her kitchen, sits me down at the table, and pours two glasses of wine. Her kitchen is immaculate but slightly disjointed. Faint seams in the walls slightly bulge beneath the paint where one wall had been removed and another added during a recent renovation. Everything is neatly labeled on the shelves. Angelina runs a tight ship and knows her kitchen probably as well as she knows herself.

I run my fingers along the smooth edge of the wood table, dipping into the grooves along the way. Two tall shelves stand at the opposite end of the kitchen filled with recipe books. Angelina says she doesn't use them very often because she makes up her own recipes as she goes along.

Angelina sits down next to me and takes a large gulp of her wine. She places her hand on my arm and looks into my eyes. "I'm going to make you a nice vegetable lasagna tonight, and you can tell me anything you want that's bothering you. In fact, I'm gonna start making it right now! I'll even teach you how to do it. Have you ever made vegetable lasagna?"

Poppy's most famous recipe was vegetable lasagna. He used the vegetables from his garden to make all of it, including the sauce from the tomatoes he grew. Poppy never followed a recipe; he naturally knew what to do and added things as he went along. He had a keen sense for which spices mixed well with others and often experimented, changing it just a little bit each time.

I remember one day when I was spending the weekend with Poppy and Nonna—I was about twelve years old—I asked Poppy if he would ever share his famous recipes with anyone. He smiled at me and said maybe one day he might. On my thirteenth birthday, he gave me my own recipe box and inside were ten of his most special recipes, the first one being vegetable lasagna. He'd actually taken the time to write them all down for me. It was my favorite and most treasured gift, even now. Having those recipes is like having a small piece of Poppy.

"My grandfather used to make that all the time. It was one of my favorite meals, but I've never made it myself."

"Oh, I bet he was a good cook! Well, mine will probably be a little different, but I think you'll still love it," she says.

"Love what?" Jamie asks from the doorway. Angelina waves her over to join us and pours her a glass of wine.

"Ella was just about to tell me what's gotten her so upset," Angelina says.

Jamie furrows her brow, taking a sip of wine.

I tell them both what happened with Marco and then how Nico saw us together and left. The way Marco looked at me leaves me feeling very uneasy. How could he think I had feelings for him?

"I knew it, El! I knew Nico liked you!" Jamie says. "But Marco, too?" She throws her head back and laughs. "What are you going to do? Who will you choose?" she says, placing the back of her hand across her forehead dramatically.

I try to laugh, too, but it doesn't come out right.

"I need to find out why he left so quickly. Does he really think I'm involved with Marco?"

"I tell you what," Angelina says, "you call Nico and tell him to come to dinner tonight. Okay? Then you can tell him everything. Even how you feel about him."

"I don't know about that," I say, knowing that my reddened face is betraying me.

"Ella, I know I'm not your mother, but just do as I say," she smiles, pretending to scold me with a pointed finger.

"I'll think about it."

"Don't think too long," she says.

"El, did you ask Angelina about what Marco said in the vineyard?" Angelina looks at me, confused.

"Oh, no," I say, "I'm sure now that he made it all up. After what happened on the veranda, I'm convinced he's just a creep. A philanderer. Just made the whole thing up to get closer to me."

"What story?" Angelina says.

"It's nothing," I say.

"Ella!" Jamie snaps. "You're not serious." Then she turns to Angelina. "There's an old story about two young lovers who used to go to Nonna Scorno's Vineyard together every day. And then one day the woman went missing. They thought her lover had something to do with it. Do you know that story?"

"It was around World War Two, I believe, yes," she says, leaning into her elbows on the table. "That's all people talked about. They'd watch them come and go, holding hands. So romantic. They were like a bright light in a dark time."

"Why's that?" I ask.

"Well, the fighting had begun—Italy's involvement with Germany." She shakes her head. "It was a dark time. Heavy. No one around here wanted the men to go, including most of the men. And when the young lovers started to come to the vineyard, it excited the neighbors," her eyes widen, "gave them something to look forward to, . . . until—Well, you know—until she went missing. And then the whispers among the houses were out of control."

"Did anyone see it happen?" I say.

"Some said they saw it. Others say they heard it. The gun shot. The screams."

"Did the police talk to them?" Jamie asks.

"Oh, yes," Angelina straightens up, "they went to every single house. Checked out every story. Every clue."

"Were there any suspects?" I ask, holding my breath, waiting for her to confirm what Maria said about two suspects.

"There were a few at first, and then they narrowed it down to two. Two men. The two who came with her to the vineyard. The lover, and the other man, who I think may have become her lover next. But no one knows for sure."

My heart cracks.

"But they never actually found out who was responsible, right?" Jamie asks.

"No. They never even found the body. She was just . . . missing. They said she might have left on her own—*wanted* to leave."

"That doesn't make sense," I say. "She wouldn't leave her baby."

"Oh, I don't know anything about a baby. But I do know one thing: When the police stopped their investigation, the whispers among the neighbors grew. They were convinced it was the lover, the one who went to war."

The crack in my heart widens.

"Why? Why him?" I say, my voice crackling. "How could anyone do something like that while they're away at war? It's not feasible. How could he get away without being discovered and then come back?"

"Well," Angelina pauses, leans a little closer so our faces are inches apart, "he must have used the tunnels."

"Tunnels?" My eyes meet Jamie's instantly. The air inside my neck is constricted. I lift my chin in an effort to allow any traces of oxygen to flow. *Tunnels? No.*

"Maria never said anything about tunnels," Jamie says.

Angelina tilts her head, "And you're sure you were really speaking with Maria? You're sure it was her?"

"We . . . yes, it was her," Jamie says, her voice barely audible. She looks at me. "Right, El?"

I say nothing. I'm stuck inside the tunnels.

Poppy

19 November 1938

The war has no end in sight. It is ugly, lonely, and desolate. I was denied my leave of absence, but it might mean I can go home sooner. I don't know what to believe. Northern Italy no longer resembles what it once was. All life it once breathed has been expelled. A shell of itself, not just physically, but also in the mind. Darkened by clouds of war.

I thank God that Gianna and my family are far south. But is anyone really safe? I must convince Luca to leave with Mamá and Papá and go to America soon. I want him to take Gianna and the baby, but that's impossible. Or is it? Maybe she can escape with them and not tell anyone. Maybe he can take her.

29 November 1938

Luca sent me a picture of the baby and Gianna. The baby is beautiful—she has my eyes and Gianna's smile. I long to hold them both. I keep it with me at all times, tucked deep inside my pocket. Luca said he meets Gianna once in a while near the deli and the piazza with the baby. And sometimes the vineyard. But that's our place. In my letter back to him, I asked him not to go there with her anymore. I can't imagine she would want to go there without me, but maybe she feels closer to me there?

Luca also said he follows her home from time to time to keep an eye on her for me, but he fears that her husband might have seen him hiding behind the trees the last time he followed her. I hope he didn't. I fear that Gianna's husband is more dangerous than I first thought and don't doubt he is tied to a bad group of men. Gianna told Luca she has papers to leave for America. I don't know how she could have gotten them on her own. Luca seems to think she is going without her husband. That would be very risky for her to go alone *with a baby. Now I know I will never see her again. I asked Luca in my last letter to convince Gianna to go with my family to America and not to go alone.*

Chapter 27

Ella

"E l?" Jamie says, shaking my arm.

"Y—yes it was her," I say, searching my brain for all possible reasons for why it *had* to be Maria. "The pictures—of the family, remember? Gianna was in them. And Poppy. Uncle Luca?" I hear the inflection in my voice rise and quiver as I contemplate whether or not the woman who said she was Maria was really Maria. Because Maria is supposed to be dead. I don't linger on that thought for too long, though, because what I'm really worried about right now is the last word Angelina uttered: *tunnels.*

"It must have been her. Yes, you're right," Jamie says.

"Anyone can pretend to be someone," says Angelina. "Anyone can have photos. A family member. A friend." She studies both Jamie and me and our disturbed expressions, then she softens her posture and places her hand on mine. "But I'm sure your Maria is who she says she is." She glances at Jamie and then at me. "I just want you to be careful, that's all. Remember what I said about the *maloik*? It's a real thing. And it sounds like Gianna was someone people could have been jealous of or, worse yet, coveted. So, just be aware. That's all I'm saying."

Her words don't help at all. Self-doubt invades my thoughts, but I continue to push them into a small compartment that I know I'll go back to eventually. I need to know more about the tunnels. I gently squeeze Angelina's hand and peer into her eyes.

"What you said about the tunnels: is it possible," I say, "for a soldier to leave his post and travel through the tunnels to get to another destination? And then use them again to return?"

"Traveling through the tunnels was very difficult and very dangerous," she says. "You'd need to have considerable knowledge about the tunnels before setting off through them. Knowing where they lead and what's on the other end. Which tunnels connect with others. There are several built beneath Italy's streets. From the north to the south."

"How did they get there?" Jamie says.

"Oh, some of them have been there for centuries!" she says, throwing her hand in the air. "And some were built around the war. World War One, mostly. It's fascinating. A whole secret life beneath the streets that very few were ever aware of."

"So, someone could—if they needed to—travel through the tunnels and back without anyone knowing?" I say, slightly out of breath.

"As I said, it depends on which tunnels they used and how well they knew them," she says. "Some were very wide with enormous rooms and staircases, while others were so small you could feel the walls on both sides as you walked."

I continue to stare at Angelina, wondering how *she* came to know about the tunnels, still waiting for her to provide an answer to my question.

Her eyes relax. "But, yes, it is possible." she nods. "Anything is possible." Angelina rises from the table and moves to the kitchen island where she begins to prepare dinner. She motions toward the wine bottle. "How 'bout you two take care of that while I take care of this."

****

The summer wind gently rustles the leaves of the lemon trees and jostles the winding vines on the veranda as I walk past them on my way to the table. It's a warm, sultry night, much like the night I fell in love with Jack. The flickering lights of the scattered lanterns throughout the veranda blink like a thousand fireflies dancing against a darkened sky. It reminds me of the night we were camping with friends. We'd met before on a couple of occasions when our friends had gotten together and spoke to each other within the conversations of the group, never one-to-one. Our love wasn't a love at first sight but more of a gradual developing friendship.

I remember it was very late and we were all sitting around the fire. Eventually, everyone went to bed, but I wasn't ready and Jack wasn't, either. He got up, added another log to the fire, and sat in the chair next to me. And once we started talking, we didn't stop. I began sharing things I never had before with anyone else. I remember not wanting that evening to end.

Jack started talking about his father and how much he loved him and worried about him because he was getting older, weaker. He worried about him dying and the things he still wanted to do with him. His eyes held so much love and sincerity. That's when I fell in love with him. It wasn't just his love for his father, the importance of family, and his willingness to share so much with me. It was because, in that moment, the way he talked about life and the world, I felt like I had a glimpse into his beautiful soul. I began to study his features as if I were seeing him for the first time. The way his dark hair perfectly fell against his tanned face. His soft low voice and quiet laugh. Something had changed in my heart that night as we stared into the fire. We agreed that the rising, separating sparks of the fire that night looked like hundreds of fireflies. I breathe in the memory and shake my head to set it free.

The center table is decorated with crisp white linens. A table runner stretches across the middle surrounded by golden, Tuscan-colored dishes and tableware. A crystal wine glass is placed at the right of each seating above the silverware wrapped in a white linen napkin. Several orange peony flowers bend over a glass vase in the center of it all. Angelina. Her attention to detail is impressive.

I check my phone for the third time to see that Nico has not yet called back. And, probably, after he hears my lingering awkward message which sounds as if I'm pleading for him to come to dinner, he'll most likely never call me again. But I hope I'm wrong. I want him to come to dinner if for no other reason than to explain that there's nothing between Marco and me. I'd never be involved with a married man, let alone someone of his character.

I'm quickly joined on the veranda by Angelina, Vinny, and Jamie, followed by several waiters rolling carts of food to the table. I jump at the vibration in my pocket and see that I missed two calls, one from Uncle Luca and one from Maria.

Vinny waits for the food to be dished out and then he indicates that we should hold hands. He makes the sign of the cross and begins to pray in Italian. His voice is smooth and gentle, and I enjoy listening to his beautiful Italian words effortlessly roll off his tongue. He pauses just long enough so Angelina can repeat each phrase in English for Jamie. When he finishes, Angelina stands and raises her glass.

"To friendship and family. We think of you as both. May we always find truth and may our paths cross again."

I hear a stirring from behind and then light footsteps.

"Am I too late?" says a familiar voice.

"No, of course not, Nico!" Angelina says. My heart skips. "We're so happy to have you!" Angelina motions to the waiters to add another place setting.

"I would have called," he says, seating himself next to me, "but after I received an interesting message from El, my phone died." He glances at me and tries to hide his smile.

My face heats up. I fidget with my hair and smile back.

"Well, you're here now and that's all that matters," says Vinny. "And now, let's eat!"

Jamie smirks at me from across the table, kicks my leg, and smiles. I try to remain calm and ignore the anxiety rising within, causing my stomach to shrink and reject even the sight of the delicious food before me. I'm probably nervous because I'm still thinking of what Angelina said about the tunnels and Maria. Or maybe it's the missed phone calls from Uncle Luca and Maria. Or maybe it's not any of those. Maybe what makes me nauseously push the food around my plate, pretending to take a bite now and then, is the same thing that makes my hand tremble as I raise a glass of wine to my lips. Perhaps the source of my profound sweat and the giddy uneasiness I've only ever felt one other time is sitting right next to me. I inhale deeply and gently dab my brow with my napkin, thankful to be sitting next to Nico and not across. Relieved that I can hide my expression and avoid gazing into his melted brown eyes.

I can handle an occasional side glance and elbow touch. But the moments when our legs quickly graze and I feel the heat from his body, I become dizzy and incoherent. Every now and then I see Jamie laughing to herself because she knows exactly what I'm thinking. And I think she knows I'm trying. I'm trying to step outside of the box I've allowed to hide and protect me for the last two years.

I hear the friendly chatter of dinner conversations around me, not really investing in any of it or contributing, just listening to the buzz of voices. I nod every now and then to pretend I'm with them. I float along effortlessly, sipping my wine, not caring about anything at all until Angelina's voice rises above the rest.

"This morning, Ella and I were talking about the tunnels

underneath the streets of Italy," Angelina says, looking at Nico.

"Oh?" he says. "You're interested in the tunnels?" He turns to me and my heart beats faster. I blink a few times and pinch my leg.

"Well, um, we were talking about how—" I stumble over my words. "Somehow, we got on the topic of—"

"Ella," Angelina says calmly, just tell him. We know nothing for certain."

I take a deep breath and look at Jamie. She shrugs her shoulders and raises her eyebrows. I shift my chair to face Nico.

"Remember when we were talking at the vineyard about the two men and the woman?"

"Yes," he says, "the woman was missing. Your grandmother, right? And you were worried that the man responsible might have been your grandfather. I remember."

Jamie, Angelina, and Vinny exchange glances.

"Well, I was concerned that if my grandfather *was* responsible, which he wasn't, how could he have gotten from his post during the war to where Gianna was? And Angelina mentioned the tunnels," I say, giving a dismissive wave of my hand.

Nico's expression changes slightly. "And what did Angelina say about that?" he says, looking at us both.

"Well," Angelina says, "I told her that, depending on which tunnels he used, it's possible to get from one place to another without being caught."

All eyes rest on Nico, awaiting his response. He pauses, straightens his posture, and looks at each of us, one at a time, before responding.

"There's a case I was studying recently for one of my classes, . . ." Nico says. "It's interesting that you bring this up. There's an article about an elderly man. Just before he died, he told his sister about some tunnels beneath these streets we sit on now. He said during World War Two he used to hide in them to escape the enemy. No one believed him at first. But he was very specific about the location, how and where to enter, where to go, what we'd see. And when they went to look, it was there. He was right. Big enormous hallways in some parts and small, narrow alleyways in others."

"Have you seen the tunnels? How did they get there?" Jamie asks.

"Yes. I've seen parts of it," he says. "They were originally built during the first World War for storage and hiding."

"What case were you studying?"

"The class was mostly about Italian history and criminal war cases. We even learned how the Italian mafia also made tunnels for drug use and hiding for their own purposes. I'm sure you've learned similar things about your country when you studied law?"

"Yes, we did. But nothing as interesting as this," she says.

"That's when I came across the article about the elderly World War Two veteran. What's incredible about these tunnels is that, until this story came out, the only confirmed tunnels were thought to be in northern Italy near Milan. A few in the middle near Florence, but none in southern Italy, especially not as far as Tropea. Can you imagine? All these years and no one ever knew the tunnels existed here?"

I nod, still wrestling with the possibility in my head that Poppy might have used the tunnels to get to Gianna. Did he use them to visit her? Or was there something else?

"So, if someone was away, let's say as a World War Two soldier during the war, up further north," I say, "would it be possible or likely that he could leave his position, travel through the tunnels to see someone, and then go back without being noticed?"

Nico looks up at the sky and then back at me, stroking his chin, his brow furrowed.

"Well. It depends how far north he was. He couldn't have done it alone," he says. "He'd probably have to work with someone.

Someone who could cover for him, watch out for him. Be in communication with him. Get him in and out safely."

"But the likelihood of that happening is probably low, right?" I say. *Say it's low, Nico.*

"I wouldn't say it's a high likelihood," he says, "but I wouldn't say it's low."

"What *are* you saying, then?"

He places his hand on mine and I shiver. "I'm not saying I think this happened with your grandfather," he says, softening his eyes, "but what I'm trying to explain is that, yes, with the right timing and the right help, it could happen."

"Time for dessert!" Angelina interrupts, and I'm glad to end this conversation. But I don't want his hand to leave mine.

Poppy

28 December 1938

I finally received a letter from Gianna today and she enclosed a picture of the baby! Bella is the name we've chosen to call her. She has brown wavy locks of hair just like her mother and chubby cheeks like mine when I was a baby. She is so beautiful and has grown so much. I can't believe she's nine months old. Almost a year and I still haven't held her or seen her in person. I try to imagine what it would be like, how heavy she might feel, how she might rest her head on my shoulder, how her voice might sound. Gianna says she's very curious about everything.

Gianna tells me that she plans to travel with the baby to America to see some of her relatives. I know this is her secretive way of saying she's running away from her husband. I'm glad she's remembering that they'll check every letter before they give it to me. I need to find a way to stop her from going alone. I'll need to talk to Luca about it.

I love hearing about all of the great things Bella is doing now. Gianna talks about everything happening in her life. Except she still hasn't told me she's been going to the vineyard with Luca. That hasn't come up at all. I wonder if I should bring it up?

15 January 1939

A package came today with all kinds of things from Mamá! A blanket she knitted, some comic books, a deck of cards, some snacks. She also enclosed a letter telling me how proud she is and how much she misses me. She signed it from both Papá and her, but I know better.

She also included a letter from Luca. He met a pretty girl named Lena and they've now started going steady. I'm happy for him. Luca is a good brother, but he's not always very smooth with women. So, that he actually found someone who likes him beyond his charming looks and continues to stay is something!

Luca said that Gianna has been acting strangely. She's fidgety and nervous and almost manic at times, making sense one minute and talking in circles the next. He says they went to the vineyard again. Again. And she kept talking about the last time we were there and had to say goodbye. He said he asked her what was wrong but she couldn't articulate it. Couldn't get it out. He's worried that she might do something unsafe to herself. It's strange how he acts as if he knows her more than I do. Maybe it's just my own insecurities.

Chapter 28

Ella

A bright morning sun breaks through the seams of the blackout curtains in my room. I rub my eyes and stare at the ceiling fan above me. Its soft, circular path releases a gentle, relieving wind. I retrieve some of the memories from last night's dinner, particularly Nico's smile and his occasional lingering stares I'd catch. The way he said my name, the way he smelled, the presence of his body next to mine. How he said goodbye, leaning toward my face and then offering an awkward hug. "Can I come by tomorrow?" he asked. "Yes, of course," I replied, waving from the doorway before proceeding to float to my room.

Pleasant thoughts are quickly pushed aside by others, especially the conversations between Angelina and Nico about the tunnels—how it *was* possible for someone, with the aid of another, to actually sneak through them, hide for a while, and make it all the way out and then back again. How long would that take? Who else might have known about it? Who would have helped? A weight presses hard on my chest as I fear what this means. I push away these thoughts as well as thoughts of Uncle Luca probably knowing what happened and helping to cover it. That's what brothers would do for each other, isn't it? What family members do for one another? Watch and protect, no matter the cost?

My phone buzzes on the nightstand, a reminder notification of the calls I missed last night. I notice that Maria left a message.

Ella, It's Maria. There's more about Gianna that you need to know. I know you leave soon. Please come tomorrow if you can. We shouldn't talk over the phone. Just come.

I throw on the nearest clothes and run a comb through my hair while texting Jamie, hoping she's awake in the next room. She comes to my door groggy but ready.

"I don't know if I trust her," she says, leaning against the door jam and tightening her ponytail.

"I don't, either. But I can't not go."

"What could she possibly need to tell us?"

I shrug my shoulders.

"No idea. But if it's something that will help us or give us direction, some kind of closure, I need to know."

"You realize we leave the day after tomorrow, right?"

"Uh huh," I say, closing the door behind us.

****

As we embark along the uneven cobbled road of Via Rosa, I notice something is different from the last time we visited. Nothing physically *looks* different. Same narrow road. Same unkempt walls and rickety doors with flickering lights above them. Some of the house numbers are loose and crooked while others are straight and neatly painted. The plants outside of some houses are well-watered while others lie dry and withered in their pots. The air has the same denseness and stillness it had before. But among this familiar scene, something is amiss. I stop walking and turn to Jamie.

"Do you notice anything different?"

"What do you mean?" she says.

"I don't know. Something's different from the last time we were here."

Jamie stops to study the houses on the street surrounding us.

"No, I don't notice anything," she says, shrugging.

"Maybe I'm just over-analyzing again."

We reach Maria's house and I pause before knocking. I have the same nervous feeling I get when I'm on a rollercoaster sitting in the first car as it slowly crawls to the peak, waiting for that last quick jolt just before we're thrusted over the top. I take a deep breath, swallow, and knock three times. An eye appears in the crack of the blinds. I hear a soft shuffle and then the door slowly opens. Maria looks behind us to the left and then to the right before smiling and motioning for us to come in.

Her tiny house smells of coffee mixed with something sweet and traces of something foul. I glance at Jamie. Her lip is curled and she looks as though she might vomit. We sit on the sofa as Maria fills our mugs and then sits across from us. She leans in, propping her elbows on top of her knees.

"I'm glad you came," she says. "When do you leave Italy?"

"Day after tomorrow," I say, not at all satisfied with what I've accomplished on this trip. Feeling a little sad and disappointed that I probably haven't done what Poppy wanted me to do. Wishing I had more time.

"So soon," she says, glancing at the floor and then at me. "Well," she reaches into a bag, "I found this." She places a sheet of paper in front of Jamie and me and we examine it together.

"Is this . . . real?" I ask, looking at Gianna's birth certificate. I trace the scarcely raised seal with my finger and read the name: Gianna Russo, born on 27 July 1920, Scilla, Italy.

"Yes. *Si*," she nods frantically.

"How do I—"

"How do we know," Jamie interrupts, "that this is real? How do we know that anything you've shared is real? How do we know if you're even Maria?"

Maria gasps and puts her hand over her heart, and then she waves them fanning her face. She reaches into her bag and takes hold of something else, pausing for a moment as if to contemplate her next decision.

"Who else would give me this?" she says. Her eyes are wild as she pushes another sheet of paper in front of us. The words are written in the same delicate, flowy handwriting I've come to know so well. It's written as a certificate and reads:

Today, as we stand atop the cliffs of this castle, with God and the deep blue sea as our witnesses, we pledge our unending and undying love for each other. Our hearts and souls: Gianna Russo's and Franco Perri's, forever intertwined. You are mine and I am yours. And no matter what shall come, that truth remains and cannot be undone.

Beneath the pledge are Gianna's and Franco's wispy signatures. Jamie and I look up at each other with the same surprised expression.

"I remember reading about this in Poppy's diary," I say, reflecting on the specific entry. Poppy described their visit to the monastery and then to the castle before he had to leave for the war.

"I do, too," Jamie says.

We examine both certificates. I try to imagine a young Gianna and Franco facing each other on top of Ruffolo Castle, hands held, the sea surrounding them, staring into each other's eyes and pledging their love. I feel Maria's hard gaze on me. When my eyes meet hers, she looks as if she might spring forward out of her chair.

"Gianna gave this to *me*!" Maria yells, furrowing her brow. "Only me! I was the only one who could be trusted with her secrets." Spit gathers on her lips as she sharply enunciates each word. She wipes it away with the back of her hand and slightly softens her posture. "I've never shown anyone. Until now. I made sure the police wouldn't find it either." She proudly motions to her breasts, "I hid them in my bosom when they came."

"They came looking here?" I say so loud my voice echoes in the tiny space.

"Oh, they did! They checked all the places Gianna usually went. They were particularly interested in Luca for a while, convinced that he was the last one to see her."

"But you're not convinced?" Jamie asks.

"I just don't know," she shakes her head. "I can't imagine he would, but—"

In the momentary silence, I reread Gianna's and Franco's pledge of love over and over. Then I lift the certificate to my nose and inhale deeply the paper, the ink, their essence, as if I might breathe it all in. Be with them for a moment. Maria breaks the silence first.

"I wanted you to have these papers because you should," she says. "You came all this way for your grandfather. Not many people would do that. But you wanted to understand what happened all those years ago. To find something he couldn't find. These belong to you now," Maria says, lightly tapping the papers. As I'm about to thank her, she leans in again, her face is grave and inches from mine. "But that isn't the only reason I called you here."

"It's not?" I say, glancing at Jamie.

"No, it's not." Maria takes a sip of her coffee and adjusts herself in her chair. Then she wipes the gathered sweat above her lip and leans forward. "After Gianna went missing, Nina was frantic. She became very close to Sienna and me. We were all grieving her loss and came to depend on each other. We saw each other daily. We needed each other." She takes another sip and repositions herself on the chair before continuing.

"Before Nina died, she asked me to keep a secret. She told me that while your grandfather was stationed up north during the war, he was moved a couple of times. Eventually, he was moved down into the middle region of Italy. No one knew. Not even his mother. Some of the people he used to trust he no longer did. Only Nina. And beside me, she was the closest thing to Gianna. I think he trusted her more because she *wasn't* family, even though that sounds strange.

"Nina helped your grandfather a lot. I don't know exactly how, but I know she was very much involved in his life at that time. Just before she passed, she shared all of this with me. I think she had to get it off her conscience.

"I remember it well," she says staring at the ceiling, "that day she told me she still had all of Franco's letters he'd written to her. She saved them all, but she was afraid to keep them with her so she hid them. She was so anxious about telling me and I think she almost didn't. Do you understand what I'm telling you?" she says, raising her voice. "She hid them! In the bricks of the monastery! I don't know if you have enough time, but I'm afraid you're not done with this just yet."

My mouth hangs open but nothing comes out. This could be it. This could be everything.

"Why didn't you tell us about this when we first visited you?" Jamie asks. Maria looks offended at first.

"Well, I wasn't sure I could trust you," she says. "I wasn't sure if you were telling me the truth about who you were or why you were digging into the past."

"What changed that?" I say.

"At the end of that visit, as we said goodbye in the doorway, I knew you were who you said you were. There was just too much that you knew about Gianna. Then, yesterday, when I called you, I decided that if you came back again today, your intentions were true."

"Yes, they are," I say. "But how are we supposed to know which bricks she hid them in? There must be thousands."

Maria gives a confident smile.

"When you get there, go to the old part of the church. The original part, not the new construction. Then go to the altar. The letters are behind the brick that says 'Proverbs 3:6.'"

Poppy

17 February 1939

I'm frantic. Out of my mind. I don't know what to do or who to tell. I opened Luca's letter today and cannot believe what my eyes were reading. A baby carriage was left on the front porch of our house very early in the morning. The wheels were locked so it wouldn't roll away and the carriage faced the front door so it would be the first thing you would see when you opened it. The top of the carriage was pulled down to shield things from getting in. Luca noticed the carriage right away as he was leaving early in the morning to go to work. He lifted the cover back and inside was a baby soundly sleeping. Upon closer examination, he saw that it was Bella! My Bella! She was wearing a light knit sweater and a hat and surrounded by soft blankets. My baby girl. There was no note, no other information. Why would Gianna leave our baby? If she had to go somewhere, she would have left her with her sister or Nina. Where would she go without her? Luca knew Papá wouldn't like this and might do something careless, so he told Mamá right away. Mamà pretended that her friends' granddaughter needed to be cared for while she went away for a while, which isn't unusual in these times. It's very risky, but it's the only choice we have to keep Bella safe. Thank God for Mama. But WHERE IS GIANNA? I'm distraught and don't know what to do.

10 March 1939

    Luca finally replied to my letter. I asked him dozens of questions but he didn't answer them all. He said Bella fusses a lot and Gianna hasn't come back for her. She hasn't even called, not once. Luca seems to think that Gianna just couldn't take it anymore and left. He says she probably figures Bella is in good hands with Mamá and she won't have to deal with her abusive husband anymore. I was wondering for a while if she might be coming to find me somehow and didn't want to take Bella with her. As much as I would love to see her, it's too dangerous for anyone, especially a woman, to go anywhere alone. But why would she do this? Luca said that maybe she went to America. But how? I feel so helpless. My heart does not want to be here in this place anymore. It never did in the first place. Thank God I have Luca. He is my lifeline to everything important to me.

Chapter 29

Ella

I stumble down the steps, then turn and wave at Maria who is standing in her doorway with a partial grin. Very different from our last teary departure from Via Rosa. On our walk down the narrow street to the main road, the hairs on the back of my neck stand up and a chill runs down my spine. I can't shake the feeling that someone is watching us. A quick look around reveals nothing unusual, but I pick up the pace, leaving Jamie slightly behind. She gives me a puzzled look, so I slow my steps so she can catch up. I link my arm in hers as we continue walking and whisper in her ear, "Something is giving me the creeps. I just want to get to the car."

She looks behind her and we walk-run the rest of the way.

Once inside the car, I ask our driver to take us straight to the monastery while it's still early enough in the day. He agrees and we settle in for the hour drive to Scilla. I pull out my phone to look up Proverbs 3:6 and see a text from Nico saying that he's on his way to the villa. I text him back right away to tell him we're not there and invite him to meet us at the castle, which is supposed to be near the monastery.

"What was going on back there?" Jamie says as we pull away from the neighborhood.

"I don't know. I just had this weird, creepy feeling that someone was watching us," I say. "It gave me a chill."

"I didn't see anyone, did you?" she asks.

"No, just a feeling. I can't describe it. Not like before on our way to Maria's when I said something was different. This is more . . . specific. Like a strong presence," I say, shivering from another chill.

"It's probably nothing," Jamie says. "Maybe you were freaked out about what Maria said and it made you paranoid."

"Maybe."

Another text comes through from my mother, and my heart sinks. I feel guilty that I haven't kept in touch with her very much during this trip. And for knowing what I know and not sharing any of it with her. I text her back to let her know everything is fine and, yes, we're having a great time and I will call her before we leave Italy. But right now, I need to call Uncle Luca.

He picks up on the first ring.

"Hello, Ella!" he says, sounding very upbeat and happy to hear from me.

"Hi, Uncle Luca!"

"How's everything? Find any more clues to the family history?" he asks in a teasing, friendly way.

"Everything's good!" I say, laughing more from nervousness than replying to his joke.

"That's great, sweetie. So glad you called. I was thinking about you. I know your trip is almost over and I'm looking forward to hearing all about it when you get home," he says.

"Yeah, that will be great. But . . . um . . . Uncle Luca?"

"Yes?"

"Did you know that Poppy and Gianna pledged their love to one another before he went to war?"

"Pledged their love? What do you mean?" he says.

"Yes, at an old monastery. An old church that turned into a monastery. They made promises, like vows, to each other."

"But they didn't get married. Gianna was already engaged," he says.

"I know, but they made vows to each other. I think they knew they couldn't be officially married, so they married each others' hearts. To always be connected—you know, before anyone else. I think it's romantic, even though it's sad."

"Hmm," he says, followed by a long pause. "And how do you know all of this? Maria?"

"Well, I read about it in Poppy's diary, and then, yes, Maria confirmed it."

"You saw Maria again?"

"Just briefly, but anyway, the reason why I'm calling is that . . . I know what you did."

"What do you mean?" he coughs.

"I know about the vineyard. I know about the tunnels. I—"

"Wait. El. What do you mean, you 'know'? What do you think you know?" he says.

"I know that when Gianna went missing, it didn't look good for Poppy. Or you. I know you both were questioned. I know he must have found a way to get to her. He had to have used the secret tunnels underground. I still won't bring myself to say the words because, in my heart, I don't believe them, and—"

"So you think Poppy found a way to get to Gianna? To harm her?" he says.

"I never said he harmed her."

"Ella— Slow down. Hold on." His voice is tight.

"No, I can't," I swallow hard. "Anyway, I called to say that I know you tried to help him."

"You . . . do?"

"Yes. You covered for him. You helped him. By pretending not to know why Gianna was missing. Pretending to find the baby. Pretending to—"

"Don't say anymore. It's okay. It's time to let this go now, Ella. Can you do that for me? For Poppy? It's time to put this to rest. Let it rest now."

"I still think maybe she left. She might have just left Italy, right?" I sniff.

"It's very possible,"he says. "That's why when you first brought it up about the letters at your mom's house that night, I didn't say very much. Didn't say what I knew. It wasn't important anymore. And you remember how surprised I was when you found Maria? But still, it doesn't change anything that we already know. Or don't know. I didn't think you'd take this as far as you have, but see? We're no better off knowing what we know now than what we did then. Does that make sense?"

"I guess," I say.

"So you'll let this go, then, right?"

"I will. But there's one more thing I have to do," I say. "I'm on my way to the castle and then the monastery. I need to be where they were that day before he left and everything changed."

"Oh, Ella, why? You're just gonna make yourself feel worse. You shouldn't go."

"No, I won't feel worse. I have to go. It's the last thing I need to do before I leave Italy. I need to go to Scilla where they grew up. I need to walk through those streets before I leave. I need to walk up the steps to the castle as they did and look over the cliff. Once I have the last of Poppy's letters, I'll leave."

"I thought you had all of his letters."

"Well. I thought I did, too. But then I found out there are more letters he wrote to Nina, probably confiding in her. And she hid them in the church near the castle to protect him. I need to get those letters. I can't leave anything behind. No more traces of this story, you know? Then maybe—maybe I can put it to rest."

"Whoever it was who told you he wrote letters to Nina is probably lying. Was it Maria? I don't think you should go, Ella. What if it's a trap?"

"A trap? I don't think—hello? Uncle Luca?" Our connection is lost.

By the time Jamie and I finish discussing my conversation with Uncle Luca, we arrive at Chianalea, a small fishing village in Scilla. Known as the Venice of Calabria, this quaint little village is where Gianna and Franco visited frequently. I step out of the car, shielding my eyes from the sun, and right away I see it perched high in the sky: Castello Ruffo.

The prominent castle, still easily seen miles away, rests upon a high rocky base, jutting out into the Tyrrhenian Sea. It splits the beaches of Chianalea and the town of Scilla. And I know from reading Poppy's diary and my own research that on the other side, behind the beaches of Scilla, is the church, Chiesa Dello Spirito Santo. Poppy never called it by its name in his diary, he just referred to it as the "gem at the base of the castle" or "the monastery." Only later, after some research, I was able to put a name to the gem.

I tap Jamie on the shoulder and point. Her jaw falls and she looks back at me, smiling widely. It is impressive and majestic and I want nothing more than to be there right now. I feel strangely nostalgic, like I'm coming home from a long journey. Like a longing I haven't felt before. But an uneasy feeling from my conversation with Uncle Luca still follows me. I check my phone. Still no signal. I hope we can find Nico.

I hear the happy buzz of a town filled with kindness and watch the people talking, laughing and working together at the marina as we pass. A real fishing village is the heart of this town, and I get a sense that not much has changed here over the years. I can almost picture life as it was for Franco and Gianna all those years ago.

A text comes in from Nico and my stomach flips. He's here waiting for us in the castle. I text him back to explain that we're near the marina and he says to wait right there, he'll come down to meet us. Jamie keeps checking her phone, something she's been increasingly doing as we've neared the end of our trip. Probably work-related but still annoying. She never gets time off without some kind of interruption.

She glances up from her phone, sees me watching her, and smiles. "Work," she says rolling her eyes. Then she looks out past the marina toward the sea. "This place is amazing. I can see how easy it could be to fall in love here. You said Nico's coming down to the marina?"

"Yes," I say, scanning the area near the castle stairs for Nico. "I hope he sees us, because—"

"Because what?" he says.

I jump and make a funny noise, almost falling into him. I catch myself and laugh, embarrassed.

"Sorry, did I scare you?" He looks at Jamie and waves. She waves back.

"No, not at all," I lie.

My eyes meet his. I will them to stay there, but they travel and I can't stop them. They shift to his hair flying back slightly in the gentle breeze, to his broad shoulders that fit perfectly in the white button-down shirt, the first three buttons undone. They then move to his snug-fitting khaki shorts, down to his sandals, and then quickly back to his eyes. It happens so fast, maybe he doesn't notice. My face feels hot and I know it's red.

"No," I say, breaking from his stare and pointing toward the stairs, "I was just expecting you to come from over there."

"Oh, I came from there," he says, waving toward the front of the castle nearest the sea. "Come, I'll take you to the castle."

"How do you know so much about this place?" Jamie asks.

"My family used to come to Scilla sometimes for a holiday. I think you say 'vacation,'" he says.

"Perfect. Then, if you know so much, you'll be able to get us in and out quickly," she adds.

"Are you in a rush?" he says.

I say no and Jamie says yes at the same time. We look at each other, puzzled.

"I'd like to spend some time here, now that we're actually here," I say to Jamie. "Is there something else you want to do?"

"N—no, I just wanted to . . . actually, it's fine. Yes, let's stay as long as you'd like," she says.

I'm confused by her hesitance but I don't say anything more.

"Is your friend Marco here, too?" Nico says. "I thought I saw him."

"Marco?" I say. "He's not my friend. He's here?"

"Why would Marco be here?" Jamie says.

"Maybe I'm wrong, but it looked like him," Nico says."When I was waiting for you at the castle, I thought I saw him. But it was quick, so maybe it wasn't him."

Jamie and I glance at each other.

"That would be very strange to see Marco here," I say. And awkward. And terrible timing with Nico here.

"Probably wasn't him," Nico says. Instead of heading toward the stairs, he motions for us to follow him toward the front of the castle, near the sea.

"Don't we need to use the stairs to get to the other side?" Jamie asks.

"We can, but we don't have to. I thought I'd take you a more interesting way," he says. "When we get hungry, I recommend we go there." He points to a sign that says, "Il Pirata." "Delicious seafood," he smiles.

I notice a slight dimple in his right cheek. I'm totally fine with that idea as well as any idea involving spending more time in this idyllic town with Nico. As he leads us around the rock of the castle, I feel so small and insignificant in its shadow. We proceed to a smaller hallway that leads to a wide, arched tunnel. I hesitate just before entering and Nico nods, reassuring me that it's okay.

"A tunnel?" I say.

"Not like the ones we talked about. Just a passageway to the beach." He smiles again and then turns to lead us through the massive tunnel with people walking through it in both directions. Jamie and I follow close behind Nico until a bright light peeks through at the end meaning we've reached the other side. We emerge onto the sandy beaches of Scilla. It reminds me of a smaller, more quaint version of Tropea. I'm in awe of the picturesque view in front of me, houses neatly tucked into the cliff along the ragged shoreline facing the sea.

"I would love to live here," I say.

"Me, too," Nico says, looking back. My heart races.

I notice a few long, narrow roads each ending at the beach, just steps away from where we are, reminding me of Poppy's Italian neighborhood painting. We follow Nico into one of the neighboring streets until he stops in front of a small, pretty white building with two tall, narrow mahogany doors. One is open and the other is closed.

"This," he motions to the building, "is Chiesa dello Spirito Sancto. Do you know what that means?"

"Yes," I say. "Church of the Holy Spirit. This is it?" It's so unassuming, I would have walked right by it.

"Yes, it is small, but it stretches a bit that way," he says, indicating that the building goes further back. "The door is open. Shall we go in?"

Once inside, the musty old smell of church and wood from the pews comforts me, reminding me of the times when I'd go to church with Poppy and Nonna as a child. The soft sounds of quiet surround us as we walk slowly down the aisle. No one else is here but us. Jamie is already at the altar, looking around. I marvel at the white marble sculptures and stained-glass windows on my way to the altar. When I turn to check if Nico is still at the door, our noses almost touch and we both step back, surprised. I hadn't realized he was so close behind. He reaches for my arm and electric waves course through my skin.

"It's all marble," Jamie says with a hand on one hip. "There are no bricks."

"No, no, no, there are bricks," Nico corrects.

"Really? Where? And how do you know?" she says, her voice edgy.

I give her a "what's wrong with you look" but she ignores it.

Nico walks behind the altar and examines it, eyeing the whole thing from top to bottom, being very careful not to move anything resting on top.

"I *know*," he says annoyed, "because I've been here before. I've studied the history of these buildings in Scilla. They fascinate me."

Jamie reaches toward the top of the altar to move something out of the way, but Nico stops her.

"Don't touch!" he yells. "Please—these are sacred." She looks at him, perplexed. "Out of respect," he says more softly, "please don't touch anything." Jamie backs away.

I begin searching the walls and shelves behind the altar to see if anything seems remotely like old bricks.

"What if they covered all the bricks when they remodeled?" I say, but Nico isn't listening. He's concentrating on something behind the altar near the floor and squats down to get a closer look. Jamie and I come near, but he puts out his hand so we stop.

"If you come too close, you'll block the light and then I can't read the words," he says.

"What words?" we say.

"The scripture that's written," he whispers. "What did you say it was?"

"Proverbs 3:6," I utter.

He repeats "Proverbs 3:6" again and again to himself as he checks each brick. And then, "Proverbs 3:6! It's here!"

We hurry over and kneel next to Nico. About a foot up and running along the base of the altar, facing the back of the church, is what appears to be the original bricks from when this church was built. Etched across the face of each brick is a bible verse, a quote, or a reference to a verse. And sure enough, in between John 3:16 and "Love Thy Neighbor" is the brick that has Proverbs 3:6. As soon as I touch it, it moves just a hair. I push against it, noticing that it's not flush like the others.

"Seems strange," I say with my hand against it. I jiggle it back and forth trying to loosen it. It feels heavy and moves only slightly. Eventually, I manage to pry one side out and then the rest. We gasp at its release. I hand the brick to Jamie and peer inside the small space, but it's too dark. Reaching inside with my hand, I feel nothing. I look again: darkness. I put my hand back in, stretching my fingers along the shallow walls of the tiny space. Still nothing. After I remove my empty hand, I stare defeated at Jamie and Nico. My chest tightens and a lump gathers in my throat. My eyes water and spill over my cheeks.

"They're gone! The letters are gone!"

I get up and pace around the altar. *She said Proverbs 3:6, right?* I check the notes on my phone. Yes, that's it. Nico and Jamie take turns looking and feeling inside the space for the letters but find nothing. They walk to where I'm standing and crying. I wipe my tears with my hand.

"I don't understand," I say. "Did Maria lie? Did Nina lie to Maria? It doesn't make sense. There was a brick with Proverbs 3:6 like she said. It was loose. It had to have been true!" I say, wiping the tears from my cheeks.

"I'm sorry, El," Jamie says, gently reaching for my hand. Nico comes closer, pauses, and then embraces me in a tight hug. I hug him back and bury my face into his shirt, the smell of woodsy pine a small consolation. He loosens his hug and I step back, embarrassed by the dark wet spot of tears I left on his shoulder.

"Was I crazy to believe that after all these years there'd be secret letters from my grandfather that might have had answers to everything?" I sniff. "If they were there in the first place."

"I don't know what to think, El," Jamie says. "But think of what you've done for Poppy already. I know he's proud of you. Even if you can't figure it all out."

Nico puts his arm around me. "I don't think you're crazy at all, El," he says, looking at me with his beautiful, brown, intensely sincere eyes. They remind me of Poppy's eyes: sincere, honest, and kind. "And I do think those letters were there. At one time. But—nah," he says, waving his hand.

"But what?"

He faces me and places my cold hands into the warmth of his. "What if they *were* there," he pauses, "but then someone took them?"

Jamie and I look at each other, unsure of what to say. Who would take them and why?

Poppy

14 April 1939

Luca wrote me a letter and said that Gianna is nowhere to be found. He went to check on her after the baby carriage was left at the house. He normally follows her home after their visits, never going farther than the cypress trees at the edge of her property. He said when he stands in that spot, the wide trees at the foot of the yard block him so he can't be seen. But he can still see a lot from that spot. Sometimes he can tell if her husband's car is there and sometimes he can see movement from the windows. But on this day, there was no car in the driveway, and since it looked like no one was home, he took a chance and walked up to the door. When he peered through the window near the door he saw nothing. No furniture, no toys, nothing. Gone. Without a trace. He said he was worried and didn't know what to do. I can see it in the frantic scratches of his handwriting: fear. My stomach is in knots and I cannot sleep. Other than my own survival, I think of nothing else.

A second letter from Luca arrived a few days later. In it, he says that he has convinced our parents to get their papers processed in order to leave Italy for America. He and his girlfriend, Lena, and Bella will go with them. He said that he and Lena will get married and they can care for Bella until I arrive. Luca thinks he can get the papers processed in one or two months. I think one or two months is an unusually short amount of time, but he said he has connections. I question these connections. I will write to him and ask him to wait for me. I am due to be discharged in just a few months. I know that things are not safe in Italy right now, and it's good timing as well as a good opportunity to go to America, but if only they would wait so we could all be together. Yet, I can't imagine leaving Italy without Gianna. Maybe I shouldn't go. Maybe Bella should stay here with me. Maybe I can find Gianna.

Chapter 30

Ella

My eyes dart back and forth across Nico's face as I try to analyze the meaning of his suggestion. At the same time, my mind races around the details of everything I know and what I don't know. I'm stuck in a pause and I can't get out of it.

"Are you okay?" he says.

"You think the letters were stolen?" I say.

With his hands still holding mine, he tilts his head as if he's giving this question deeper consideration. "You said Nina told Maria she had letters that Poppy had written to her, right?" I nod. "And she hid them behind a brick with Proverbs 3:6 on it, right?" he says.

"Yes."

"It's so very specific." He runs his fingers through his hair creating several cascading waves. "And we've done everything she said. Went to the church. Found the brick with Proverbs 3:6. And when we removed it, there was a space behind, big enough to hold something small, like letters. I think everything Maria told you about the letters was true. I think the letters were really here." He breathes out a long sigh.

"Then who would have taken them? And why? When?" I say, glancing at both Nico and Jamie. Jamie looks up from her phone and puts it in her pocket.

"I don't know, El," Jamie says, scratching her head, "but it feels like we've been on a wild goose chase."

"It does feel like that," I say, "but it can't be for nothing."

"No, it can't be," Nico says. "It can't be."

****

The afternoon sun thrusts its oppressive heat upon us as we duck inside the small Il Pirata restaurant where we stop to eat before going back to the villa. Vibrant Italian music plays through small speakers on the terrace. Nico leads us to a table under an umbrella and signals for a server. He pulls out a chair for both Jamie and me and only sits after we do. Once seated, we relish in the small momentary wafts of air coming off the ocean. As Nico speaks to the server and orders our drinks and several small plates of food, he continuously glances at me with a smile as if he's talking about me. I know I'm blushing and look away.

The waiter quickly returns with our drinks and a long-stemmed red rose which he hands to me. "From the gentleman," he says, nodding to Nico as he departs.

"Oh, Nico," I say, "it's beautiful." I smile, feeling the butterflies in my stomach again.

He pauses for a moment and then looks at me with sleepy eyes. "No, you are beautiful," he says. My heart quickens and I feel out of breath. *Is this happening?*

"Um . . . I feel like maybe I'll take a walk?" Jamie says smiling, her eyebrows raised. I can tell she feels uncomfortable by the way she's shifting in her seat.

"No, that's okay, Jame. Stay," I say, but she's already up.

"I'm just going to use the restroom," she says, smirking.

And now here we are. Alone. For a moment.

The sweet music plays in the background and a strong warm breeze blows through the terrace. Most of the tables are filled with friends, families, couples eating, talking, laughing. I almost don't hear them because I'm floating. Like I was at Angelina's dinner. Nico stands and reaches for my hand. "Dance?" he says. I feel fluttery and shaky as I clasp his hand and rise to my feet.

We walk out a few steps into an open space and he takes my hand and places it in his. His other hand against the small of my back. When he pulls me close, I bring both of my hands around his neck. He brushes a piece of hair out of my eyes and we sway slowly to the music. I feel weightless in his strong arms. Our eyes lock. And then, his eyes drop to my mouth and he draws me in closer, placing his lips gently on mine. Small, light kisses become deeper, passionate. We gaze into each other's eyes and then we hug. Resting my chin on his shoulder, I stare out into the blue sea. *What have I done?* I close my eyes and wait for the song to end. When it does, we step slightly apart, smile, and walk back to our table holding hands. Jamie isn't back yet.

"Nico, I—I shouldn't have done that."

"I've wanted to do that for a while."

"You have?"

"Yes," he smiles. "Since the day I found you floundering on the beach, lost. I couldn't get you out of my mind. Still can't."

"But . . . I don't know where this can go," I say. "I don't know if I'm ready."

"Why?" he asks.

"I'm going home in two days."

"Which is why I couldn't wait any longer to tell you how I feel."

I shake my head. "How can this work? We live on two different continents."

"I will come see you."

Jamie returns looking a bit perturbed. Our server sets the food on the table and we begin to eat in the somewhat awkward silence. Had she seen me dancing with Nico? Kissing?

"So this is what I found when I looked up Proverbs 3:6," I say, reading from my phone. "'Trust in the LORD with all your heart, and lean not on your own understanding; in all your ways acknowledge Him, and He will make your paths straight.'"

"What do you think the connection is?" Jamie asks.

"I've heard this before," I say. "It's meant for someone who's unsure of their path. They don't know what to do, maybe they're at a crossroads or a challenge in their life. It's meant to remind them to not worry but have faith. Maybe Nina purposely put the letters there because of what was happening with Poppy. Maybe he needed to 'lean not on his own understanding.' Maybe he was scared or worried."

"Makes sense," Nico says, and Jamie nods her head in agreement.

Before we leave Il Pirata, I turn back toward the open space between the tables where Nico and I danced and watch us there once more. I wonder if I'll ever dance with him again. Jamie calls for me a few steps ahead and Nico slips his hand in mine as we walk to the spot where our driver waits. The shadows lengthen as the sun descends a little lower in the sky and we exit the little town of Scilla.

****

As my head rests upon the soft pillow, I stare beyond the blades of the ceiling fan and ponder the events of the day, meticulously analyzing each minute detail. Our visit with Maria. Finding the church but not the letters. Where are they? What should I do about them? What *can* I do? Dancing with Nico. Kissing him. Then there was tonight's dinner that ended later than I expected, which gave me more time with Nico. And he never left my side. Not once.

It was sweet of Angelina to invite us to another dinner at the villa. She mentioned a couple of times how she's going to miss us and how much she's enjoyed our time here. She was so happy to cook again

239

for us. But I couldn't figure out why she was so jittery when we first arrived. She was happy but also frazzled and preoccupied. Later, in the middle of dinner, she burst out with, "Sophia was looking for you this afternoon. Did she find you?" I was thinking how strange that was for Angelina to bring it up like that. And that Sophia of all people would be at all interested in finding us. No, actually Sophia did not find us. In fact, I don't think I've seen her since the vineyard.

Then I start thinking of Poppy. And Nonna. And my mother. And my whole family. How can I bring home the truth about what I've discovered here in Italy? How can I do that? It might be devastating for my mother. And Nonna would have to explain why she never told her about her real mother. And Uncle Luca lied to Aunt Lena and to Nonna and to my mother. And then what would I say about Poppy? That he's a passionate man who became passionate enough to harm someone he loved? My heart denies that vehemently. Yet almost everything I've found leads to this possibility. Maybe it's better not to say anything. Let them all think Italy was a big waste of time for me. But can I really keep all these secrets? I don't even know if I'm ready to leave Italy. Not yet.

Then I think of Nico again. His wavy hair blowing in the wind. His hand in mine. His lips on mine. And immediately I see Jack in Nico's face followed by a pang of guilt and a wave of panic.

A sadness grows within me that I can't quite define. I breathe in the salty ocean air blowing through my window and close my eyes.

> *The wind blows hard and fast becoming gusty and unruly. Rain pours relentlessly, like a waterfall. I'm repairing a broken vase with papier maché. It's filled with dead flowers. The wet papers fall as I press them to the vase. They become loose and stick to my fingers. When I shake them off, more stick to my hands. The papers have words written on them. How hadn't*

*I noticed before? Thousands of words that I can't read. What
are they saying?*

*A sharp wave of rain splashes in through the window and
swooshes up all of the papers with the words, swirling them
high into the air. No! I begin to cry. I leap to catch them but
my feet are anchored to the ground. I stretch my arms but they
are liquidy and loose. My hands are weighed down with glue.
I cannot control them. I become free for a second and grab one
of the papers, trying to read the words through the rain, but as
I do, they begin to disappear one by one until the paper is
completely blank.*

*I shrink into a corner that is filling with water. I see the
papers swirling up above but they're too far now. Suddenly the
rain is as loud as thunder. Will I die here? Something breaks
through the deafening rain. Something on the other side. I
can't make it out. Music? A song? A voice? Where is it coming
from? A crash of lightning. Pounding. Louder. So loud. Where
is it coming from? "El!"*

I tell myself to breathe. It was only a dream. And then I hear heavy
knocking on my door. "El?" says a voice. A female voice. Not
familiar. I peek through the peephole in my door and see Sophia
standing there. She seems agitated, shifting from one foot to the
other. Opening and closing her fists.

"Sophia?" I say through the door.

"Yes. Please let me in."

I cautiously open the door and she lets herself in.

"Close it and lock it," she says. So I do.

"What's going on?"

"I know you went to the church today. And I know what you
were looking for," she says panting. "It was something important."

"How do you know?"

"I don't have a lot of time. Marco told me. Actually he didn't come out and tell me. I caught him in a lie."

"Marco? But how—"

"He followed you today. Everywhere. Via Rose, the castle, the church. Everywhere."

"But why . . . ?"

"He took what you were looking for. All of them. He acted so suspicious yesterday morning. I knew something was off when he left for the market. I watched him closely when he returned. He was nervous and distant. Had papers in his hands but said they were for work when I asked. I pretended I was taking a shower and I spied on him. I saw where he put the papers in his briefcase.

"When he left again, I quickly got them. They were letters from someone named Franco. I remembered you talking about your grandfather and said his name was Franco. You had some of his letters. I knew they had to be what you were looking for. I don't know why he took them or why he kept them."

I can't believe this. Why? "My God. Sophia. I need to get those letters."

"No, you don't," she says. She reaches into her purse and pulls out several opened envelopes and hands them to me. "Please don't tell Marco I came to you. I don't want to betray him, but it's wrong to keep them from you." She stares into my eyes with a yearning. An ache. "And—Marco and I—we're not . . . what people think we are. He is not who I thought he was. I hope you find what you're looking for. I really do."

Poppy

8 May 1939

After what seemed like forever, a letter from Luca finally came today. It was very brief. He said that the police went to every house in our neighborhood and in all of the surrounding neighborhoods asking questions about Gianna. Did they know her, have they seen her, where were they on the nights of February 14th–20th, could they verify this information? He said this was their second visit. The police first questioned the neighbors after they received a call from Maria stating that Gianna hadn't come home after her walk. Luca never mentioned this to me before. He never said anything about Maria calling, but it makes sense that she would. That was one of the first things I asked him in a letter I'd written back to him after he shared the horrible news of the baby carriage being left on our doorstep, but he never answered it.

Now he says the police are back and they're questioning everyone, including him. He also said they asked him, Mamá, and Papá about me—where was I, how long had I been serving in the Royal Italian Army, had I been home for a visit, in what capacity did I know Gianna? He said they will probably come here to ask me questions. They want to know what I've been up to and where I've been. I hope they don't question my friends here, especially one. I don't like the way this is sounding or the direction it seems to be heading. I don't like any of this. I don't like not knowing.

Chapter 31

Ella

"Sophia. . . I don't know what to say. I can't tell you what this means to me." I'm so happy I want to cry. I go to hug her but she dips out of reach.

"It's okay. I have to go," she says, opening the door. She pokes her head out, quickly looks both ways, and departs, closing the door behind her.

I lock the door, sprint to my bed with the letters, and devour them one by one.

Dear Nina,

The police still think I did it. After hours of questioning, they finally let me go. They don't have any significant evidence against me but they're still watching me closely. I feel them examining every move I make. I already feel like a prisoner. Nothing seems right since I returned home. Nothing. Even Mamá doesn't seem herself. I still don't know if I can leave for America without Gianna. Only you would understand how I can say that while still being engaged to Olivia. What have I done?

I don't know how I would have coped without you. I'll never be able to thank you or repay you for helping me find a way to see Gianna before everything happened. I needed someone I could trust and I couldn't rely on anyone in my family for many reasons. But you—you are a true friend. I will never forget what you did. What you continue to do.

    Sincerely,

    Franco

Dear Nina,

    My heart is restless. I'm feeling nervous and afraid. I love Olivia. I really do. But I don't know if my heart is prepared to accept someone else into it while Gianna has already filled it. How do I put my love for her aside? I know I must. It's not fair to Olivia who is leaving everything she has in Italy to embark on a new adventure with me to America. I know it happened fast between us and I know you're unsure about her, but she really is a good person. She trusts me and she loves me deeply. I see it in her eyes. I want to give her that same love in return, but I fear I'm not free to do that. I think I've been given a second chance at love and it's right there for me to take. Should I take it? I know Mamá and Papá expect me to marry soon. They keep asking if I'll consider Cecilia again. Remember her? How did I lose Gianna? How did I let her slip away? Please tell me what you think.

    Sincerely,

    Franco

Dear Nina,

    What if what Olivia said the other day is right? What if Gianna appears one day and I'm engaged or married to Olivia? My mind and heart would be at war and I wouldn't know which to trust.

    Sadly, it's unlikely that Gianna will ever come back. But, because we've never found her, I feel like there is still a possibility that maybe she's out there—alive. Maybe she's okay but she can't get to me?

But if Gianna doesn't return? Then I've wasted my life waiting for someone who will never come and miss out on a second chance at love. My head hurts with confusion. What should I do? I know you're busy, but perhaps we can talk soon.

Sincerely,

Franco

Dear Nina,

I finally figured out why Olivia has been on me constantly about Gianna. She found the love letters between Gianna and me that I had tucked inside an old book. She said when she was cleaning, the book fell to the ground and the letters fell out. I know what you're thinking: books don't just fall off shelves. You think she's been snooping, but why would she do that?

Those letters were very personal to me. They held all of the secrets of our hearts: our love and desire for each other, longing to be together and vowing to never love anyone as much as we do each other. She read them without my permission yet she is angry with me.

She'd been acting insecure and emotional all day and I asked her to tell me why she was suddenly questioning my feelings for her. And when she pointed to the book, I knew she'd found the letters. I was angry that she'd read them without asking me and she was angry because I was still holding onto Gianna's letters. I guess I can understand why she felt that way. We didn't talk much for the rest of the day. I pulled out my picture of Gianna (you know the one) and stared at it while the memories flooded my mind. I went to bed after Olivia fell asleep. I need to keep them in a box or something safe.

I thought you'd want to know since our last conversation ended abruptly.

Sincerely,

Franco

Dear Nina,

Luca stops over almost every day now on his way home from work. He says he likes to come over to say hello and see the family. I would normally think this is very nice of him.

Usually when he visits he brings something like lemons or bread, but today he didn't bring anything, just wanted to say hi. He finally remembered to pay me back for the money he borrowed a while back. I never thought I'd see it, the way he's been so forgetful and distracted lately.

But the strangest thing happened. His wallet was bulging at the seams from being stuffed with so much cash. While retrieving the money, his finger and thumb became stuck in the folds between the money and his wallet. When he finally pulled it out, everything spilled onto the floor. I started to help him pick it all up and thought I saw an edge of a photograph mixed within the dollar bills. It was unmistakably a woman's wavy brown hair. I swear it looked like Gianna's, but Luca swept it up so quickly and shoved it all crumpled and mangled into his wallet. Maybe I'm crazy, but it reminded me of that picture I have of Gianna, the one with her hat slightly falling off her head and resting on her shoulders. I've always wanted to paint that picture.

Do you think it could be her picture? Why on earth would Luca have it in his wallet? He left quickly, saying he had to stop somewhere else on his way home. I know you've been suspicious about him lately, but I haven't seen what you have until today. Do you think I should ask him about it or let it go? Maybe it wasn't her picture? I'm probably overreacting, right? I should know what to do. He's my brother, but something doesn't feel right.

I'll say this much: Luca is not the same. Yes, I agree, we should try to talk in person.

Sincerely,

Franco

Dear Nina,

Ever since Luca's last visit, he's been acting more and more peculiar. He won't look me in the eyes when he speaks. Partially mumbles when he talks. It's almost as if he's talking to himself and not to me. When I ask if he's okay, he says yes, he's just got a lot on his mind at work. I say, "Let's talk about it," but he's vague, talking only in generalities, not really saying anything specific. I tell him to be honest with me, and he reassures me that everything will eventually work itself out, but for now he's just feeling stressed. That's not what I mean. I want him to tell me what's happening in his mind, but he doesn't get it. I'm worried about him. I agree with you that it seems like he's hiding something. He's been very secretive lately. He looks over his shoulder a lot, too. He reminds me of Papá—always paranoid and untrusting of others. I hope he doesn't become like him.

You're a good friend to me, Nina. It's obvious why Gianna chose you to be her best friend and confidant. But you don't need to worry about me. I'll be fine. He's my brother, for goodness sakes. He would never do anything to hurt me. Never.

Sincerely,

Franco

Dear Nina,

Luca stopped by again on his way home. You won't believe what happened . . . well, maybe you will. He went to use the restroom and laid his jacket across the bench in the hallway, probably not realizing that part of his wallet was sticking out. I think he assumed it was covered.

As soon as I heard the door close and the lock click, I grabbed the wallet and opened it. Everything was crammed in so tightly, and I tried to look for the picture. I heard the toilet flush which meant I still had a couple minutes while Luca admired himself in the mirror. Unfortunately, he returned sooner than I expected and I still had the wallet in my hands. He asked me what I was doing with his wallet and I said I accidentally knocked his jacket off the bench while hanging my coat on the hook right above, and the wallet fell with it. (I know you're comparing this to what Olivia said about finding those letters, but it's not the same.)

Right away he accused me of stealing from him. Then it got ugly. I asked him why he would think that. What would I steal? A picture of someone? Why would I do that? Is there a picture of someone in your wallet that you shouldn't have?

"Go ahead!" he said! "Open it up! There's nothing in there, see?" He opened the wallet, tipped it upside down, and dumped everything on the counter, spreading it all out in front of me. There was only money, receipts, and a few lists. He stared at me with fiery eyes like he was staring right through me. It made me uncomfortable. Then he grabbed his wallet and everything on the counter and left screaming things I couldn't understand because they didn't make sense.

I was upset with him and at myself for losing control. I noticed he left his jacket behind, so I grabbed it and ran to catch him, but I was too late. He was already gone. I figured it was just as well; he probably needed to calm down anyway.

As I held his jacket in my hands I just couldn't stop myself. I searched both side pockets but found nothing. It wasn't until I put the jacket on the hanger that I noticed an inside pocket on the right side. So I reached inside and guess what I pulled out? The picture of Gianna. I couldn't believe my eyes. Why would he have a picture of Gianna? Why would he keep it with him? You were right, Nina. You were right. He is hiding something about Gianna. I agree with you on that. But I don't agree that he's the one who did something to her. Although I think he definitely knows something about what happened to her, I don't think he did that.

Sincerely,

Franco

Dear Nina,

Luca didn't come back for his jacket so I stopped by his house to bring it to him. When I arrived, he was getting ready to go out with Lena. I almost wasn't going to ask him about the picture, but I did. He acted confused, pretending not to know what I was talking about. When I showed it to him he said, "Oh that! That's an old picture she gave me when I was looking after her for you." I told him it didn't make sense that she'd give him a picture of her. He insisted that she did. I said I noticed it in his wallet the other day, so why was it now in his jacket pocket?

Of course, then he got mad, asking me if I was purposely going through his things. And I said, "Actually, yes, Luca. I can't figure out why you'd have a picture of Gianna in the first place or why it would be in your wallet one day and your jacket the next." He got very sarcastic and said, "Is it illegal to have a picture of a beautiful woman? Are you the only one Gianna could have given a picture to? The only one she loved?" I lunged at him but stopped myself. He said Gianna tucked that picture next to the baby the day he found the carriage on his doorstep. He said this: "I even had it with me while everyone looked for her after I—after she went missing." I said, "Luca, you just lied to me right now. You just said she gave it to you, but now you're saying she left it in the carriage. For you?" And then I started laughing. He charged at me and we wrestled to the ground. He's much stronger than I realized, but I was able to push him off of me. I got up and threw his jacket at him. Eventually, he'll realize the picture is gone. I have it now. I can't believe that happened. We've never fought like that before. We've never even fought.

Nina, something's not right. He never mentioned finding a picture of Gianna in the baby carriage until now. He said there was nothing else with the baby.

On my way home I recounted everything that had happened in my head, especially the last thing he said. I almost missed it, when he said, "I even had it with me while everyone looked for her after I—after she went missing." Did you notice that? "After I—after she went missing." After I what? What did he mean by that?

The brother I've always known would never raise a hand to me. I used to think I could depend on Luca for everything. That he had my back. That he loved me and would do anything for me. He was my rock. Was. I don't know what he is now. I have an ominous feeling in the pit of my stomach.

Nina, I think you might be right. I think he did it. Oh my God. I think it was him.

What do we do?

Sincerely,

Franco

PART 3 - Truth

Ella

Chapter 32

I feel it. A profound throbbing in my heart. It rushes through my veins, up my neck to my head. I hear a whooshing sound. A loud, pounding heartbeat in my ears. I feel it pulsing. Each powerful beat. Every single one. It pounds faster and faster. How can I calm my racing heart?

Breathe. Focus.

I've got to tell Jamie. Do I wake her? Do I tell her what I've found? Should I text Nico? Poppy said to be careful who I trust. Did he mean only Uncle Luca? Poppy's letters to Nina prove that Nonna knew about Gianna, so why did Nonna act as if she'd never known her?

I'm jumpy and I need answers. I text Jamie to see if she's awake but get no reply. At 5:00 a.m. I throw on my robe and slide out into the hallway, being as quiet as I possibly can in an old creaky villa. Just as I near Jamie's door, I hear it close and see a man rounding the corner toward the lobby. I quickly follow, but he exits the villa before I can catch up. But not before I realize who it is. There's only one person I've met in Italy who has that kind of confident, assured gait, flowing hair, impeccably dressed. Marco. Was he coming from Jamie's room? I watch as he crosses the street and turns a corner, and then I race to Jamie's room.

As I'm about to knock on the door, I hear a muffled voice as if someone is purposely talking quietly. It sounds like Jamie's talking to herself, or maybe she's on the phone. I strain to decipher the words but can't make them out. The conversation ends quickly and I rap hard on the door three times.

"Jamie?" I hear movement—quick, sporadic shuffling of feet that stop just before the door, but she doesn't open it.

"El?"

"Yes, it's me. Open the door."

The lock slides slowly and then she cautiously opens it. Her hair is a mess and she's rubbing her eyes as if I've awakened her.

"What's wrong?" she asks.

I brush past her and she closes the door, following me to her bed. I sit on the end of her bed. My hands are shaking.

"I don't know. You tell me," I say, my heart galloping fast.

"El, it's five o'clock in the morning. I don't know what you're talking about. I was hoping to sleep in a little since we've got a late flight tonight,"she says, annoyed.

"Jamie. What's going on? Please tell me," I say. She stares at me blankly. "I know you know something. Don't act like you've been sleeping. I heard you on the phone just now." Her eyes scrunch up and she tilts her head. "I saw Marco leave your room."

All the color in her skin drains away, and her upper lip twitches like it does when she's nervous. She combs her fingers through her hair and walks over to the desk chair, but she doesn't sit down. She turns slowly, facing me again, but stares at the floor instead as if gathering her thoughts. Then she lifts her gaze to me.

"It's not what you think," she says. "I wanted to tell you but he said I shouldn't—we shouldn't."

"What? Who told you that? Marco? That slithering snake. Do you know what he did?" I fold my arms and stand right in front of her.

"It's complicated, El. I didn't want to keep it from you."

"But you did. You did keep something from me. How could you

do that?" As I spit out the words, my heart breaks a little from her betrayal.

"I meant to tell you earlier but—"

"Meant to tell me what? And what stopped you?" I say, shaking my head.

"I just—"

"Marco doesn't care about anyone but himself. I knew someone was watching me that day coming from Maria's. I felt it. You pretended not to know what I was talking about, didn't you? You probably knew he stole the letters from the church."

"Stole them? How do you know?" She seems genuinely surprised, but I don't believe her.

"It doesn't matter who told me. He got them before I could. It must have been Marco who Nico saw that day at the castle. I knew I shouldn't have trusted him. I knew it. It *wasn't* a coincidence that we kept running into him and Sophia. When we saw them at the villa and the vineyard, did you know they'd be there?" Jamie tries to answer in between questions but I don't let her. And then it dawns on me, an epiphany forming in my mind. "Oh my gosh. Wait. It was *you* who told them, wasn't it? Every time. It was *you*."

"No, it wasn't me," she says, shaking her head.

"Had to be. There's no other way. It all makes sense."

"No, El. You don't know anything."

"Tell me, then. What is going on, Jamie? I need to know."

"He was just worried about you, that's all," she says with downcast eyes.

"How did it happen that you and Marco became so close that you knew he was worried about me?"

"It wasn't Marco who was worried," she says.

"Then why did I see him leaving your room?" She looks confused and doesn't answer. "I was on my way to your room to show you the letters, and just before I got there I heard your door close and saw a man leaving. I know it was Marco because I followed him."

"Wait, you followed him? Did you talk to him?"

"No. I didn't get to him in time."

She puts her hand over her mouth and her eyes are wide. "You have the letters? So then you know everything." She stares at me, her eyes bulging.

"Yes, I know everything."

"I'm so sorry, El," Jamie says, slouching. "I'm sorry that you had to find out it was him. Poppy." She shakes her head and then places her forehead in her hands.

"What? What do you mean? That's not what the letters say." She furrows her brow and begins nibbling on her lip. "What makes you so sure it was Poppy? Where's this coming from?"

She fiddles with the hem on her shirt and starts to talk but then stops herself.

"Jamie, what do you know? How do you know it?" I say as anger courses through me.

She rolls her neck and begins massaging the muscle in her shoulder.

"I promised him I wouldn't say anything. He's so protective of you. He didn't want you to find out about Poppy. He pulled me aside before we left and asked me if I would keep an eye on you while we were in Italy. And let him know what was going on. He told me that he's been keeping this secret about Poppy for decades. He wanted to protect the family from, you know, the truth. He said it would devastate them. That Poppy lost control one day and—and killed her."

I try to put it together in my mind but it doesn't fit. My thoughts are a mess.

"Wait. Slow down," I say. "Who are you talking about?" But I know.

She closes her eyes as she answers, "Uncle Luca."

And then the heaping pile of mess in my mind becomes clear, straight lines of thought. I see it perfectly. I recall on our trip when Jamie received a few phone calls from Uncle Luca because he was "worried" about me. Her strange behavior at times that didn't make sense then makes sense now.

"Jamie. That's not true at all."

"He said you'd say that. He really didn't want you to go to Italy, thought it was a bad idea. He didn't want you to, you know, regress after all the progress you've made since Jack. He knew you'd be in denial. That's why he involved Marco."

"Marco?"

Jamie sighs as if she knows she must relinquish the rest of what she's been told to keep secret. "Marco is Uncle Luca's great-nephew on your Aunt Lena's side. Uncle Luca got in touch with him as soon as we planned our trip to Italy."

Rage twists inside of me. "I knew it wasn't a coincidence," I say through clenched teeth. "Jamie, you've been deceived. We both have." I reach for her hand. "Come with me. I need to show you something." I lead her to my room and place the letters in her hands.

"I'm not reading those," she says. "I've read enough."

"Jamie, please." I say. "Do this one thing for me."

She breaks eye contact with me and looks down at her feet. When she looks at me again, I can tell that she's not sure what to believe— whether she's right or I am.

"Read these. Then you'll know."

She takes them reluctantly and sits on the edge of my bed. Her eyes grow increasingly grave as she reads through the letters one by one. She pauses only for a moment to look up at me when she finishes one and moves on to the next. After the last letter, her watery eyes lock on mine.

"Oh my God, El. What a fool I've been." She wipes her eyes. "I don't know what to say. I'm so sorry. I didn't mean to betray you. I thought I was helping to protect you. How could he do this?"

"I don't know."

"What are you gonna do?"

"Well, I have to confront him," I say as I climb onto my bed and gather a pillow to my lap. "I can't just let this go. I won't."

"Then he'll know I told you," she says, but then adds, "but that's okay."

I squeeze hard on the fluffy pillow. "I can't believe how he tried to fool us both. The fact that he pretended and continued to pretend that he was the loyal brother who wanted to protect his brother from being blamed for a terrible crime. Protect me from being hurt. Protect the family honor. The only person he wants to protect is himself." I wipe my tears with the pillow as my heart breaks over the love and admiration I had for my favorite uncle. "How will I tell Mom and Nonna?"

A peculiar, almost uncomfortable expression spreads across Jamie's face. She pushes her hair back and rubs under her eyes. "You know how I said Uncle Luca pulled me aside and asked me to watch over you while we were in Italy and report to him how things were going and to keep you from digging too deep?" I nod yes. "Well, just before that I accidentally walked in on what looked like a private conversation between him and Nonna. I couldn't really hear what they were saying, but I knew it was serious by their expressions and the way they were talking close, waving their hands.

"Uncle Luca kept looking over his shoulder as he talked, and that's when he spotted me. I paused in the doorway, not sure whether to walk away or stay and eavesdrop. I was curious so I stayed, but as I said, he saw me. He waved me in as if there was nothing they'd be talking about that I couldn't interrupt, so I just passed through. Later on, after dinner, that's when your uncle pulled me aside. He seemed very concerned."

"What are you trying to say?"

"What I'm trying to say is," she stops for a second, "I think Nonna might know more than she's letting on."

"No, I don't think so. They were probably just talking about not wanting me to go to Italy. You know how Nonna worries about everything. She didn't want me to go alone. Remember?"

"Yes, but it didn't seem like that kind of conversation. I don't mean to worry you, El. But when I walked into that room unexpected, I definitely had an uncomfortable feeling like I shouldn't have been there. It wasn't just a conversation over worrying about you getting lost in Italy. It seemed deeper than that."

Chapter 33

I hear a soft shuffling of feet in the hallway outside our door and then a knock. Jamie and I exchange worried glances. I tiptoe to the door and peer out the peephole to see Angelina's plump, smiling face looking back. She's wearing her robe and slippers and stands patiently with her hands in her pockets, waiting for me to answer the door. "Angelina," I mouth to Jamie as I unlock and open the door.

"I thought I heard some commotion coming from your rooms. Is everything all right?" She gathers her robe around her more tightly.

"Y—yes. Everything's fine," I say. "We couldn't sleep so we thought we'd get up early today."

"I can't believe it's your last day with us already," she says, frowning. "It went so fast."

"I'm not going anywhere," I blurt, surprising myself along with Angelina and Jamie. "I mean I can't. Knowing what I know."

"El, what can you do about it?" Jamie says while Angelina looks on. "And what about your residency? Are you giving that up?"

"I can't go back yet," I say. "I need to talk with Uncle Luca. I still don't know what happened." Jamie rolls her eyes and looks down at the ground. "Unless there's more you're not telling me?"

"No. You know what I know," she says.

"Know what?" Angelina says with her hands up. "What are you girls talking about?"

"It's a long story, Angelina. Yesterday I went to that church near the castle to look for some letters that Poppy wrote to Gianna's best friend, Nina."

"More letters?" she says. I nod as I continue to tell her the rest. About Maria telling us to find Poppy's private letters to Nina hidden in the old church proving that he never had anything to do with Gianna's disappearance. How Marco happens to be Uncle Luca's great-nephew who he purposely sent to run into us and keep us from finding out too much. How Marco followed me and stole the letters before I could get them. That Jamie knew about Marco but thought she was doing the right thing to protect me. And finally that Uncle Luca is the one responsible for Gianna's disappearance, but he may have had help from Nonna, of all people. By the time I'm finished, Angelina's face shows a look of disgust.

"Marco." Angelina says, shaking her head. "I don't know much about Marco, except he has this look in his eye which makes you wonder if it's a sparkle or a sneer. As you know, he's a flirt. He comes across as outgoing and generous, but I think it's for his own need to feel superior. I've caught on to him. He can't fool me. But his wife Sophia? I've known her since she was a young girl. To look at her, you'd think she's standoffish and snooty, but she's at least real. You know what you're getting with her."

"It's a lot to take in," I say. "I still haven't grasped it. I can't believe he tried to frame my grandfather for what happened to Gianna when he was the one responsible all along." The thought of it makes me queasy.

Angelina covers her mouth with her hand and shakes her head again. "*Diablo*," she says.

Jamie stands with her arms folded and she's staring at me with a scowl on her face. I give her a "what's wrong?" look.

"I can't believe you're not coming home tonight," she says. "You're doing it—never mind."

"No, say it. What am I doing that's wrong?" I say.

She sighs and gives me a concerned look. "You're stopping yourself from what you should be doing. You're not following through on what you planned. You worked hard for your medical career and you're so close to seeing it become a reality. Something you've always wanted. You're avoiding it because you're afraid to move on. Without Jack. Because those were the plans you had when Jack was here. I think you truly believe that if you go through with your medical career and continue with the plans you both meant to have together, that it will mean you *can* go on without him. And I don't think you want to admit that. This mystery, this unfinished business, gives you permission to keep pushing everything out further and further. It's self-sabotage. And I can't stand by and watch. You found out the most important thing about Poppy: he's not a murderer. What else is there to do? Here? In Italy?"

I stand, facing Jamie, hearing her words as they shoot through me like daggers. A combination of hurt and confusion spreads from my heart to my head. She's always been more black-and-white about things, not grey like me. Am I upset because Jamie, of all people, should be the one who understands and supports me when I need it whether she agrees with me or not? Or am I upset because she's partially right? Why is she always right? I look away to collect myself and then look back.

"Jame, I know you mean well and I—"

"You don't know what it was like," she says, her eyes watery. "To hold you up and watch you every minute for hours because you took too many sleeping pills after Jack. Or to drive you to an emergency counseling appointment because you couldn't stop screaming. Or talking you out of wanting to die. I've seen this play out before. You step forward and begin to do things and then you stop because something else pulls you in. Then nothing at all happens because you're stuck."

I feel my eyes fill as I recall that dark time when I felt I had nothing to live for. I remember tiny healing steps forward and then, because I was afraid to move on, I'd do something to make myself fail. I know I do that and I don't know how to stop. I don't know what I would have done without my family and Jamie. I just don't.

"So please don't tell me," she continues, "that you know I mean well. You know I'd do anything for you. Any time. I just want you to give serious thought about not coming home tonight and truly know the consequences. Are you prepared for that?"

"Maybe I can still have both," I say, knowing that I probably can't. But the pull and need to see this through is just too strong. "Or maybe I'm going in a different direction now. Maybe different things are important to me now," I say with more conviction.

"What about Nico?" Angelina interrupts. I almost forgot she's still here. She's been quietly watching Jamie and I go back and forth.

"Nico?" I say.

"Well, you must be healing and moving on a little because you like him. I can see it," she smiles. "You're letting yourself like him. That's progress."

I smile at Angelina and look at Jamie.

"I don't know, El," Jamie says. "Just please at least give it some thought over the next couple hours and then let me know if I'm flying back alone or not."

"I promise to do that," I say. "Will you stay in the room with me when I call Uncle Luca in a few minutes?"

"Maybe," she says.

A text comes in. It's Nico. He wants to come and see me before I leave tonight. My heart flutters as I text him back yes.

I'm wobbly and almost can't breathe as I pull up Uncle Luca's number on my phone. I briefly pause before pressing the green call button. It rings right away. My stomach is one tight knot. After the third ring, he answers and I jump at the sound of his voice.

"Ella, what a pleasant surprise," he says. "I wasn't expecting to hear from you until you were home. Everything all right?"

I'm silent. I can't get the words out. Where do I begin?

"El? You there?" he says. It sounds like he's shuffling papers or something.

"Y—yes," I say. "Hi." He's waiting. I know I need to say it. "Uncle Luca?"

"Yes?"

I search my thoughts. What am I going to say? "Um, I'm not coming home tonight as I planned," I say. "Something's changed and now I can't."

"Are you okay? What's changed?" he says, sounding more concerned.

"What's changed . . . is the truth," I say, trying to sound calm. "I know everything now. Even though you didn't want me to. Even though you tried hard to keep it from me."

"The truth about what?" His voice is higher.

"Poppy," I say.

He makes a strange, twisted noise in his throat. "I'm sorry you had to find out about that. I only kept it from you to protect you. From . . . learning something that's hard . . . to know about him. Hard to accept." He coughs.

The built-up anxiety in my chest suddenly dissipates and is quickly replaced with fire. A betrayed, wild, and angry fire. It rises high into my throat and then spews out all over the place. "How could you?" I yell with a voice I don't recognize. "*You* took away the love of Poppy's life, *and* pretended that *he* harmed her!" My breath is ragged. "How could you do that, Luca?" I pant. "He loved you and trusted you more than anyone else in his life. He wrote that in his diary! I can't believe this!" I say, my voice catching.

"He stood by you, taking the brunt of your father's rage to shield you from it. And you became the favorite son. Poppy never did anything right in your father's eyes. But you did! I bet you loved every minute of it! Watching him suffer while you got all the praises!" My eyes are wide and I'm out of breath. I catch the drool from my lip. "He thought you had such good intentions when you said you'd watch over Gianna. How nice of you! While he lay awake thousands of miles away wondering if he'd live or die or ever see his family again. And you wanted to play house with Gianna and the baby. The baby—*my mother*! Pretending it was your family. But it wasn't, Luca!" I stop to catch my breath and regain composure. I hear nothing on the other end except for short, quick breaths.

"Ella—"

"No! You don't get to talk. I'm not done. I need to know, Luca. What happened on the last day you and Gianna were together?"

"Ella—"

"Admit it. You were the last to see her. Did you force yourself on her when she said no to you? Did she scream it? Did you listen?"

"Ella, wait—"

"Did you even care that she was married? Or that her heart belonged to Poppy? She could never love you. Is that what you thought? That she loved you? Or was it a competition? Your brother wanted her, so you did, too. You wanted to prove that you could have her, right?"

"No. I—"

"And then you took her to the vineyard. Where she and Poppy went. Why? So you could spoil their special place? Why, Luca? Why?" I'm breathless but I feel empowered. Like my words were my grandfather's. Words he never got to say because he never really knew for sure. I glance at Jamie. I hadn't noticed that she'd been with me. Her face is awestruck. I listen intently but hear nothing on the line.

KRISSY BACCARO

"Luca?" I can no longer refer to him as an uncle. "Luca, are you there?" Silence.

"Ella, this is your Aunt Lena. I took the phone from Uncle Luca in the middle of your rant." Her voice is flat, defeated.

"So then you heard—"

"I heard enough. Uncle Luca just drove off. I don't know where he went. Honey, why did you call to tell him those things? He's an old man. Don't you know he loves you dearly? He doesn't need this right now. And neither do I." And then she hangs up.

What? Where did he go? What did she hear me say? Has she known about all this, too? I'm not done. There's still more I need to say. More I need to know. What did Luca and Nonna talk about that day he pulled Jamie aside?

About an hour later I receive a strange text from my sister, Liv:

Ella Perri! Answer your phone! Mom's flipping out. You butt-dialed her during some phone conversation. It recorded on her voicemail. Something about Gianna and a baby. She keeps playing it back. I heard it. It does sound like you're saying that. IDK what's going on but you better call me! Don't you come home tonight?

Chapter 34

An overcast morning sky casts a dim light in the room. It's almost as dark as night. I look outside the window at the ominous clouds hanging above us, knowing at any moment the sky will open up and unleash its fury. I can smell the unfallen rain. I know a storm is coming. I lean my throbbing head against the cool window glass. My body is light and shaky since the phone call with Luca. Time escapes faster and faster and I'm not even close to being done. I hesitate before punching in Liv's number. She picks up immediately.

"It's about time, El."

"Liv."

"What the hell's going on?"

"What happened with Mom?" I say.

"I stopped by Mom's earlier to drop off some groceries for Nonna and she pulled me aside to tell me about the weird voicemail she got from you. She kept replaying it to see if she could figure out what you were saying about Gianna and a baby. She was very OCD about it. Then Uncle Luca showed up and went on this wild, out-of-control rant. I barely understood him." Without even taking a breath, she continues. "He kept saying he was sorry to Mom and that he should have told her. He was irrational and angry. Had this crazed look in his eyes. I've never seen him like that before."

"Told Mom what?"

"He kept saying Gianna loved him, too, and it wasn't meant to be this way. What the hell does he mean by that?" I try to jump in and answer, but she persists, not pausing once. "He paced back and forth in front of Mom, who was trying her best to calm him down. He said something about a necklace breaking and apologized again. He made absolutely no sense. Then Nonna came in the room and—"

"Nonna?" My heart sinks.

"Yes. She stayed the night. She's been doing that lately."

"What did Nonna do? Did she know about the voicemail?"

"I don't think Mom told her, but Nonna definitely understood what Uncle Luca was talking about."

"How do you know?"

"Well, she kept saying, 'That's enough, Luca. It's over now.' Then she'd shake her little head and say, 'Too many lives destroyed.' I know she sometimes can get dramatic, but she looked like she saw a ghost."

"Oh, God. What did Mom do?"

"Ella, why is all this happening?"

"Oh, Liv, there's so much to tell. For now, I'll tell you something Mom doesn't know, so please keep it between us."

"You're making me nervous."

"I know. Sorry." I squeeze Jamie's arm for moral support. "It's Nonna. She . . . isn't . . . Mom's biological mother." She doesn't say a word so I add, "Gianna is."

She gasps. "How do you know?"

"Trust me, it's true. It's even in Poppy's diary. Nonna and Poppy raised Mom together as if she were their own. But they never told her."

"What the—"

"And remember the letters? When Gianna went missing and no one knew what happened to her?"

"Yes," she says.

"It was Uncle Luca. He did something to her. And then he let people think it was Poppy."

"No. It's not possible," she says. "How can that be true?"

"There's a lot more you don't know." Silence. "You there?"

"Barely."

"There's something else I need to tell you," I say, pondering the words I should use. "I can't say it."

"Just say it!" she shouts.

I let out a deep sigh. "It's Nonna. She might have been involved."

"Involved? In *murder*? Are you saying she and Uncle Luca murdered Gianna? No way. You're wrong, El. You're just wrong." Her voice is edgy.

"I know it's hard to believe, Liv. But it doesn't look good. Something's not right where Nonna's concerned. I'm still trying to sort through it all. Just please, please promise you won't say anything to anyone until I talk to you again."

"I don't like any of this. If you're right, when this comes out, it's going to be bad. Will you be home tonight?"

"I don't think so. With everything that's going on, it doesn't feel right to leave yet."

She makes a clicking noise with her tongue. "Why? What else can you do?"

"Go to the police. Tell them I have information that will help them solve an old case from a long time ago. Maybe even . . . get them to search."

"For her body?" she bellows. "Oh my God, El. Are you serious?"

"I've never been more serious." A warm hand links into mine and I look up to see Nico standing beside me. A smile spreads across my face. He must have snuck in quietly while I was talking on the phone.

Liv begins to speak, then hesitates, then sighs. "Okay. But you better make sure you're right about everything before you start pointing fingers and sharing your stories."

"Not stories, Liv. Truth," I say.

"I just thought of something I didn't mention before," she says. "Something else happened when Uncle Luca was over. It was so weird. Right after his rant, I saw Mom leaning against the doorway in the kitchen with this glazed look in her eyes. She was playing with her necklace like she does when she's thinking. Then suddenly she yelled, 'Luca!' He immediately stopped in his tracks and walked toward her quickly. I wasn't sure what he was going to do. He didn't even look like himself anymore to me."

"What happened?"

"Mom asked Uncle Luca to describe the necklace. He seemed nervous and fidgety and he wouldn't speak, but he pointed to Mom's necklace and said, 'It hung on a chain like that one.' Mom opened the locket around her neck and took out the scripted *G*. Uncle Luca dropped to the floor and started crying like a baby saying, 'That's Gianna's! Where did you find that? It was hers! It was hers!'"

"Oh my God, Liv!"

"I know! Then he got up and threw his hands in the air like he does when he's out of things to say and yelled, 'It was an accident!' and ran out of the house. No one even went after him. We were all in shock."

"Where'd he go?"

"I have no idea. I looked at Mom and she had taken off the necklace and was examining it with Nonna. Nonna kept fanning herself with a magazine. It got really quiet and then Mom said, 'This whole time I thought the G was for Gabriella.' She looked so sad and confused. I felt sorry for her. She just sat there in a daze.

"I sat next to her and asked her to tell me about her necklace. She said it was something she found when she was playing in Nonna's jewelry as a child. It was beneath several other necklaces and it was broken. She said she loved how sparkly the fancy G was and since her name began with G, she took it and kept it hidden in her dresser drawer for several years. Nonna never asked her where it was, so she assumed it was meant for her to find and keep. It wasn't until much later that she bought a necklace with a locket. She placed the G inside the locket and has worn it every day since."

"Did she ask Nonna about it?"

"Not that I know of."

"I can't believe it. Poppy gave something like that to Gianna," I say as the fragmented pieces of a story slowly come together, a new form taking shape.

Nico waits by my side patiently for the next hour as I explain everything to Liv. I begin with the contents of the box, to the secret letters through the hidden tunnels, all the way to my conversation with Luca just a few hours ago. She devours every detail and makes me retell how I found Maria who was supposed to be Nina, and how I danced with Nico. Before we hang up, she tells me how proud of me she is and that she loves me, and it makes me glow inside.

Jamie comes to my side and says she'll extend her time in Italy with me for another couple of days and that makes my heart a little lighter. I agree not to stay longer than that, especially now that my mother knows something terrible is unraveling right before her eyes and she can do nothing to prevent it. I need to be with her to help her cope with the truth about her family. Our family. Jamie leaves the room to help Angelina pull together some ingredients for a last-minute lunch.

Nico embraces me in a warm hug and then he lifts my chin and kisses me softly on the lips. "I'm so glad you're not leaving Italy yet," he says. The warmth he creates in my heart quickly disappears as I wonder where Uncle Luca went after he left my mother's house. Did he go back to see Aunt Lena? Does she know about any of this? Nico pulls me to the sofa and puts his arm around my shoulders. I melt into his strong, muscular body. He starts to say something but my phone rings.

It's Uncle Luca. My heart stops. I pick up.

"H-Hello," I stammer.

"Ella," he says, his voice frayed, his breath uneven.

"What's happened?" I say.

"I—I—" he sputters.

I don't wait. I say it. "What happened to Gianna." It's not a question. It's a demand. He holds his breath. "Please tell me where she is. So we can put this behind us. Please?" I feel the pulse in my neck. "Is it the vineyard?"

"I. —I just—" he says with a catch in his voice. The rhythm of his breath changes. Becomes heavier with gaps between breaths. Like he's crying. A whispered cry. "I'm sorry," he moans.

"Uncle Luca—"

"I never meant to hurt you. Or anyone." He begins sobbing.

"I know," I say, but I really *don't* know. I need to keep him with me. Keep him on the line. Get more information. I can't lose this opportunity. He blows his nose and steadies his breath.

"Okay. Yes," he says. "I'll tell you. Where to find her," he sniffs.

My chest squeezes in against itself. "Where? Please tell me where?" I plead. But he doesn't say a word. "You're doing the right thing, Uncle Luca. You can tell me. Where is she?" I feel hope, excitement, fear.

"We went to the vineyard that day. I—I wanted to tell her how much she meant to me. I knew Franco couldn't make her happy. But I could," he says, his voice a little stronger. I wanted to interrupt him and defend Poppy. Tell him he could never make her as happy as Poppy did. But I don't. I let him go on. "She was in a terrible marriage. I made her laugh. Forget what she didn't have. I wanted to show her what she did have. Could have with me. She must have felt the same because she gave me a look. When she smiled I knew I needed to kiss those lips. And then she ran."

"Ran? Why did she run?"

"I don't know."

"You don't know?"

"I ran after her. To try to explain. But she—she hit me. And then I—" He stops himself, and then small, almost inaudible whimpering breaths follow. Breaths that work their way into a bellowing, thunderous cry. And that's exactly what he does. When the crying finally subsides, I interject.

"Did you . . . hurt her? In the vineyard?"

"In the wooded area!" he yells. "Behind it," he says, deflated. The normal softness of Uncle Luca's voice is long gone. The sweet uncle who took care of me as a child. Brought me to school, took me for ice cream, comforted me after Jack. Gone. The man on the other end of this phone is someone I no longer know.

"There are some things you can't possibly understand, Ella. It's not always what you think. You weren't there. You couldn't know how I felt."

"There's nothing that I need to know, Luca. It's simple. Gianna loved my grandfather. She wanted him. And you prevented a family from being together. You know they would have waited for each other."

"You don't know what you're talking about!" he barks.

"You said she was in the woods," I spoke slowly, intentionally. "Where in the woods?"

"What does it matter? Deep in the woods behind the vineyard. That's all you need to know."

"You called me," I say, trying to keep my voice level. "You must have wanted to tell me, right?"

"And I told you. It was a long time ago," he sighs. "Don't you think I think about it every day?"

"No," I say. "And I think you would have kept it a secret forever."

He makes a grunting noise. "You're ruining everything, Ella. If you think telling the family is a good thing, you're dead wrong. This wasn't meant for you or anyone to know. But you can't seem to keep to yourself. I should have stopped you from going to Italy. I could stop you from coming home. You think you're so smart. You should be more like your sister. This is none of your business. It's no one's business."

"It became my business the minute Poppy told me to find the box. He told me that for a reason. And I intend to see it through to the end."

"Not if I can help it," he says, and his tone sends chills down my spine. I want to hang up the phone but I can't just yet.

"There's something else I need to know," I say. "It's about Nonna's involvement in this. And don't tell me she isn't because I know she is." I really don't want to know, but I must find out.

"Nonna? She's got nothing to do with this."

"You were talking with her about something secretive at the dinner Mom had a few weeks ago. Jamie said she walked into an awkward conversation between the two of you. You were whispering about something and you stopped when she walked in."

"Nothing. Nonna's not involved," he grumbles.

"I don't believe you," I say. "Something's not right. I know it."

"Listen to me—"

"You can't tell me what to do, Luca. If you have nothing to say about Nonna, then I have nothing more to say to you. I have what I need for now."

"What do you mean by that?"

"I'm bringing Gianna home," I say slowly and steadily. The words feel good as they slide off my tongue and into the air. I hang up and ignore his next three calls.

Chapter 35

Nico watches from across the room. I left his side once I heard Luca's voice. I'm still captured, analyzing a conversation I didn't want but needed. Like I'm in another universe; here, but not. Am I capable of bringing Gianna home? Nico's expression is confusing. He rushes to me and holds me at arm's length. He doesn't speak, but his eyes do. They are deeper and richer than usual. A chocolate, earthy brown exuding kindness, warmth, compassion. There's something else within his gaze. Something that causes his beautiful eyes to water. Pride? Is he proud of me? He blinks but continues to stare, and then he pulls me close and wraps his strong arms around me. I feel his heartbeat against me. Tension and anxiety seep out of me, and for a moment I am light again.

Nico releases me slowly and brushes a piece of hair from my eyes. "What you did just now—was amazing," he says. "You're so . . . strong. And determined. You didn't let him intimidate you at all. I can't imagine how difficult that was—to confront someone like that. Someone you once admired, loved. It must be so disappointing." He cups one hand against my cheek. "I've never known anyone like you. I would never want to disappoint you."

I swallow hard, trying to stay composed. A tear escapes and I quickly swipe it away. I want to tell him I know he wouldn't disappoint me. That I feel something stirring within my heart and I can't control it. I want to scream it out loud, but instead I mutter a quick, "I know, thank you." And look away.

A long, low rumble of thunder yells in the distance, and the wind gently rustles the edges of the curtains. A storm is coming and I don't have time to wait for it to pass.

After a quick lunch, I gather the letters to Nina, Gianna's birth certificate, and my phone, happy that I'd thought enough to push record when I started talking to Uncle Luca. It's not a full confession, but I hope it's enough. Now the thunder roars loudly, coming closer, faster, and the wind swooshes through the window throwing the curtains high into the air followed by cold splashes of rain. I rush to the windows to close them and turn to Nico and Jamie. "We have to go."

I kiss Angelina goodbye as she insists we wait it out. She says it's bad luck to leave in the middle of a storm. We explain our need to use the time we have left. We can't stop now. Not until I've been to the police station. And the vineyard. She nods and wishes us good luck and makes us promise to be careful. We dash from the villa to the car, dodging the pelting rain.

Jamie shoots me a look just before we pile into the car and yells, "Want me to drive?"

I hesitate momentarily and then yell back, "No, I'm okay!" Jamie looks worried but sits in the back. Nico meets me at the driver's door.

"I know where I'm going. I'll drive," he says.

"No—it's okay, I'll drive," I say, opening the door. An eerie feeling of déjà vu overcomes me. Instead, I climb over the driver's seat and into the passenger seat. Nico slides in and takes the wheel.

"Oh, thank God," Jamie says as we pull away, the worry visibly draining from her face.

The windshield wipers push waves of water from side to side, only allowing a clear view for a few seconds at a time. After about a mile,

Nico does the smart thing and pulls over to the side of the road, something I had replayed again and again in my mind since the crash with Jack. If only I had pulled over back then. If only I'd waited out the storm. Maybe he'd still be here. *No, don't think it.*

It's not long before the storm clouds recede, revealing small rays of light poking through. The rain subsides to a light sprinkle as we pull onto the road that leads us around a bend toward an immense brick building surrounded by police cars. I feel a combination of nausea and anxiety. Will they take me, a foreigner, a girl from America, seriously? Will they believe me? Will they care after all these years?

Once inside the precinct, a desk officer directs us to a small area just outside of the main offices where we sit and wait for our turn. He hands me a clipboard with paperwork to be completed. I have a hard time answering some of the questions related to times and timelines. I give vague answers, hoping my evidence is enough to offset my lack of details. After about a half hour, an older gentleman ushers us into his office and motions for us to sit. He seems like he's in a hurry.

He looks at me and smiles, "What brings you here today?" he says.

My words jumble inside my head. I push them out.

"Well . . . um . . . I have some information about a missing person," I say. "A woman who went missing. Fifty years ago."

He raises his eyebrows and tilts is head. "That's a long time ago. Do you know if there was a report filed?"

"Y—yes, there was," I say. "Her name was Gianna Russo. She was about twenty years old. Her mother and sisters reported her missing. Her sisters are Maria and Sienna Russo. I don't remember the exact date, but I think it was in February, 1939." As I spit out the information, his fingers dance across the keys. He looks up when I say "Gianna" and then again when I say "1939."

"And why are you here now?" he says.

"I have information about who was responsible for . . . her death," I say.

He raises his right eyebrow. "What kind of information?"

I pull out the birth certificate, the letters, and my phone from my purse and place them on the desk in front of him. My heart races.

"The person responsible—his name is . . ." I hesitate briefly and glance at Jamie and Nico before continuing. "His name is Luca Perri. He's my uncle, great-uncle," I say. "Gianna was my grandmother."

His eyes jump to each of us. "And how is it that you got all this information? How do you know she's dead?"

I take out my phone, pull up the voicemail conversation, and press play. He listens intently, scribbling across a notepad and then typing on his computer. His eyes are glued to something on the screen; he shifts them only once to look at me. Then he begins typing again.

He calls another officer over to look at his computer. The officer strides over and leans in toward the screen. He taps his pen against the counter as he reads what's there. He looks at the chief of police and whispers something. The chief replies with, "That's what I thought." The chief excuses himself for a moment and Nico, Jamie, and I watch him leave. He says nothing about what was on his screen or where he's going. A few minutes later, another officer calls my name and motions for us to follow her to the back.

We enter an old office, the door partially ajar. She leads us in and then leaves, closing the door behind her. In front of us sits the chief of police behind a large desk. It's hard to read what's behind his expression. The nameplate reads Officer Cal Rizzo. I notice a box sitting on top of the desk right in the middle.

"You said Gianna Russo was your grandmother," he says. I nod. "And that she went missing in February of 1939." I nod again. "February fourth, to be exact," he says, and my stomach tightens. He takes the lid off the box and pulls out the contents. A stack of papers, a file, and a photograph of Gianna. He hands me a report stating that Gianna's parents and sisters reported her missing on February 14 at 6:30 p.m. Two more reports beneath it show details of the investigation, primarily the visits to the neighborhood and surrounding area including the vineyard, and notes about suspects. He leans in and slides his index finger down a list of names and stops at Luca Perri. "And this is your uncle? The one talking on the phone?"

"Yes," I say, staring at his name.

He moves his finger to the next name, Franco Perri. "And this is the one who wrote the letters? Luca's brother, your grandfather?" I nod. "It looks like he was questioned, too, at a later date. I think they arrested him or they were going to. There was a lot of speculation at the time."

"I know there was. That's another reason why I'm here. To prove he didn't do it."

A long discussion ensues about Uncle Luca. Where is he now, do I think he'll do anything stupid, could he hurt someone in the family, like me? Have I ever been threatened by him? My mind is a swampy mess and I don't know how to answer his questions. Uncle Luca did threaten me on the phone—when I told him I'd see this to the end. He said, "Not if I can help it." That's a threat. I mention this, too. He turns to me and says, "And what is it you would like us to do about this?"

"What would I like you to do?" I say, not quite sure why he's asking something that's so obvious to me. "For one thing, I'd like this case to be no longer unsolved. We *know* who kidnapped her. We *know* he probably killed her." I stare at him and then at Jamie and then Nico. "I want justice, for Gianna's family and for mine. That's what I want."

It can be complicated, he tells me. The length of time that's passed and the fact that Uncle Luca no longer lives in Italy and hasn't for years can be problematic in cases like these. And there's no body. You can't solve a case without a body. It's not that it *can't* be done. But it makes it much more difficult.

My neck and arms are sweaty. I grow more frustrated by the minute. Everything begins to bother me. The incessant ticking of the clock. A woman across from me, seated in a chair next to another officer, is crying. I see her through the glass door. I imagine Gianna's mother explaining that her daughter is missing. Showing her picture, telling important things about her. Crying for her. Begging for help. I have to do something. *Say it. Say what you came here to say.*

"I—I was hoping," I stammer, "that we could . . . excavate . . .an area in the vineyard?"

The chief's eyes bulge. I think they might pop out of his head. He leans in close to me. His breath smells like coffee and black licorice. I try not to breathe.

"Miss? Do you think we can just go to the vineyard and start digging up dirt everywhere? Do you know how much land is on that vineyard?"

"No—I—" I stutter. "I mean, yes. Yes, I do know. But it's not just anywhere. It's a specific location. The wooded area behind the vineyard. Like Luca said in the recording. What about that?"

"It's still not specific enough," he says.

I sigh and feel my body slump. I rest my forehead in my hands. Nico's fingers caress my back.

"Is there anything you can do?" Nico asks the chief.

I peek up from my hands. The officer's eyebrows relax and he strokes his beard.

"Here's what I'll do," he says, leaning across his desk again. "I'll reopen this case and assign a team to it. They'll review the files and the new information you've brought us. If they think there's a reason to go into the vineyard and dig it up, we'll do it. But you have to promise one thing"—he continues—"that you won't go back to the vineyard. This is our job now. You'll need to stay out of it if you want us to do our jobs. Don't go looking for things that aren't there." He eyes us suspiciously.

"But that could take a long time. Maybe weeks," Jamie says.

"Well, unless you can bring in your uncle and he can lead us to her, or if you have something more specific as to where Gianna might be, then yes, we'll have to wait a bit. But reopening the case is a big step."

Jamie, Nico, and I stare at each other. I want more than this, but it's all we've got for now. "Thank you for your time, sir," I say. "Thank you for reopening the case. It's a start. We'll take it."

Jamie and Nico stand and shake his hand. He downloads the conversation from my phone and hands us his business card before we leave.

"Call me if you have any questions or if you find more information," he says as he walks us out.

Just outside the doors, I turn to Jamie and Nico. "We need to go to the vineyard," I say, but their eyes reflect what I already know: it's getting late and darkness will soon settle upon us. "I know what you're thinking," I say. "But if we leave right now, maybe we'll have enough time."

Nico shakes his head. "By the time we get to the vineyard," he says, "we might have an hour at the most before it's dark. It's just not enough time, El. I'm sorry."

"And we don't know our way around," Jamie adds.

"We'll go first thing in the morning," Nico says, reaching for my hand.

"I guess you're right," I sigh. "You're both right." But I wish they weren't.

Chapter 36

Standing at the crest of the hill near Maria's street the next morning, the once beautifully rolling hills of the vineyard now appear jagged and fierce, no longer welcoming us in, but daring us to enter. A sadness gathers deep in the pit of my stomach as I imagine the carefree love and happiness that was once shared here, shadowed by the darkness of one person. Who was close to my heart. Whom I trusted with my life. Someone who altered the courses of the lives he said he loved and protected. I catch a tear that falls to my cheek.

"You don't have to do this," Nico says as he reaches for my hand. Jamie stands close to us.

"I have to do this. I've come this far."

Nico squeezes my hand.

We walk the winding path toward the vineyard, the cool wind nipping our necks. Somber clouds hover low above our heads. Their shadows loom upon us. The winery is smaller than I recall and farther out than I remember. We follow the path that leads to the woods.

At the edge of the woods, I stop and turn toward the vineyard again. I wonder where it happened. Did Luca take advantage of Gianna closer to the winery or did he lure her into the woods? We walk silently as we enter the dense woodland, stepping first on a brown needled path, easy to see, but it quickly disappears under the wild brush. What stands before us next is a mess of overgrown vines and more trees. We push through as best we can until we can no longer walk without tripping or becoming entwined in branches and vines. The sun fails to break through the trees and I can scarcely see beyond where we stand. I look at Nico and Jamie who have faithfully followed me without complaint.

"She could be anywhere out there," I say.

"Did Luca say anything more specific about where she was?"

"No," I say. "It's like he didn't want to give me everything."

"What are you hoping to find?" Jamie asks while pushing aside branches.

"I'm not sure. A sign? Anything really," I say. An eerie feeling creeps through my skin but I brush it aside as paranoia.

For the next couple hours, we search the area that Luca described as the woods directly behind the vineyard. He said he didn't go far back but far enough to be hidden. I begin to lose hope but continue looking, sweeping my arms back and forth through the brush, again and again, pushing my fingers through open spaces until my sleeve catches on a broken branch and it tears. I lose my balance and stumble to the ground. Nico and Jamie hurry over and reach for me. As I grab hold of them, something catches my eye. I steady myself and squat back down to see what it is, but I've lost sight of it.

"What is it?" Jamie asks.

"I'm not sure," I say, "but I think I saw something."

Gently, I drag my fingers through the dried branches and dead leaves, watching them pop up as I go across. I see it again: a small space of wild grasses and moss partially covered by vines. It strikes me as unusual, not quite looking like the rest of the surrounding woods. With care I separate small branches from the vines, loosening their grip from the earth. I press my fingers into the soft moss and start gripping and removing clumps of dirt.

286

Without a word, Jamie and Nico come beside me and begin digging, too. As I pull my hands across the damp soil, they catch on something. I pull and dig at the earth all around it. Soon, I'm able to see what is entwined within. A chain. Tarnished and slightly discolored. Anchored to the soil and buried beneath it. I dig my fingers deep into the earth, pushing and scooping around the chain, careful not to break it. I slowly remove and untwist the tangled parts of the chain from the earth until it's free. Sadly, it is broken. Its tiny links no longer complete what might have been a necklace. A small design that could have been its middle is hard to discern. I raise the chain to show Nico and Jamie, hardly believing what I'm holding in my hands.

"Do you think it's hers?" Nico asks.

Jamie's eyes are wide and she's nodding her head.

"How can it *not* be?" I say.

"After all this time," Jamie adds. Twigs snap in the darkness behind us. No one says a word but our expressions are the same: fear. We quickly run in the direction we came. I look behind me but see nothing. Probably just an animal.

Out in the open, among the hills of the vineyard, we stop to catch our breaths. I frequently look over my shoulder, scanning the woods until we're out of the vineyard and back on the neighboring streets of Tropea.

We speed back to the police station. Officer Rizzo is on his way out, but I beg him to wait just for a minute. I promise him it's important and related to why we were here a couple of hours ago. He reluctantly agrees and leads us quickly to his office. I lay the chain on his desk and flecks of dirt fall from it. Next to the chain I place the picture of Gianna with the necklace on. It really could be the one.

"You see," I say, pointing to the middle of the necklace in the photo and then to the chain, "I think this might be the necklace she was wearing in the picture."

The chief squares his glasses on his nose and compares the broken necklace with that of the photo. He furrows his brow, squints his eyes, and scrunches his mouth as he deeply examines both.

"Hmm. It's possible," he says scratching his head. "You said you found this in the vineyard?" We nod. "Even after I told you not to go there?" His eyes narrow. I begin to speak but he cuts me off. "You don't listen!" he chides. "I specifically said not to go back to that vineyard if you wanted my help. You gave me your word you wouldn't." He pushes his chair back and glares at me. "Why should I help you now?"

"Please. I'm sorry," I say, leaning forward in my chair. "You're right. I didn't listen. I—I just needed to go and see for myself before I went home. I didn't think I'd find anything. I just want . . . to do this for my grandfather." I trail off, feeling defeated. This was a bad idea. I should have known better than to think they'd believe me or even care. I look down at my feet. The room is awkwardly quiet.

He clears his throat and pulls his chair up to his desk. He picks up the necklace and the photo and examines them both. "I'd like to hold onto this if I may?" he says.

"Um . . . ," I pause. Is he reconsidering? I don't want to give him the necklace. I want to keep it. Take it home with me.

"We may have to process this as evidence," he says.

I look at Nico and Jamie for guidance. Nico just stares and Jamie shakes her head no.

"It's my only chance to figure this out," I say to them as I reluctantly hand over the necklace to the officer very slowly, releasing it into his hands. I snap a couple pictures of the necklace before I leave it behind.

"If needed, would you be able to take us back to the exact location where you found this?" he says.

"Yes," I say. "Will that be soon?"

He smirks, "Probably not that soon, but we'll be in touch." He gives me a stern look and points his finger. "And no more visits to the vineyard. I mean it. Let us do our job this time." He stands, pushes the door open, thanks us for coming, and firmly shakes each of our hands as we exit his office together.

A few feet away from our car, something blocks my peripheral vision. A dark figure slowly approaches. I grab both Nico's and Jamie's hands and hasten my steps. The darkness also hastens. The hairs stand on the back of my neck and my knees feel weak. We're almost near the car but fear grips me hard.

"We're in trouble," I say.

We reach the driver's side, and over the top of the car, on the opposite side, we see him.

Luca.

Chapter 37

The wind rushes through the trees, rustling the leaves. Some break free and swirl above us. Luca stands tall on the other side of our car, a sports coat draped over his right arm, a suitcase in his left.

He waves as if nothing has happened and we've just spotted each other after a long time apart. *As if he hadn't revealed to me just two days before that he did hurt Gianna all those years ago and that I'd find her in the woods behind the vineyard. As if he hadn't threatened me when I told him I was bringing her home.* A chill runs down my spine. Would he harm me to protect his secret?

"Abriella," he says, panting. He takes a step forward.

"Stay where you are," Nico warns, but Luca continues to walk, the car no longer a safe barrier between us.

"Luca . . . what are you doing?" I say. I wonder if security cameras will catch him standing here. Maybe a police officer will step outside and see us. Should I run to the building and alert someone that he's here—the man who admitted to harming Gianna all those years ago?

Luca stops. He's shivering. He rubs his hands over his head and looks to the sky. Then he lowers his eyes to meet mine.

"You were right," he says. He drops to his knees and begins swaying back and forth, his hands clasped tightly as if in desperate prayer. "It's true! What you said, Ella. Oh God, it's true!" he cries.

"Please forgive me, Jesus. Please forgive me for what I've done." He continues swaying and looks up at me with wet eyes. I don't know this man in front of me. He wipes his eyes with the back of his sleeve, and then his posture changes from slumped over and broken to straightened and sharp. He stands.

I step forward but Nico takes my hand and whispers, "No, El."

"Don't believe him," Jamie says. "After everything he's done. Pretending to be someone he's not. Don't fall for it, El."

"Please," Luca says through clenched teeth. His face is scrunched up tightly and sweat beads across his brow. "I *need* to show you something. Let me show you."

I look at Nico and Jamie who are shaking their heads and mouthing no.

"What is it you need to show us, Luca?" I say.

"Well if . . . if I could drive with you . . . I could tell you how to get there."

"No," Nico growls.

"Then you'll see, Ella," he continues. "You'll want to see . . . you should . . . see."

My stomach tenses. *See what?*

"Where is this place?" I say.

Nico shoots a warning look.

"Luca!" Jamie blurts. "You've already done enough! We're not listening to you anymore."

I give her a side glance. I know she's being protective. But I need to know what else he's hiding.

"Ella . . ." she says quietly.

"*If* we go," I say to Luca, "you won't be driving with us. We'll drive our car. You'll call a driver and we'll follow."

Jamie and Nico are visibly upset, hands waving, mumbling something under their breaths.

"It would be easier—better if I could—" Luca continues.

"You heard Ella," Nico snaps, cutting him off. "It's that or nothing." His eyes are narrow and dark.

Reluctantly, Luca agrees.

"Where is this place?" I ask again.

"Not too far from here." Luca says, his voice scratchy.

The afternoon shadows lengthen and expand across the roads and grasses, and a murky dusk descends. Nico drives slowly, keeping several feet behind the car driving Luca. None of us has spoken since we got in the car. Their grave faces and lack of conversation creates an impenetrable tension making it hard to breathe. But how do I stop when we've come this far?

"We can always turn around," I tell Nico and Jamie after twenty minutes of driving. They don't reply. I keep thinking we'll be there in just a few minutes.

Our car climbs the quickly narrowing road extending through the mountains as wispy gray clouds float beside us.

"I don't like this," Jamie says. "It doesn't feel right." Nico glances at Jamie through the rearview mirror. I feel uncertain as well. I begin to tell Nico to turn around when Luca's car drastically slows down almost to a crawl. Nico slams the breaks and we're bumper to bumper.

"What's he doing?" I say.

Luca's driver signals left and we follow down a long, narrow road with few streetlights. We pull up to a series of small brick buildings with metal doors, no windows. Luca's driver pulls into a parking spot. Luca gets out, says a few words to the driver, and walks toward the building closest to us. He motions for us to follow.

We park our car a few spaces away, closer to the road. I stare at Nico and Jamie. They look back at me with fear and regret.

Once we're out of the car, we take small measured steps toward

Luca. The menacing trees behind the building twist and wave as if teasing, luring. *Do you dare step inside?*

Do we dare?

We stand side by side, holding hands a few feet behind Luca. Jamie's on my left, Nico on my right. Our hands are sweaty, my heart is racing. Luca fiddles with the lock. Metal on metal. A loud click and the door slides open.

A sick, sinking feeling pools in the pit of my stomach as we inch our way up the walkway behind Luca. *Where are you leading us Luca? Is this a trap?* Maybe one of us should have waited at the door. Just in case. What secrets are inside? Upon entering the musty smelling room, I see hundreds of boxes from floor to ceiling, lining the walls.

Luca turns to us and says, "Stop right there." He then faces the boxes in front of him and spends a few minutes moving and shuffling things around. He lifts some boxes and stacks them on top of others and continues doing so until he finds the one he wants. He pulls it forward and places it in front of us. From a small bag he removes a pair of scissors and begins cutting carefully along the taped seams of the box. He opens the flaps and bends them back. Luca stares into the box but doesn't take anything out.

I want to jump into that box and pull out what he's hiding, but I don't. I wait, hardly breathing, while my heart drums against my ribs.

He reaches into the box and grabs something, but I can't see what it is. Something white? He lifts it out an inch at a time. A sweater. Soft and thin. Delicate. My heart stops. Next, he takes out a sun hat similar to one I've seen in Poppy's painting of Gianna. A hat she wore often in several photos I'd seen.

Luca isn't done yet. He scoops up something from the box and then turns his hand over to release three blue buttons, not from the sweater. Not once does he look at us.

No longer able to contain myself, I run to the box and kneel on the other side of it across from Luca. The tears that pour from my eyes don't stop. Jamie and Nico gather beside me. I touch the soft sweater and look at Luca.

"What have you done?" I say.

Luca continues to stare blankly at the remaining contents inside the box. I follow his eyes and see hundreds of photos of Gianna. Gianna pushing a baby carriage. Gianna sitting on her porch swing reading a book. Gianna in her garden. Photos she had no idea were taken of her. He keeps his head low and finally looks up after he's taken out her sunglasses and small brown leather purse. The box is now empty. He peers into my eyes. More creases than usual surround his droopy eyes.

"That's everything. All I had of hers," he says, deflated.

I clutch my stomach and mouth at the same time.

"Oh my God, Luca!" was all I manage to get out as the weight of this crashes upon me.

The man in front of me is small, frail. His face careworn. A shell of the man I once knew.

"Why?" my voice cracks. "You of all people. Why?"

He sighs. "I didn't mean for this to happen. I loved her. I thought she loved me." He shakes his head. "She could have loved me. We should've been together. Not Franco. *Me.*" His voice is unsteady, ebbing and flowing from fear to sorrow to anger. "I held her. Tried to kiss her. Show her how much I loved her. She . . . swung her arm back and hit me in the face!" His eyes narrow. "So, I held her tighter. Maybe she misunderstood me. I would show her I loved her," he says, his eyebrows pointed. "She pushed me away and ran. I . . . ran after her. I just wanted to talk to her. She said I was a fool. She could never love me. Only Franco was worthy of her love. And that's when I—" He paused and looked first at me, then at Nico and Jamie.

"When you . . . ," I say encouragingly.

"I . . . grabbed her neck," he says, relenting. "I wanted to shake some sense into her. I gripped her necklace in my hand and scratched her neck . . . by accident." He screws up his face, his mouth is twisted. He's there again, remembering. Reliving. Spit forms at the corners of his mouth. "I wanted to break that necklace that *he* gave to her. I squeezed it in my hands but it wouldn't break. I yanked it down and she . . . fell to the ground," he says softer, wiping a tear from his cheek. "Something was wrong. . . . Her skin was . . . darker. She wasn't breathing. I pulled my hand away from her neck. But it was too late. The necklace broke but it was too late." He laments. "Oh God, what did I do?"

"Luca . . . what happened after that?" I say, my voice catching.

"What did you do with Gianna?" Nico interrupts.

"I panicked," Luca says. "I didn't know what to do. The vineyard was closing but I stayed . . . with her. We should have stayed on that bench where we were, near the woods. The sun was setting. It was a beautiful sunset. We should have stayed there." He rubs his neck and winces. "But she loved the trees and wanted to walk in the woods. That's when it all went bad." He slumps over. His shoulders begin shaking.

"What did you do next, Luca?" I ask again frantically.

He lifts his head. "We were already near the thickest part of the woods. I dug out a shallow pit and . . . gently laid her there."

"You just left her there?" Jamie asks.

"I laid her on top of the soft dirt and pine needles and covered her with leaves and vines. Pulled as much as I could all around her until she could no longer be seen."

I cannot believe what I'm hearing. I steady myself against Nico and pull myself up.

"And all this time you let everyone in Italy think it was your own brother. Why? Why are you telling me this now?" I say.

"It's time, Ella. The secret is out. I can no longer keep it." He pulls out a handkerchief and wipes his eyes and face. "You're a smart girl, Ella. Smarter than I realized. I know you'll want to tell your mother. You'll think you need to tell the police. I'll go away. You won't need to worry about me anymore. I wrote a letter to Lena. Please just let me be."

"I'm sorry, Luca, but I can't do that." He gives me a crazed look that begs for explanation. I sigh, preparing for what I want to say next.

"I need you to tell me something first," I say. He raises his eyebrows. I look him squarely in his eyes. "How was Nonna involved?" He shuffles his feet and rakes his fingers through his hair. "Just say it," I say.

He stares back at me, his eyes softening. "Nonna didn't like the idea of Gianna. She didn't like raising a child that wasn't her own by another woman that your grandfather loved. Oh, he loved Nonna, but not the way he loved Gianna. She knew that." He pauses, as if considering his next thought. *Where is this going? Nonna, what have you done?*

"Nonna grew to love that child—your mother—as if she were her own. But she always worried about Gianna coming back and she didn't want her to come back. Ever." *No, Nonna, no.* "I reassured her that she didn't need to worry. Gianna wouldn't be coming back." *I don't want to hear this.*

"She knew you killed her—and she kept your secret!" I spew.

Luca tilts his head. "Yes, you're right, she did keep a secret."

All the air in the room escapes. I don't know what to do.

Luca waves his arm to break my stare. "Nonna kept a secret, but not what you're thinking," he continues. "While Poppy was in the army, I left for America with your great-grandparents. He came later with Nonna." I recall reading about this in his diary. "When your mother was a baby, she was left in a carriage on our front porch when we still lived in Italy," he continues.

"You mean *you* put the carriage there and pretended she was left—"

"Yes," he says. "Before Poppy brought Nonna to America, he told her about Gianna and about Bella. Nonna didn't like having her husband's love child in the same house with her at first. I told Nonna that Gianna ran away with someone else. That Gianna no longer loved Poppy and wanted to begin a new life far away. Nonna thought Gianna confided in me and left her baby with me. That's the secret she kept from your grandfather."

A rush of relief sweeps through me followed by guilt for thinking the worst about Nonna. She was keeping secrets, but nothing at all compared to what I feared. I begin to cry. A furious cry I hadn't had since Jack. Nico and Jamie try to comfort me. Luca stands aloof.

I break away from Nico and Jamie and get right up into Luca's face. "I need you to take us to the vineyard *right now*," I say between breaths. "You need to show me where you left Gianna. And when I say show, I mean we're bringing a shovel. That's the only way. Otherwise I'm going to the police and they'll dig up the vineyard anyway and arrest you. You show us and you can go anywhere you want, because, honestly, I don't care if I never see you again."

"I—I can't do that," he says.

Footsteps on gravel come from behind. A dark figure emerges from the doorway. A man. He's holding something in his left hand. A gun. He raises the gun and aims it at us. The late afternoon sun breaks through the clouds revealing his face. Marco. We raise our arms and back away. Luca seems as surprised as we are.

"Marco," Luca says. "Put the gun down."

Marco takes a step closer. Nico steps in front of Jamie and me.

"You don't have to do this," Nico says.

"You see . . . thing is," Marco sneers, his Italian accent no longer charming and sweet, "Luca said to do whatever I have to . . . didn't you, Luca?"

Marco looks at me. "Sophia and I got in one of the worst fights we ever had. About you, Ella. She asked me why I've been following you. Why I'd steal the letters." He looks at Luca, "And why I'd ever associate with *you*. Said she'd leave me if I keep working for you. Been saying that for a while. I didn't believe her."

He looks back at me. "When I saw you at the vineyard I called your uncle." He motions with the gun toward Luca. "He said keep following you. I was tired of it but did it anyway. The money was good and I was afraid of what would happen if I didn't. I went home first. When I got there Sophia was gone. Took everything. Gone." Marco shakes his head. "Been your spy long enough, Luca. And for what? Look what it cost me." His voice is ragged. "You're both not worth my time anymore. Or money," he says, looking at Luca. Then he grips the gun with both hands and aims it at us hard.

My heart drops to my stomach. Nico stands firm with his back against us and his hands out, his muscles twitching through his shirt.

"Put the gun down, Marco," Luca says, enunciating each word slowly.

"I actually liked you in the beginning, Ella. Probably more than I should. Your uncle said you felt the same, but . . . you played me. You both did. And to think—I *almost* told you what Luca's been up to. Because I thought we might— You should have stayed in America and minded your own business. I don't know what I was thinking. Sophia loved me. Now she's gone. Now you're both gone." He shifts his aim fast at Luca. I gasp. "And you lied, Luca. Oh, how you lied."

"Put the gun down," Luca repeats. "Let's talk."

"It's too late for that," Marco says. "We *will* go to the vineyard. You'll do some digging until I say stop. If there's a body like you say,

I might let you go. If not, if you've been lying to me this whole time, I'll bury *your* body. *Capiche?*"

Marco walks up to Luca with the gun pointed at him. He motions for us to step aside. Luca's driver is long gone, so Marco makes Luca get in his car. I grab the box of Gianna's things and put them in the trunk next to the shovel and garden shears we'd purchased after our first visit to the police station. Marco watches closely and, with his gun still aimed at Luca, he steps forward to block me from getting in the car.

"We drive together," he grins. "I'm not dumb enough to think you won't go right to the police."

I'm caught off guard. "I wasn't—"

"Tell you what," he says, his lip curled. *"You* drive with us, and your friends can follow."

My heart sinks.

"No," Nico says. "She stays with us."

Marco laughs. "You don't bargain with me," he barks, waving his gun. "She goes with us. You follow." He glares at Nico. "And I'll be watching. If your car turns off the road for *any* reason, she dies. I got nothing to lose."

Nico, Jamie, and I stare at each other with fear-filled eyes. They watch helplessly as Marco grabs my arm and pulls me to his car. I steal frequent glimpses from the back window to make sure they're still there. They drive closely behind Marco's car all the way back to the vineyard.

It is dark except for the bright glimmer of the moon. Luca leads us to the woods behind the vineyard. Marco is right behind him with gun aimed. Jamie and I shine a path before us with flashlights while Nico carries a shovel and large garden shears. Shoes squeak across wet grass, clouds of breath hover above our lips in the cold air. I shiver, but not from the cold.

We walk into the woods until Luca stops and surveys the area around us. The vines, low and winding, weave together tightly and cover the ground making it difficult to walk. As we pass the area where I found the necklace, Luca begins pacing back and forth. He's panting like a dog, quick, shallow breaths. He tells Jamie to shine a light on the bark of a large oak tree and then another and another. He touches the bark of the trees, examining around the base and near the top.

All at once, he stops in front of one particular tree and begins trembling and crying. He studies the surrounding area and then bends low to the ground and vomits. His arm shakes as he points to an area just beyond. "There," he cries. Without words, he begins digging. After some time, Nico takes over. They open up the earth in all directions and find nothing. They dig deeper, still finding nothing.

"I don't understand," Luca says mostly to himself. He runs his fingers through his hair. "This is it. This is where I laid her. I marked the tree," he says, pointing to a branch where something metal still clings. "She was here. I know she was here."

"You *sure* she was dead?" Marco mocks.

"Yes, of course," Luca says. "She had to be." He scratches his head. "Wasn't she?" he mumbles. Nico, Jamie, and I stare.

"Stupid old man," Marco says. "After all this and she's not even here. You know why she's not here? Because she's probably not dead! I mean, maybe she's dead by now 'cause she'd be old like you. But I bet you didn't kill her. I bet she *did* get away from you!" Marco begins laughing hard. Luca is silent and still. He looks dumbfounded and lost. He takes a flashlight and retraces his steps, examines the trees again. Shakes his head.

"What a waste of time. At this point," Marco continues, "you might as well tell her the rest."

"Don't," Luca says.

Marco turns to me, "Like I said, nothing to lose."

"Stop!" Luca yells, but Marco waves him off with his gun.

"Your uncle confided a lot when he asked me to spy on you," he sneers. "Gianna—"

"Marco!" Luca yells.

"Enough, Luca," he says, glaring at him. He faces me again, his brow furrowed. "Ella, you know that Gianna's baby—she is your mother, right?" I nod, wondering where he's going with this. "What a special day when your mother was born, right?" He sneers. "I mean, if it weren't for her, we wouldn't have *you*." He stops talking until I look him in the eyes. "Did you know that your mother was not born into this world alone?" I stare into his cocky, jeering eyes. Eyes I once believed were generous and kind. "You see, Gianna didn't just have *one* baby," he says. "She had two! She had twins."

A low, gravelly sound comes from Luca.

I swallow hard. "That's not . . . possible," I say. I look at Luca and, as I catch his eyes, he lowers them to the ground.

"But it *is* possible," Marco says." And true."

"He's lying, Ella," Luca mutters.

"I'm not the one lying," Marco says.

Luca hangs his head and covers his ears.

"I don't know *why* they were separated," Marco continues, "I just know they were. Your mother was raised in America, and her sister— what was her name?" He taps his head, pretending to think hard. "Ah, Grace? She was raised here, in Italy," he says. "And now you know what *I* know about this dysfunctional family."

Grace? Strange, yet familiar. I thought I heard Maria say the word "grace" at our last visit. Had she mumbled it in prayer as she'd said when I asked her? Or did she slip and say the name Grace? Marco lowers his gun for a moment and strokes his chin, fully satisfied with himself.

Suddenly, Luca bolts into the woods. Marco shoots his gun and takes off running after him. Jamie and I shine our flashlights in the direction Luca ran but we don't see him or Marco anywhere. Nico shouts, "Let's go!" and we race in the opposite direction toward the car. Fear grips me hard and I can't feel my legs, but somehow they carry me all the way. My head is a messy clump of twisted vines. One thought tangled among the others, stuck between Gianna getting away and twins.

Chapter 38

Standing at the edge of Castello Ruffo, looking down, I spy a perfect view: beautiful beaches of Scilla to the left and scattered cafes and restaurants near the fishing village of Chianalea to the right. Directly across is the Messina Strait and Sicily. A glistening sun wakes up, still low on the horizon, and casts an orange-pink glow stretching across the sea. I imagine a young Franco and Gianna spying the same beautiful scenery and reminiscing about their childhood. I ponder their last day together.

I try to shake the feeling of impending doom that's hovered above us since we left the vineyard. I watch the crowds of people in fear that Luca or Marco may emerge. My mind remains troubled, but I don't allow it to cast darkness on this moment.

Our last moment together. Nico leans against the brick ledge looking out at the sea. His hair moves with the wind. One strand stays against his cheek and hovers just above his lips. The thought of saying goodbye leaves a dismal feeling in my heart. How is it possible, after three short weeks, to feel this way about someone I hardly know? What will happen when I go home? Will we go on with our normal lives and not be part of each others?

Nico faces me and brings my hand to his lips. When he pulls me close I try to commit to memory every part of this moment: how it feels to be in his arms, the smell of his cologne, the warmth of his body.

I wonder if this is how Poppy felt before he left Gianna for the army. Uncertain of whether he'd see her again. Was he fearful of letting go from her warm embrace? Would he forget the softness of her skin, the smell of her hair, the touch of her lips? Would time erase these things from his mind? Or did he know that it would never leave his heart?

I still remember everything about Jack, and I still long for him. But I notice that I'm loosening my grip and allowing myself to release the pain of a true love lost. My heart will never be exactly what it once was, but maybe it doesn't have to be. Maybe it can hold a place for special people. Maybe it can create space for love to grow again. But what does this mean for Nico and me? Will the distance be too much for us?

Waves crash below us and we're caught in the warmth of the wind's embrace. Our bodies slightly part but our eyes lock. I know I've glimpsed his soul in these eyes. He brings his hands to my face and draws me in, kissing my lips gently and then deeply. My body tingles at his touch. Our hands are wild against each other. I cannot get enough of him. He kisses my chin, my neck, my shoulder, my fingers, and then he steps back and takes my hands.

"I don't want you to go," he says with a sad smile.

"I don't either."

"You could stay?" He grins.

"I can't, Nico. I—"

"Shh. It's okay. I know," he says. "It's just that I—I feel like I've always known you. And I don't want to say goodbye."

My stomach flips.

"I know," I say. "I feel the same."

"You do?" he says, grinning wide.

"Of course. Can't you tell?"

"I thought so, but . . . maybe there's someone waiting for you in

America," he says, half joking, but I can tell he's not sure.

"No. No one. I wouldn't have kissed you if there was," I say. I look out at the blue below. "There *was* someone once. But that was a long time ago."

"I like you a lot, Ella Perri," he says. "I think I might even . . . love you," he says, blushing. My heart rapidly drums inside my chest. "Do you think someday you could—"

"Yes," I say smiling. "I think I could." I could love this man. "What do we do now? Because I—"

"Well," he says, "it'll be torture not being able to see you every day or hold you when I want. I won't deny that." Is he changing his mind? "But I'm willing to take a chance with you, Ella. See what happens."

The smile on my face widens and stretches into something that hardly resembles a smile.

He gives me an odd look. "Are you willing to take a chance with me?"

In my heart, the answer to this question is easy, but is it real?

I place my hands on both sides of his face and kiss him. "Yes," I say. "I do want to take a chance with you."

****

A gentle breeze coming off of Skaneateles Lake whispers through trees surrounding the home that once belonged to Poppy and Nonna. I stand steadfastly at the foot of the hill on West Lake Road, the entrance to their yard. I study its structure, note its flaws, and make a silent promise to give it the care and attention it needs. And it beckons once more, just like before.

Come in El. Come home.

This time I don't resist. I long to go inside this home. To step beyond the chipped pillars and through the entrance. To be embraced in the structure of the home that raised me and the grandparents who saved me. I need to be here. I kick off my shoes and step barefoot through the long, soft grass, the blades tickling my feet as they did when I was little.

I traipse up the cobbled path and stop at the cozy white porch, my mind filling with memories, love, warmth—everything my grandparents exemplify. Three weeks ago, I stood in this same spot under a cloud of darkness, uncertainty, and loss. A secret letter tucked in my pocket and a mystery to unravel. I promised Poppy that I would do anything for him. When he said to find the box, it became my destiny to find it. I wasn't expecting to discover what I did, one secret leading to another. So many lies. So many lives were altered because of one person. The biggest heartbreak and disappointment of all.

And I almost didn't go. If I hadn't pursued those secrets, I wouldn't know what I know. Wouldn't have seen where Poppy grew up. I wouldn't have met Nico. Sometimes I wish I could pretend it didn't happen. But then I'd be part of the secret. And I want nothing to do with that. Poppy wanted the truth out in the open. And he whispered those words about the box to me and only me. And now I realize why. He knew that *I* understood that the heavy sadness and depth of losing true love is like losing part of your soul. He trusted our bond and knew that, once I found the box, I'd uncover the truth. I hope that in doing this for him I brought him peace. What I wasn't expecting was that this journey has also brought me peace.

Now that we know the truth, we have to deal with it, and that's not going to be easy. Today the darkness is not gone but different. Our family is different. We'll need to adapt our lives and what we once believed to a new reality. I dread telling my mother that Nonna isn't her biological mother or telling Nonna that the secret she thought she was keeping is far different than the actual secret itself.

Or telling Aunt Lena that I don't know where Luca is. Telling everyone what he did. Maybe they won't believe me. Maybe I shouldn't tell them.

While standing at the front door, a butterfly lands on my hand and turns to look at me. It stays there even when I wave my hand to free it. "It's okay, you can go," I say, but it doesn't release its grip. I gently pry him from my hand and let him go. He lands above the door and stays there.

When I swing the door open I'm greeted by the familiar and much loved scent that is known only to Poppy and Nonna. I breathe it in as I walk down the hallway, through the house, sliding my hand across the door to the study as I pass, reminiscing all the way to the other side of the house. I see them through the glass door leading to the backyard. Everyone is there. My whole family, except for Luca. They're waiting for me and they know I have a lot to tell them.

They sit patiently and talk quietly under Storybook Tree just as I asked them to. The same spot beneath the branches where made-up stories were shared with little eager eyes and where broken hearts were mended. The same spot where our sweet Poppy came to breathe his last breath of fresh air. I feel him all around us now. I open the door and walk down the steps leading to the tree and hug and kiss each member of my family, one by one. Nonna's face shows signs of worry and regret, my mother's eyes reveal deep concern, and Aunt Lena's carry doubt. They wait for me to tell one more story under the tree: Poppy's story.

After quick conversations on what everyone has been doing over the last few weeks, I begin to tell them everything I know. It isn't all a surprise. My mother had informed those who didn't know the latest about Uncle Luca. No one has seen or heard from him since that day he ran from my mother's house. Aunt Lena said she never received the letter he told me he'd left for her. I wonder if she's telling the truth.

I tell them about my encounter with Uncle Luca in Italy and share what happened in the vineyard. My mother believes that Gianna may still be alive and wants to find her. I haven't decided whether I'll tell her about her alleged twin or if I'll try to find out on my own first. I tell them about Angelina's and Vinny's open invitation to come back and stay with them again.

They're shocked to hear about Maria, that she was alive and well. I explain how she helped us, how she showed us Gianna's birth certificate and all the pictures she had, especially of my mother as a child. And how Maria was elated when I told her Luca confessed. But we hadn't found Gianna's body in the vineyard where Luca said he left her, so perhaps there is still hope for Gianna.

I retrieve the necklace I found in the vineyard and show it to my mother. Her eyes widen and fill as she holds the broken chain in her hands. She takes an edge of her sweater and rubs away some of the black from the chain and then flips it over. She strains her eyes at something and rubs it a little more.

"Look," she says. With her phone on camera mode she hovers over a thicker part of the necklace which looks like a stretched out heart, zooms in to the tiny print on the back, and reads what's inscribed: "'With Love, Franco.'" Then she pulls out the locket that was tucked in her shirt. She opens the locket and reveals a small scripted *G*. "This must have been part of the necklace that Poppy gave to Gianna," she says. "I found it in Nonna's jewelry box when I was little," she whispers.

"His diary says the necklace had "F & G" with a little heart attached," I say. "You've had the *G* all this time." We examine the broken chain for signs of the *F* but can't find it. It's the only piece that's missing. "Poppy knew something wasn't right." I hold the necklace in my hands again. "I hope you can be at peace now, Poppy. I hope I made you proud."

I feel an arm reach around my shoulders. It's Nonna. She sits beside me on the bench and wraps her arms around me. She tells both my mother and me the story about the day my mother had been left on the front porch in her baby carriage. She'd been swaddled tightly and covered with blankets. Poppy's mother had been caring for the baby and noticed the scripted *G* tucked beneath the padding. She put it aside and showed Nonna when she and Poppy came to live with them right after they arrived in America. Nonna, having been told by Uncle Luca that Gianna took off with another man, pretended to go along with the story that Gianna was missing. She didn't want Poppy to see the *G* so she took it and hid it in her jewelry box, not ever thinking that one day my mother would explore that jewelry box.

Nonna begins to cry and apologizes to my mother, who offers a half-hearted hug back. What a mess. Even though she lied for all those years, I actually feel a little sorry for Nonna. I don't think she ever realized the true depth of this lie.

When I tell everyone about Nico and how I plan to go back to Italy in a few months to see him, my mother says she'd like to go, too. Nonna stares off.

I look at Nonna and think of all the wonderful memories with her as my grandma. How she listened, nurtured, and loved us so deeply, and I can't imagine not having her even for one minute in my life.

"I love you, Nonna," I say.

She leans against my shoulder, her soft hair tickling my chin. Her little head pops up. "You know what, Ella?"

"What?" I say.

"You made us both proud. Poppy and me," she says. "I know you did this for Poppy because you love him. And I'm sorry I disappointed you," she says in that soft, sweet voice I love so much.

I squeeze her hand and kiss her forehead. After a few moments, we follow the rest of the family out of the chilly air and back to the cottage. Nonna, Mom, and I stand together with me at the center and we walk arm in arm toward the cottage.

When we reach the back door I stop. "Nonna," I say. She looks at me. "If you're truly planning to sell this house, please don't sell it to anyone but me."

Tears fill her eyes. She nods her head and squeezes my hand as we enter the warm cottage.

Now I am home.

Acknowledgements

The idea for this book has nagged at me for years, ever since my grandfather, Poppi passed away. Fragmented ideas and thoughts have surfaced or emerged at the oddest moments. I'd jot down an idea, a song, a quote or anything that came to mind in a little notebook that an old friend once gave me until one day when I finally sat down to write it all out. The first person I'd like to acknowledge for providing the foundation for Buried Secrets is my grandfather, Poppi whose love, quiet strength and devotion to our family had an enormous impact on me throughout my life. His real-life character provided the inspiration for the fictional character of Poppy in my book.

I'm deeply grateful for my husband, Jimmy for his constant encouragement from the beginning to follow my dream as a writer. I'm thankful for his patience when I'd spend hours working on revisions or other writing decisions that would often occupy my time away from our family. His thorough examination of my story and his valuable feedback and opinion whenever I needed it will always mean so much to me.

I am forever grateful for all of my "muses", the beautiful people in my life who have taken the time to share their thoughts, opinions, advice, and guidance on my story. My friends, family members, and fellow writers, I am so appreciative that they took the time to read my entire manuscript and provided detailed honest feedback on the questions I asked about it. I'd like to give a special thanks to my parents Dennis Parnell and Yolanda Parnell and my in-laws Gary Baccaro and Corrine Baccaro who were always ready to read anything I put before them and lovingly offered advice and guidance almost instantly. My children Sarah and Michael for encouraging me to keep going and for reading my story and giving their opinion on a variety of things related to my book.

I would like to thank The Write Practice for giving me the courage to finally start writing stories and sharing them with a writing community. Alice Ludwig who was the first professional editor who read it and provided invaluable feedback to guide my story in the direction it needed to go. Through The Write Practice, I found my writing tribe, an incredible group of writers whom I've grown close to and learned so much about the craft of writing, critiquing stories and supporting each other. Many from this group also helped me tremendously with Buried Secrets.

I would like to thank my editor, Megan Basinger who immersed herself in my story and polished it up to make it stronger and sharper than ever.

Thank you to my readers who have followed along, read my newsletters, and cheered me on as we all waited for Buried Secrets to be completed. I am grateful to you all.

If you enjoyed reading Buried Secrets, please consider leaving a review to spread the word on Amazon, Bookbub and/or Goodreads.

About The Author

Krissy Baccaro writes mystery and suspense. Her short psychological thriller, LUCA, was recently published on Amazon. She also collaborated with authors from around the world to publish two anthologies, *Once Upon a Story: A Short Fiction Anthology* and *The Rearview Mirror: An Anthology* which feature her short thrillers "Luca", "Monster", and "In the Shadows".

As a child, she picked up the book, From the *Mixed Up Files of Mrs. Basil E. Frankweiler* by E.L. Konigsburg and became enthralled in mysteries forever.

She is currently working on the soon-to-be-released sequel to *Buried Secrets*.

For 25 years, Krissy taught Kindergarten through fifth grade. Currently, she teaches writing and reading to 5th-grade students and loves to share with them all she knows about writing. The author resides in upstate New York not far from Skaneateles, where the puzzle of *Buried Secrets* begins.

Ella Perri Mystery Book 2 will be released late summer/early fall - be the first to know when! Plus get free thrillers & Mysteries when you visit my website and join my mailing list:

https://krissybaccaro.com/

Amazon Author Page:
https://www.amazon.com/Krissy-Baccaro/e/B0862CXFFP

https://Twitter.com/BaccaroKrissy

https://www.goodreads.com/author/show/18891057.Krissy_Baccaro

https://www.instagram.com/krissybaccaro/

https://www.facebook.com/Krissy-Baccaro-Books-100566741650751

Other Books By Krissy

LUCA

Once Upon a Story: A Short Fiction Anthology

The Rearview Mirror: An Anthology

Made in United States
North Haven, CT
20 January 2024

47695682R00193